Campus Cravings

A NOVEL

CANDY QUINN

PATHFORGERS  PUBLISHING

Preface

Sign up to my newsletter to receive free, exclusive
stories:
http://candyquinn.com/newsletter

⚮

Book Themes: bimbofication, virgin, breeding, titjob, blowjob, ff, mff, teacher/student, age gap, multiple partners, older man/younger woman, hypnosis
Word Count: 85,163

⚮

One

C asey stood by the door to her dorm room, the sound of thumps and moans resonating from within. She was looking up and down the hall, in case any of the teachers or resident 'narcs' came by. It wasn't exactly glamorous, and definitely not what she had in mind when she was first sent to the prestigious institute of learning but...

A squeal and a gasp emerged from her room as Casey shifted, one of her dainty hands fidgeting with the hem of her pleated skirt.

She was a pale girl, with a few freckles peppering her lovely, delicate facial features. And while she was a sweet girl, who dressed nice and preppy, she was no longer a flat chested girl. Instead, her bust had swelled dramatically over the past year, until her blouses were nearly bursting, and the round, bubbly swell of her backside created a looming crisis of exposure whenever she walked too fast or the wind picked up enough to lift her skirt.

But she made due, in her high-heeled Mary-Janes, her

thigh high stockings neatly in place. Of course, the sound of her roommate with her... boyfriend? She wasn't sure what to call him, since Dahlia was with a lot of guys, and never with one for too long. And she certainly never seemed to get too hung up on any of them.

Regardless, the sounds of her moaning and gasping and crying out were a distraction. It made it hard to keep a good watch, especially as she heard the guy Dahlia was with grunt and groan, his deep voice masculine and pleasured. Something about that, more than anything else, sent a shiver down Casey's spine, and caused a tension in her already too-tight bra as her nipples stiffened.

Though the worst was the way her tiny panties seemed to grow oh-so-sticky when he muttered a low, strained, "Fuck yes!"

Boys weren't allowed in the girls' dormitory usually, which was why Casey was on guard. Their spot was on the opposite side of campus, with the school's main hall and the staff's homes in between the two groups. But somehow, Dahlia never seemed to have trouble sneaking her boyfriends—or whatever they were—over, when she wanted to.

Casey felt so lost in her new school, Ceresian Collegiate.

Not knowing what was right or wrong, confused about all the conventions of things, from teachers and other students. But Dahlia? She seemed to have no trouble, fitting in, finding her way, doing as she wanted and having fun.

Casey couldn't help but be envious.

The sound of her gasping and crying out, in that intense way that meant she was about done, didn't help. Casey didn't know squat about boys, or men, or how to have fun with them, like Dahlia did. She was jealous of her best friend, especially as that guy's long, low groan filtered through the door.

Yeah, they were definitely finishing up. Casey knew that much, from experience watching for her friend. Luckily this time had been easy, and she hadn't had to work to keep anyone away, or invent excuses. She hated doing that!

She was left there, alone with her thoughts as the heat betwixt her own thighs distracted her. Until finally, the door opened, and a very tall, handsome, darkly dressed guy came out. Casey hadn't seen him with Dahlia before, but with his lower lip and eyebrow piercing, his school jacket dyed black—how did he get away with that?!—he looked... surprisingly handsome as he nodded to her.

"Thanks for that," he said to Casey, in his deep voice, his tie hanging loose from his undone shirt collar. He looked like one of the group who hung out, wearing dark clothes, sneaking in cigarettes and generally being loathed by everyone. Only underneath it... Casey saw the striking handsomeness in him, and how easily he could've looked like the most preppy, in control guy on campus if he wanted to.

Casey flushed as he looked at her, and she felt as if he could see just how wound up she was. Sure, he had no way of seeing the slickness between her thighs, though maybe he could get a glimpse of how stiff her nipples were beneath her bra. Still, she felt transparent as her emerald gaze desperately avoided catching his.

"Yea, of course. What are friends for, right?"

He looked at her curiously, his brows raising a bit at that. But then at last he cracked a wry smile and reached out, brushing a finger along her cheek, as he tucked back a lock of strawberry blonde hair behind one ear of hers.

"Well, if you ever want a new friend, come find me some time, huh?" he said in his charming way that exuded a lack of concern for what others thought of him. He seemed so intensely... comfortable with his own self. Something Casey did not understand at all.

Especially since it took every ounce of self-control she had not to squeal like a school girl at his touch, at his strange, intoxicating words. She couldn't stop the way her neck lifted, to hold onto his caress a moment longer, or the heat of her blood as it rushed to the surface, painting her pale cheeks crimson.

"Find you where?"

"Well," he said, rubbing his chin thoughtfully as he cracked a hint of an uneven grin, "you can find me at the boys' dormitory by asking for Damien. Otherwise, ask your friend Dahlia how to get to The Pit. You'll find me there," he remarked so casually and confidently. As if he was from a whole other world than Casey.

"The Pit?" she asked with her nose crinkling in distaste, though her brows were lifted with curiosity. It sounded so... seedy. So dirty. Somewhere good girls didn't go.

But she was so *tired* of being a good girl. She'd been at the school for over a year, and it had been weird from the very first day. Who would've been able to guess that a pandemic would put the whole world in lock down, making her universe so small... She'd never really had a chance to adjust to normal school life before the *new* normal became a thing.

"Yeah," he said in his deep, low voice, so rough and

4

masculine compared to most of the other guys around. "It's where a bunch of us hang. You need someone to vouch for you to get in. But just tell 'em I sent you," he remarked with a smile that highlighted his piercing.

"Damien sent for me," she rehearsed, muddling up just a little bit. Her brain was a fog of desire and longing, and it filtered out in little ways. "Okay, I can do that," Casey said with a smile that revealed the dimples in her cheeks. She honestly felt like he could say anything and she'd do it like an eager puppy, desperate for affection.

Damien's grin grew and he gave a light little chuckle at her slight flubbing of the line.

"Perfect. That'll do the trick," he remarked, reaching up to brush his thumb along her cheek before he started to head off. "Don't forget," he said with a wink as he headed down the long, old corridor, with its intricately carven wood panels.

She stared after him, totally lost in childish fantasies that didn't have much more than sounds and soft caresses to go by. Sure, she knew that whatever Damien and Dahlia did before that door was a lot more than just curses, grunts, and tender touches, but she didn't have the experience to fill in all of the blanks.

And given the lack of internet—and the no cell phone rule—it made it almost impossible to do independent research.

She didn't hear the door open up and Dahlia say her name. She didn't fully snap out of it until a hand was in front of her face, waving back and forth.

"Oh! Ah! Hi, Dahlia. No trouble today."

Her dark-haired friend was looking much the same as

when she first went in again, though her cheeks were more flushed and her hair didn't have quite the same meticulously cared for look. But she smiled at Casey as she adjusted her skirt and blouse. She hadn't rejected her uniform as much as Damien had, but she got rid of the tie, and jacket, and just had the blouse undone three buttons, showing some cleavage.

"You're a doll, Casey," Dahlia said with a warm smile. "So, what are you up to now?" she asked casually, stepping back, letting Casey come in if she wanted.

Casey took the offer, slipping into the room and leaning against the door frame. There was that *scent*, another piece of the puzzle that ignited some animalistic part of her that she didn't understand or have control over, and she inhaled deeply.

"I don't know. I was thinking of wandering around later for a bit. Why, what are you up to?"

"I dunno," Dahlia said, shrugging her shoulders, which made her breasts jiggle. Until Casey had her miraculously sudden flowering, Dahlia had been the bustiest girl on campus. And she wasn't afraid of flaunting it, unlike Casey. "I know they want us to study this afternoon, or consult with the teachers in their offices, but..." she rolled her eyes and stuck out her tongue.

She could seem so serious and severe at times, but Dahlia was always nice to Casey. And Casey couldn't help seeing her as a harmless friend, with freckles on her cheeks that matched her own. They were almost like sisters in a way.

They were opposites in others, though. Dahlia was always so confident and she knew exactly what she wanted, and more importantly, how to get it. Casey couldn't even put into words what she wanted. She just knew it had something to do with men and closed doors.

"I don't think I can study today. My mind is going a million miles a minute. And all my homework is caught up on. Hm... I could go see Mr. Alder, I guess. Have you heard anything about when the new uniforms are gonna be here? I put in a request, like... forever ago and still nothing."

Dahlia looked a bit amused at that as she looked in her mirror on her side of the narrow room, adjusting her thick black hair.

"I doubt it'll be any time soon. At least... I hope not. It's nice having some freedom with how I dress," she peered back in the mirror at Casey, "Oh, of course I know it's different for you. Sorry, Casey." But she puckered her lips, sizing them up as she applied some more lipstick, Casey had noticed it had seemed to lose its luster during her time with Damien. "Mr. Alder, huh? Aren't you already like... acing his course?"

Casey fidgeted with her blouse, the strain becoming far too much for the delicate buttons. If she gained even a pound, she was sure it'd burst.

"Huh?" she asked, looking up at Dahlia. "Oh. Well... yea, but that's because I really enjoy it. I feel like I'll never learn enough about those old romance languages. And he's fluent in, like, all of them. Well... almost. He knows more Classical Latin than Popular Latin, given the fact that Popular Latin ironically wasn't passed down," Casey said before realizing she was being embarrassingly nerdy. "Anyways, I like talking with him, but it feels weird being alone with a teacher when my shirt is trying to undress me."

Dahlia laughed at that, then smacked her lips again as she finished with her lipstick. She moved onto her mascara.

"Some teachers would love that, I'm sure," she said with that deviously playful voice of hers. But she peered back at Casey. "Well good luck. I'm gonna go hang with some other students for the rest of the day, I think. Take it easy," she said casually.

"You won't need me to keep guard anymore?" Casey asked, twirling a strand of strawberry blonde hair around her index finger. Her ringlets were immaculate, even though she couldn't help but play with them when she was nervous, which was a lot.

"Nah I'm good for now. Thanks though," Dahlia said as she finished up, then reached down, purposely rolling her skirt up, hiking it another inch higher, so that it sat scandalously short. She turned and smiled at Casey, "Have fun with Mr. Alder," she said with a light airy giggle at the end.

Casey's brows furrowed, and her full lips turned down.

"He doesn't even think of me like that. He's, like, different from other guys. A perfect gentleman," Casey said, with both respect and disappointment mingling in her voice.

"Oh, Dahlia, where's the Pit?"

Two

"The Pit...? You wanna know where the Pit is?" Dahlia asked, sounding quite surprised and in a bit of disbelief that her wholesome roommate would even ask about such a place.

"I mean... I should know where things are in the school. It's been so hard figuring out this place with all the lock downs and..." Casey trailed off, her gaze trained onto her polished Mary-Janes, feeling a little embarrassed for even asking.

Dahlia shut the door again, studying Casey. She smiled, just a tiny hint of a smirk to it.

"Well, sure... but it's not where you go for school stuff, like study and that. It's a secret spot, where we go to hang out, without the staff up our asses," Dahlia said. "So you can keep it a secret, right?" she asked.

"I've kept all your secrets," Casey said earnestly, meeting her roomie's gaze. She might be a bit of a good girl, but she knew the value in keeping some things private. People had a right to that, even in an overly strict campus.

Dahlia softened, losing that smirk entirely.

"Yeah, you're a good friend," she said, coming over to Casey, and giving her a kiss on the cheek. "Alright. You know the big main hall running north to south, from the boys' dorm to the girls? Well, you go along that in the center building. And you know that old stairwell by the storage closet? Well... head down there. Beyond the first door, it looks just like an old, dinghy storage room. But if you move aside the box by the north wall, where the pillar is... you'll find an old hatch. Go through there. But... be warned, if you go snoopin' around without someone there to vouch for you... they'll probably think you're a narc."

Casey bobbed her head, mentally mapping out the path she'd have to walk. She had an excellent memory for such things, and felt pretty confident it'd be no problem.

"Thanks, Dahlia. I won't be dumb about it, I promise. I just... I don't know. I want something..." she trailed off, letting out a sigh. "It doesn't matter, it's silly. I might not even go. I just want to know that I could, if I wanted to."

Dahlia studied her for a moment, then smiled once again.

"Maybe I'll meet ya there sometime," she said with a smile. "Alright, I'm heading out. You have fun!" Dahlia said, kissing her lips lightly then blowing it to her friend before she headed out the door.

Casey shut the door behind her, going to Dahlia's mirror, and looking herself over. Her waist was still so tiny, but her breasts were almost comically large on her slender frame. The white fabric was strained to the limit, and it made the edge of her lace bra even more apparent. That wasn't even the worst part, considering the bra was also at least two cup sizes too small, and couldn't hope to contain all her tits, so they bulged a little at the rim. Casey tried to fix it, but as usual, the second she moved, so did her breasts, and so they pulled out of the cup instantly.

Casey sighed. The skirt wasn't doing much better. It kept slipping up to her belly button, desperate for the narrowest part of her torso as her hips and ass kept up their shapely development. It really was quite cruel that of all the things the pandemic was screwing up, getting new uniforms seemed to be top of the pile. Maybe she could find someone who lost a lot of weight during the pandemic and wanted to swap?

That was probably a long shot. They ate well on campus, after all, with lots of delicious, healthy foods. Part of the campus even had a farm, to teach students all about animal husbandry and agriculture. It was hard to turn down fresh food when the rest of their lives were so tightly controlled.

Casey looked at the lipstick Dahlia had used, and for a moment, she really wanted to put some on. But she couldn't break her friend's trust by using her things without asking, so she went to her side of the room, and grabbed her clear lip-gloss that tasted lightly of vanilla. She swiped it along her full lips and gave her youthful face a fleeting smile.

She ignored the wetness between her thighs, and her untended-to-needs, as she always did, and headed out her dorm room to go visit Mr. Alder.

During study days, as they were called, the campus was

a bit odd. Equal parts quiet and chaotic. Students didn't crowd the halls generally, because that was an easy way to get caught and be forced to sit in detention hall where you actually had to study. But you still tended to see people going about in the midst of strange little missions of their own making.

But this time, there was a curious sight. Crossing from the girl's dormitories to the main hall, she saw a clustering of people at the corner of the building. It was too far away to make out any faces. She got so distracted by it, she didn't see the guy in the long black coat, hood up, who was rushing by... not until they bumped into each other and she fell down.

"Fuck," came a muffled curse from the dark stranger, as he quickly rebounded.

Casey was a *lot* slower to come out of her shock. Her skirt had flown up, and she was certain she'd flashed everyone. She was less certain that a button on her shirt had popped off, but she thought that was pretty likely. And in her high heels, there were not a lot of graceful options for getting back up.

So instead, she prayed that the ground would just swallow her up as she tried to regain her breath.

Instead, a gloved hand grasped hers, and she found herself being pulled back to her feet by the tall figure in black. Their hood dipped low in front, and they were wearing a black face mask, so she couldn't make out who it was at all. Nor even recognize the voice.

"You okay?" they asked, concern in their muffled, indistinguishable voice.

"I... are you okay? Sorry, I didn't see you, I should've

moved..." she said, still flustered by the shock. "I'm not hurt, I don't think. Maybe a bruise, but..." she trailed off. She wanted to say that it was the first time she felt thankful for her curvy ass, but she'd *never* say something like that, especially not to a stranger.

It wasn't normal to see someone wearing a mask here, they'd had no direct contact with the outside world since it all began, so it simply wasn't necessary. But the anonymous figure got her on her feet, looked her over with concern before saying.

"Forgive me," they said, and they reached out, touching Casey's milky thigh before she realized... they were tugging her skirt back down for her, as it had flipped up and clung to the waistband, leaving her panties exposed. "Don't worry about me. I want to make it up to y—" they began to say, before some shouts from around the corner of the building drew their attention, and they looked off for a moment. "Shit, I gotta go."

"Oh, uh... okay! Of course. Uhm, have fun!" she said, before once more willing the ground to swallow her up whole. Why would she say that? This was clearly something serious, why would she tell them to have fun?

The masked figure turned and left, but not before peering back at her again from beneath that hood. And soon he was sprinting off around the other side of the building, as the voices from the other direction grew.

"That was weird," Casey muttered to herself, frowning as she realized she did indeed lose a button. She glanced back at the ground, finding it and picking it up. Now she'd have to find some thread, but until then, her overfilled cleavage was presented through a new keyhole that was created in her blouse.

She had a choice. Return back to her dorm room, and hope that she had a sewing kit laying around, which she was pretty sure she did not, or continue on to Mr. Alder. It seemed safer than waiting for whatever ruckus was happening with the mysterious stranger.

Though she was curious about that...

She slipped in through the doors, but she paused there, peering out the glass from the corner, to see who it was in pursuit.

A few people came by. But only one was she really familiar with. The big form of Claud. Everyone knew Claud.

Casey had arrived shortly before the pandemic broke out, so one of her first classes was interrupted by a school meeting. Everyone gathered together to hear the dean tell everyone that with the way things were, the students were all safer there than back at their homes. There had been no breakouts in the secluded rural area of the campus, and strict lockdown measures would keep it that way, unlike the cities and towns they all came from.

At first people were tense about that, but as news trickled in—mostly through papers, since the school had a strict policy on no internet except for specific classes, and there was literally no cell service in the area—everyone began to feel safer at school than anywhere else. But an unintended consequence of this was that... when the supply lines began to get interfered with, the school was particularly hard put.

No, there were no shortages of food or necessities. The

school had ample stock of those just in case, and they were prioritized. But things like uniforms weren't being restocked. And pretty soon the students began to realize: if they tampered with their uniforms, there was no way to replace them.

So, a school of everyone dressed the same slowly began to diversify. Claud was one of the first to get out of the traditional uniform, but in his case? It was totally by accident. He was the biggest guy in school, strong as an ox! And had a tendency to tear his school jackets and shirts, because they simply didn't make any big enough for him. So finally, he tore all but the last of them that fit at all, and... they let him stick to wearing his workout top. A V-shaped black top, that wrapped around his waist, then went up between his pecs to his neck and shoulders. It left him pretty bare, but seeing as he was such a sweet guy—and absolutely hunky—nobody seemed to mind.

From there the goths figured things out, and began to dye their uniforms, knowing that unless it washed out, the school would just have to let them stick with it. And more and more students began to follow suit in big or little ways.

Casey, however, was another case of inadvertently stumbling into it. When she'd first arrived, she was still rather petite. But the sudden spurt of growth in her butt and breasts—probably brought on by the much richer diet of the campus than she got from living at home with her poor mother—meant that she was struggling to keep from flashing everyone with an upskirt, or her top bursting open.

And now it felt kinda full circle: her outfit was more tenuous than ever, and here was Claud, the guy who helped kick off the whole trend to begin with.

But why was he leading a crowd and chasing the stranger?

She lingered long enough, and turned about, briskly walking towards Mr. Alder's office, temporarily forgetting the new boob window that had been formed in her blouse.

Three

The instructor offices were spread out along a series of halls at the back and front of the building. Mr. Alder's was at the back, and she went that way. As she almost got there, she found herself having another close collision with a tall guy, but was luckily more careful this time.

"Whoa," he said, as he reeled back. His own uniform looked perfectly fitted, albeit worn a bit carelessly. He hadn't done anything to tweak it, unlike so many other students, except for failing to do up his tie tightly. But his handsome face was drawn to her chest for a moment, before he looked to her. "Sorry about that," he said, giving a light, nervous laugh. "I must be a real klutz today," he remarked. "Of all days no less."

He had blonde—in fact, almost platinum—hair, cut short but with a hint of shagginess, his eyes intense and steely looking. But a warm, casual smile on his face.

"I just fell on my butt, like, two seconds ago, so I think you have some work to do if you want that klutz of the year award," Casey said, her giggle just as nervous. "I don't know, maybe I'm just in everyone's way today. Or like... I'm the invisible woman and I only appear once someone bumps into me. At least I saw you coming this time."

He arched a brow at her reaction, sizing her up.

"I don't think anyone should miss you coming, but then... I guess I did," he said with a light laugh as he held his satchel bag to one side. "I'm uh, in a bit of a rush right now... but my name's Aeron," he said, extending a hand to her with a smile.

"Oh, uh, hi Aeron!" she said a little too eagerly, putting her dainty palm in his. She had had a hard time making friends outside of Dahlia, and so she was feeling quite excited to have met someone all on her own. "I'm Casey. Are you in any of Mr. Alder's classes?"

His hand was big compared to hers, firm, and he gave her a squeeze as they shook.

"Uh yeah. Just went to see him, but uh... forgot something," he remarked, raising his free hand to his tie, and straightening it a bit. "But... I owe you. For nearly sending you on your butt. These hard floors wouldn't be kind if I had," he remarked before releasing her hand. "So, mark me down as owing you one, okay Casey?" he remarked as his eyes were drawn back towards her chest before he tore them away.

"Everyone owes me one today. It'll be a fun day when all those debts get paid," she teased, feeling a rush as he checked her out. It made her squirm with embarrassment, but also, desire.

"It was nice meeting you."

"Really nice meeting you," he said with emphasis on

'really' as he ran a hand back over his platinum hair. "And I hope to do it again soon," he said, blatantly flirting with her as he backed away down the hall, staring at her with his lopsided grin and running a major risk of bumping into someone else. But he didn't seem to care this time. "I'll come for you, Casey!" he called out with a grin.

It sent a shiver down her spine and she let out a soft whimper as she stared after him. It felt like such a tease, and by the time he disappeared from view, and she was knocking on Mr. Alder's door, she felt that slickness between her thighs once more. She squirmed, tugging her skirt down.

It wasn't long before the tall, dashing figure of Mr. Alder was unveiled before her as the door swung open. His face lit up with a bright smile as he swept a hand back through his thick, medium length dark hair.

"Ms. Casey," he said, in that lightly accented voice of his, that sounded quite English but not in a snobby way. "Come on in," he gestured, in his finely tailored suit. He certainly didn't have her concerns, as he ushered her in. "And how could I possibly help my top student today?" he asked.

"Oh, well, I just finished all my homework, and I feel prepared for all my tests, but it's study day, so I thought maybe I could do some extra credit for you or something," Casey said. She wasn't really sure why she went to him. She just felt comfortable with him, and as much as she was dying to break out of her shell and explore all that life had to offer, she still felt trapped by what she thought she should do.

Get good grades, have her teachers praise her, be that good little girl.

He shut the door behind them, as he then pulled out a seat for her.

"Ahh, extra credit? You know, it's usually students desperate to pass that come here for that. But I guess you want to see if you can get a grade higher than one hundred-percent, is that it?" he teased as he then went around his desk, plucking up a leatherbound tome. He had such a natural grace about him, seeming so refined, so in control, so casually confident and capable at whatever he was doing. But studies like this were where he especially shined.

It put her a little at ease that he didn't immediately reprimand her for her missing button. Or stare at her chest, though the throbbing between her thighs told her she was equally disappointed by that.

She crossed her legs at the knee, but quickly found that did little to quell her desires.

"Well, maybe I could do some advanced coursework that I could use to try to get some scholarships?"

He seemed to ponder that, getting lost in thought a moment. But then... maybe he was staring at that open hole instead, at her supple young breasts showing through. Whatever the answer, he licked his lips and tore his gaze away.

"Tell you what... Ms. Casey," he remarked, rubbing his chin thoughtfully. "I have some papers by first years to grade. But you absolutely obliterated that content. So... maybe you could grade some of them for me. And tomorrow evening, meet me here—in my office—and I'll see how you did? I'll have a little reward prepared for you.

Something I know you'll appreciate," he remarked with a wry, growing smile that was quite warming.

It made her heart pitter patter, and she was thrilled by the assignment, let alone the promise of a reward.

"I would *love* that," she said eagerly.

He smiled and leaned forward, resting a soft, gentle hand on her shoulder.

"I thought you might. You'll be my unofficial Teacher's Aide, how's that sound? Of course, you can't go spreading that around, or you might get yourself a reputation as a teacher's pet too," he jested warmly.

"I Ieh, I don't think anyone would be surprised by that," she said, her gaze lifting from her hands in her lap to his face. "I think my roommate's called me a teacher's pet more than once, just because I choose to come talk to you on study days instead of... studying like she does."

"Does she now?" he asked, as his hand slid from her shoulder, and he flipped through some folders on his desk. He put one in particular on top, then looked back to her. "Well... we'll keep this assignment and tomorrow night's little tête-à-tête between just you and I, non?" he said with a wry smile and a playful wink.

"Okay. I'm good at keeping secrets," she said with a bright smile. "What time tomorrow night? After dinner?"

He looked thoughtful for a moment then spoke softly.

"How about at dinner time? I'll have something here for us to snack on as we work. Help it go by more smooth-ly," he said. "Of course, if your friends would be missing you, we can meet right after instead," he said, reaching his hand to her cheek, and lightly brushing back a stray, curly lock of red hair.

"Dinner will be more than fine," she said eagerly, but when he touched her, her heart began to pound in her chest, the excitement and budding desires welling to the surface so readily.

"I promise, I'll grade them just like you. Fairly, and always ready to see potential."

He looked so warm at her words.

"You didn't even need to say that for me to know it, Ms. Casey. Thank you. I'm sure you'll be a big help. And it'll be great practice for you. Since I seem to recall you mentioning once that you hoped to become a teacher one day," he remarked with a playfully sly expression.

"It would be a dream," she agreed. "I've just always thought it's one of the finest professions, filled with selfless people who want to help the younger generation learn everything they need to know to be a success as an adult. It's amazing..."

He paused, his constant buzz of energy seeming to still as he gave her a poignant stare, then a sweet smile.

"Teaching could certainly use more of those types. And you, dear Ms. Casey, are indeed a selfless and wonderful young lady. You'll make an exceptional teacher," he said, before taking up the folder and handing it to her. "You won't need me to tell you anything more about the assignment, I'm sure. You know how I grade. And if it's too much to get all done by tomorrow night... don't worry. It is just an extra credit assignment after all," he said fondly.

She held it to her chest like a precious gift as she smiled up at him.

"I can't wait to get your feedback, all the same. Thank

you, Mr. Alder. This is really an honour. Better than anything I could have expected."

He sat on the corner of his desk, one leg raised. He smiled at her.

"No, thank you, Ms. Casey. You're a pleasure to teach. And frankly, I enjoy your company too. So, it'll be nice having you help knock this grading out of the way," he said. "If you need anything, you know where to find me," he said. "Either here, my class, or in the instructor's hall out back."

She made a mental map of that as well, before giving him an enthusiastic nod. She stood up, her body so near to him as he sat on the edge of the desk. "I'll get it all done, I'm sure of it. Thank you, Mr. Alder. I'll see you tomorrow for dinner."

They were oh so close. She could smell the aroma of fresh, fragrant tea and pine from him, some mixture of his beverage of choice and cologne perhaps. But sat like that, they were closer to eye-level with each other than she was used to. His handsome face, shining eyes, charming hair, right before her.

"Until then. Don't overdo it on yourself," he cautioned, reaching out, tapping two of his fingers to her wrist, before letting them slide down along the back of her hand.

"I won't, I promise," she said again, filled with promises for him. And at his caress, she really felt that he could ask anything of her, and she'd promise him that as well. That was an actual concern for her, truly. School work usually helped to distract her from the nagging desires that kept popping up, but today, it really felt like it'd reached a fever pitch.

She didn't pull her hand away from him, or rush back to the door, like she might usually have done.

Instead, she lingered.

"I have another question, though. This one's more personal."

Four

"Oh?" Mr. Alder said simply, a brow raising in that endearing way of his. He always looked intrigued and eager to learn along with his students, and that one expression exemplified it more than anything else. "By all means, the door is shut, it's just us," he said softly as he folded his arms across his chest, taking on a serious look.

"It's kind of embarrassing but... do you have a sewing kit I could borrow? Someone bumped into me outside and one of my buttons popped off," she said, glancing down at her nearly obscene cleavage with a slight blush. Yet despite her embarrassment, her emerald eyes darted to his, to see if he'd look again.

And she caught him looking. A little longer than necessary even. He began to nod, as he tongued his lower lip, pulling it into his mouth before meeting her gaze again.

"I noticed, but didn't want to... say anything inappropriate," he remarked with a light smile. "I don't have a sewing kit on hand, but... I'll do something for you tomorrow night when you drop by, how's that sound?" he said. "For the time being, it might be best to undo the button above it too. Make it look... intentional," he suggested, his eyes glancing back downwards. "Want me to show you what I mean?"

"Wouldn't that just make it worse?" she asked, frowning slightly before nodding. "I guess I could always do it back up if I want to. You haven't heard anything about getting in some new outfits, have you? I know some of the students like a bit more freedom, but I swear, this shirt is not gonna last long..."

Mr. Alder shook his head slowly, then his two nimble hands went for her chest. He touched her blouse, carefully avoiding her skin as he popped the button above it through the hoop.

"Not likely to get anything soon. One of the ferries that brings in supplies to the nearest port is out of commission, and on top of all the other pandemic stuff... school uniforms got bumped down the priority list even more, I'm afraid," he said, as he peeled back the shirt a bit, adjusted her collar. "Here, take a look in the mirror and tell me what you think," he said, as he placed a hand at the small of her back, guiding her to the tiny mirror on his wall that she'd seen him use when adjusting his tie.

She let out a little gasp as she looked at herself, her face turning a bright red.

"Oh my God, I look obscene," she said, though she couldn't quite tear her eyes away. "If my mother saw me like this, she'd say I looked like a harlot, but it's not like I willed a growth spurt. Who even hits a growth spurt once they're 18?"

"You are no harlot, Ms. Casey," he said to her in his patient, smooth voice as he touched a hand to her cheek, guiding her eyes back to herself despite her attempt to look away. "I see a growing young woman, slowly realizing just how beautiful, strong, resilient and in control she can be," he remarked, and...

For a moment, she thought she could see it. That hint of a resemblance to Dahlia. Presenting herself without shame—or Casey wished.

"People judge you for having curves, though. Even if you're a virgin," Casey said with a sigh, sucking her lower lip into her mouth and tasting the remains of her vanilla gloss. She'd never noticed a ring on Mr. Alder's finger, though that didn't always mean much. A lot of married men never bothered to get a band, after all. Though he'd never mentioned having a partner, despite him being a romantic at heart.

Feeling his hand on her cheek, and the flush of heat that he drew to the surface, she found her mind wandering there, though. Wondering if he had a wife somewhere, cut off from him by the pandemic.

She stayed there, enjoying his closeness, the scent of him, the incessant throbbing between her thighs.

And she caught a glimpse of something in his eyes... something intense as he stood behind her. But he swallowed, and slowly retracted his hand from her cheek, squeezing both her shoulders.

"You don't have to do anything you're not comfortable with," he said to her, his voice huskier than usual as he murmured quietly. "But I think the look suits you well. And makes you seem more confident and in control... than if you walked around with one random button in the middle missing," he said, his eyes unable to avoid looking at her cleavage for too long.

She let out a little giggle at that.

"You're probably right. It did look a little strange. But it feels weird... letting it be intentional rather than accidental. I knew it was coming for some time, though. Hopefully the middle button doesn't go next," she said, watching him in the mirror with a curious expression on her face.

His breathing had increased, and she saw him swallow anxiously, but he tore his eyes from her chest and smiled at her in the mirror, giving her shoulders another squeeze, before letting his fingertips trail down along her bare arms.

"I'll have something for you tomorrow. Be sure to come by for that dinner, okay?" he said, smiling, as his fingers lingered at her elbows for a moment before he stepped back.

She was disappointed that the spell was broken, and she nodded a bit dejectedly. It wasn't like she *wanted* to do something with her teacher, but she certainly didn't not want to. It was complicated.

"Okay," she said softly as she turned around to face him. "It's a date, then, Mr. Alder. I'll see you tomorrow."

He smiled and adjusted his blazer and tie, tugging the jacket down before opening the door for her.

"I know you won't let me down, Ms. Casey," he said to her fondly, his hand going to her back, fingertips lightly grazing her spine down to just above her bottom as he guided her out.

She nearly moaned with desire, but she swallowed it back.

It was really getting out of hand.

"Thanks," she said, looking over her shoulder at him, her curls bouncing back into place.

He tucked his hands in his pants pockets and smiled at her backside as he stood in the door, his tall dashing figure filling it quite nicely.

"Until tomorrow, I bid you adieu," he said with a smile and a slight bow of his head.

"Bonne soirée," she returned, clutching the file folder at her hip as she began walking towards the library. It was instinctual, at that point. Dahlia had an awful habit of being... distracting while she was studying, and Cascy really couldn't handle any more of those types of distractions. She was already about to burst with a need that she didn't know how to fulfill.

She'd heard of masturbation, but... it wasn't a thing that good girls did, after all.

So, she had her full intentions on getting lost in her work and forgetting all about how good Mr. Alder smelled, or how the light hit Damien's lip ring, or how big Aeron's hand was, or how the mysterious stranger fixed her skirt.

She'd put all of that aside.

The school's library was immense, and it was three stories tall, with a big main atrium. The whole thing was made of old wood, intricately carved by master craftspeople. It looked stately and quite old, like it should've come out of the old world instead of the new.

And it was deathly quiet, thanks to the rigid standards of the librarian, a nice fellow named Mr. Dejardin that was always courteous to Casey. The only disruption she got in the first hour, was the school administrator passing through. The stern looking man in his expensive suit, swept his gaze over her, noting her prominently displayed cleavage with what she thought was a scowl... but then, he was always scowling.

"My button broke," she instinctively said in a low murmur, apologetic.

It didn't seem to do much to improve his mood, his stern, aquiline features glaring at her as he adjusted his expensive silk tie.

"That's what they all say," he remarked, before heading off and giving her no chance to respond.

But as she sat feeling bad about that, Mr. Dejardin—who had been standing nearby, filing some books—came over to her, remarking quietly.

"Don't let him get to you. He's always like that. Nothing pleases him," the bespeckled older man said with a smile.

"I wasn't lying, really," she said, clearly worked up about it and feeling very self conscious. "I even still have the button to sew back on," she said, though when she went to check her bag, she couldn't find it there.

"It's okay, Casey," said the silver haired librarian, touching a hand to her arm. "I believe you," he said, caressing her arm, until the sound of one of her only friends entering into the library was heard.

Nadir, the dark young fellow dressed prim and proper, put down his satchel bag on the top and nodded to Casey.

"Good day, you two," he said, as Mr. Dejardin backed away and nodded back.

"Afternoon, lad," Dejardin said, returning to his book sorting.

Nadir was a very smart boy, a little younger than Casey, but he made a good work partner. He was quiet, did his own thing, and never bothered her. He was also not the type to judge or be... weird.

"Hey, Nadir. My button fell off," she blurted out. It was as though she wanted everyone to know that it wasn't her fault, even if Mr. Alder had told her to make it look more natural and be confident about it. That was still a work in progress.

Nadir looked to her chest unflinchingly then nodded.

"I noticed," he said simply as he sat down and began to take out his work things. "Maybe you should just take a bed sheet and turn it into a toga, if you keep losing buttons at this rate," he remarked. And she wasn't sure if he was joking or not.

Nadir could be so dry.

"Heh, yea, maybe. Apparently, I need to just give up on trying to get a new uniform, anyways. They're not going to get here any time soon. What are you workin' on today?"

"Just a personal project," he said as he looked over at her, studying her, not making a great effort to avoid her cleavage. "I'm ahead on all my classes, after all. What about you?" he asked.

And it was true, though he was younger than Casey, he was brilliant. He'd been skipped grades and was at her same level, despite his youth.

"Oh, well, Mr. Alder's asked me for my thoughts on some papers for extra credit," she said, only a little bit full of herself. "What type of personal project? Don't tell me you're reading for *fun*," she teased.

Nadir shook his head as he peeled open a journal.

"No, no reading right now. I just finished doing some of that out in the gardens," he said as he took out a pencil and began to sharpen it. "Going to work on some writing," he remarked simply, pushing his glasses up his nose. "You won't be spending a lot more time in the library from now on, I bet."

She puzzled at that.

"Why not? Is Dahlia moving rooms or something?" she asked, oblivious to his implication.

"No," Nadir said, shaking his head, then blowing on his pencil tip before touching it to the page. "I just imagine you'll be way too popular to spend your time in here before long," he said casually.

"I've never been popular," she said with a roll of her eyes, looking back to the paper she was grading with a frown. "It's not my fault there's no more shipments coming in, anyways. I've been asking all over the place, but I can't make the ferry start up again, you know."

"I know," he said in that very calm, certain way of his. "But it doesn't change the fact that you're a beautiful girl who's gonna be very popular, very soon," he remarked as he began to write. His handwriting slow but exquisite.

She didn't know why he was making her so upset with that insinuation, but even when she tried to get back to grading, she was all worked up. Maybe she felt guilty, because she wanted to blossom, to experience more than just the library and classes. Maybe she wanted to be popular, to have men pay attention to her.

But she had a lot of ingrained preconceptions about what type of girl wanted those kinds of things.

She stared at the paper for a while longer before she

decided to skip that one, and move onto the next. But she couldn't focus on that one, either, and she knew she was fighting a losing battle with her attention span.

"Are you going to eat supper in the cafeteria today?" she finally asked.

Nadir gave a shrug of his shoulders.

"I guess. Why? Did you want to go do that now?" he asked her, peering over at her, his glasses glinting so much light, thanks to the setting sun pouring in through the large, three-story tall library windows.

"Yea, I'm hungry and can't focus. But if you're just getting into things, don't let me stop you," she said as she began putting the papers back in the folder and tucking it in her satchel.

Nadir pondered that a moment, as Mr. Dejardin came around the bookstacks and smiled to Casey.

"If you just want a quick snack, here," he said, the older man in his sweater-vest fishing out some foil-wrapped chocolates from his pocket and placing them in front of Casey.

"Aw, thank you, Mr. Dejardin, but I really want that pasta they're serving tonight. I've had a craving," she said. "But... can I keep these for later?"

"Of course you can," said the older man, smiling brightly and reaching out to lightly pet her red curls. "Stop by any time," he said with a smile and a wink, before heading back to his work.

Nadir was getting ready then, shooting a look in the librarian's direction.

"Yeah, let's go do supper," he said.

Casey usually loved spending time with Nadir, but

tonight she was a little sour at him for his jealous comments. Still, she knew it likely came out of a place of being afraid that they wouldn't spend so much time together, and it wasn't like he had a lot of friends, so she tried to be understanding.

"Great," she forced with a smile, tossing her bag over her shoulder after tucking the chocolates in the pocket. "I'm starved."

Five

Outside the library it was madness once more, students were pouring along the halls this way and that, but most of them were headed towards the cafeteria. If she was annoyed with Nadir, the crowd helped her, because she got separated from him pretty quickly, though she could see him back a distance, looking for her.

But up ahead, she saw the thick, muscular arm of Claud, waving in her direction as he stood in front of the cafeteria door, a warm smile on his face.

That was... weird.

Sure, she knew him, but it wasn't like they were buddies.

Still, curiosity got the better of her. Maybe he needed help with his homework again. That wouldn't be surprising. He was pretty smart, but sometimes he needed some help getting his thoughts together.

"Hi, Claud, everything alright?"

"Wow," the big guy said, looking her over from head to

toe without wasting any time on civility. "You're lookin' amazing, Casey," he said with a bright grin on his broad, chiseled face. He had the looks of a stunning old-fashioned footballer, and it helped that his top left his broad shoulders, biceps and... well, a whole lotta muscle visible. "I wanted to ask you about somethin'. Mind sittin' with me?" he asked, jerking a thumb inside as students flooded by them.

"Oh, sure. My friend's with me... somewhere back there, but I'm sure he can join too, right?" she asked, not cold hearted enough to abandon Nadir entirely.

Or maybe just feeling extra guilty about what he'd said earlier.

"Sure! The more the merrier," said Claud, as he put his giant, strong hand on her shoulder then guided her on into the cafeteria. Luckily, despite being a bit slow to beat the crowd, the friendly giant was very good at getting people to clear out of the way.

It didn't take long before they got their lunch trays and were through, heading over to a table together.

"So, tell me, Casey... you hear about what happened earlier?" he asked, trying to look very serious, but the big handsome guy's eyes kept straying back to her breasts. Even as Nadir came and sat beside them.

She smiled at Nadir before looking back at Claud. She'd almost forgotten all about him chasing that masked stranger after being around Mr. Alder.

"No, what happened this afternoon?" she asked, not entirely lying about not knowing. She didn't know most of it, after all.

Claud began to eat, his own helping several times hers,

since the cafeteria workers knew to cater to the school's prized athlete and his need for extra protein.

"So you never saw nothin' in between the girl's dorm and the academy earlier today? Some weirdo in a black getup, runnin' off?" he asked, brow furrowed a little as he gave Nadir a nod while he ate.

"Oh, someone bumped into me and knocked me down, but I didn't know them. They helped me up then said they were in a rush, so I went to Mr. Alder's office after that. Why?"

Claud's brows remained furrowed as he thought, but Nadir piped in.

"Wait, does this have something to do about the story of people saying that Declan finally got the crap beat out of him?" Nadir asked.

"Yeah," Claud responded, but Casey was reminded of how the rich brat Declan had made her life so miserable for so long. He was one of the prestige students, here because his parents qualified, not him. And he was hell to be around. He'd taunted her as scrawny and stick thin when she first arrived. Then started comparing her to a cow and remarking on her 'udders' after they grew.

There was no winning with that vile prick.

"About time. Good," said Nadir.

"Wait, what happened? Who beat up Declan?" Casey asked, suddenly very interested in the story.

"Well," began Claud, taking another big bite and finishing it before he launched into the story. "Declan was outside, you know... being a big jerk as usual, hangin' out with his crowd. When he got up on the old statue of the founder," he explained. "He was spoutin' a bunch of nasty stuff as usual when... someone threw a bottle of... somethin' at him. Hit him in the back of the head, broke. Covered him in some kinda stinky stuff, and made the guy fall off the statue."

"Wow," Nadir said, his eyes wide as he ate at a much more reasonable pace. "Okay, even better than I thought."

"Oh. So who was the guy in black? The guy that threw it?"

"That's not funny, Nadir. Declan had to be rushed to the clinic. They say he might've broken a bone in his leg," Claud chastised the younger guy, before looking to Casey. "I dunno," he said with a shrug. "I just know I wanna catch him. Whoever it is. I mean, I know Declan was a big jerk, but he could've gotten seriously hurt. And whoever did that might do it again. Only worse next time."

Casey didn't want to say what she really thought about it. It'd be too cruel. But Declan needed to be brought down a peg, and maybe next time, he'd think about what he was saying before saying it.

"That sounds scary. Sorry I can't help more. Did you think I could or something?"

"Someone just said they saw you in the area around the time," Claud said with a shrug, before his eyes drifted back to her breasts. "You're not an easy one to miss," he remarked, before eating some more.

"I say it was an unmitigated good for the whole world. Declan was scum," Nadir said definitively.

"I didn't see anyone around," she mused lightly, not disagreed with Nadir, but not encouraging him either. Still, she decided that Claud's interrogation of her was probably satisfied. She began to eat the chicken alfredo pasta with a great relish. The pasta was all freshly made, and the cream was from the cows on campus, though most of the chicken had to be bought from town, given the massive quantities needed. Still, it was a simple, divine dish that she never had back when she lived with her mother.

It was definitely one of the reasons for her sudden growth spurt.

The meal went by quietly after that, but for a point where Damien—the handsome, pierced dark boy—sang a song with his goth companions. Something about *ding dong the dick is gone*. It got a lot of glares from the rich kid's table. And Aeron, the handsome boy she'd run into earlier, got up on the table and belted out a surprisingly mournful song to Declan, but she couldn't help but notice the playful way he seemed to ham it up in mockery.

By the time the food was all done, Dahlia entered into the hall, looking so utterly confident in a way that Casey wished she could.

"Hey, good look there, sis. You hear the news?" she remarked, leaning over the table, grabbing the formerly monopolized gazes of Claud and Nadir for her own ample cleavage. "Declan is being shipped off campus. He seriously broke his leg. So, you know what that means?" she remarked with a grin, hiding none of her own glee.

"I won't be getting called a cow for a week?" Casey asked, some bitterness creeping into her usually gentle voice.

Nadir looked to Casey sympathetically. While Dahlia placed a hand on her shoulder.

"At least. No more having my butt pinched either...

when I didn't invite it," Dahlia declared, before some girls at the next table cheered at that, and Dahlia wandered off.

Everyone began to disperse then.

"I'm sure his leg will heal anyways. His parents can afford the best doctors, after all," Casey said, mostly to herself, since she was feeling a little guilty about how relieved she felt that he was gone.

"You're right," Nadir said, touching her arm lightly before he gathered his things. "Nothing to feel bad about at all. Whoever did it deserves thanks, not to be hunted down," he insisted, shooting a look to Claud.

But the big handsome himbo just grimaced a bit.

"If I had known he was such a terror, I would've set him straight. With words, not force," Claud naively insisted, before getting up and heading off as if on a mission.

Casey let out a sigh before she stood up as well, gathering her bag.

"Good luck with the writing, Nadir. I'm going back to my dorm to finish up for the night," she said, but even then, she knew that wasn't all she was going to be doing.

It had been a long, exciting day, and she was looking forward to doing a little sleuthing and finding out just *what* happened at The Pit after dark.

Six

The hallways were still walked by students and staff after supper, but it was less intense than the meal time rush. And Casey was able to follow Dahlia's directions, heading off down the big main corridor, following along with other people, until she saw that dingy supply closet and made her turn.

Her high heeled Mary-Janes made some loud sounds, especially once she went inside the room proper. There was nothing there but some old boxes and furniture not in use, and everything sounded so much louder there.

But she flipped the switch and searched in the dim light of the dangling bulb, until finally she found the thing Dahlia had mentioned. The box in question, was luckily empty and easy to push aside. And the hatch—while too short for some—was tall enough for her to fit through with just a bit of ducking.

Once through, she found herself in a warm mainte-nance tunnel, with pipes around. It headed in two directions, but one was barred with a grate. So that left... just the one way.

Following along in the dim lighting—for it only seemed to come from dim little emergency lighting hidden amidst the pipes and wires—she carried on and on. And she very soon got the feeling of being in some kind of hidden under-world, beneath the school itself. It gave her chills.

The sound of a door opening and closing up ahead didn't help, and made her pause a moment.

But once she came to an intersection of sorts, she looked around. The tunnels branched off in four direc-tions, including the one she came from. Two of the remainder were wide open, but the final had an old, rusted metal door. It must've been the one she heard open earlier.

She was so nervous, but so excited. Her curiosity had been eating at her ever since Damien had mentioned it to her. She felt the rush of blood as her heart began to pound, and for just a second, she entertained the thought of turning back. Of going to her safe dorm room, and hiding under her sheets, ignoring the throbbing need between her thighs.

But if ever she were to take a chance, now was the time.

She went to the door, putting her hand on the lever, and began to pull.

The old, rusty lever moved with a loud high-pitched sound. Her gentle touch only seemed to draw that out in fact. But once it was open, she could hear the distant sound of music coming from further down the tunnel. So, she stepped in, letting the heavy door swing shut behind her.

But she had barely begun to walk, when a voice disturbed her.

"Hey," he said, as a cigarette lit up in the dark. "Stop right there," he said, stepping out of the dark alcove. The guy was done up in all black, his skin pale, but he wore black eyeshadow and lipstick.

Casey instinctively put her hands up, as if she were under arrest, before realizing how silly she must look.

Immediately, she blushed.

"Oh, hi. I'm not a narc. Damien actually sent for me," she said, as if that were the password to get in. She wasn't quite sure why she was whispering it, though.

The guy looked more than a bit amused by her and was laughing before she even got to the part about Damien.

"Yeah, I'm sure you're not," he said, stepping out, a hand in his pocket as he sized her up, staring at her tits for a while. "Tell you what, suck my dick and I'll sponsor you in. What do you say?" he asked, grinning as the cigarette dangled from the corner of his lips.

Her eyes widened in shock at that.

"Wh-what?" she sputtered, uncertain if he was joking or not. What had she gotten herself into?! She barely even knew what a dick *was* let alone how or why she'd suck one!

"C'mon. It'll be real easy, I promise. I'm about ready to pop as is," he said as he reached down, unbuckling his thick, studded belt.

But as Casey was stunned into shock, a voice arose down the tunnel.

"Fuck off, Trent," came a familiar voice, as she saw Damien's silhouette coming towards her. "Keep that nasty thing in your pants, unless someone asks for it, huh?" he said, as he came to Casey, putting his arm around her, resting his hand on her shoulder. "You okay?" he asked, as he led her down the corridor.

"Yea but... that was weird, right?" she asked, still too in shock about what Trent had said and done to even really appreciate his sudden touch. It was just so casual and smooth, so it didn't take her long to warm right back up to him.

Looking to the taller man, she saw he'd changed his look a bit more himself. He still had on his dyed-black school jacket, but the shirt beneath... well it was no longer beneath, he was bare there. His six pack abs and pecs on display, with some black ink marked there in strange, ominous patterns as he guided her towards the source of the music.

"Yeah, it was. Sorry you had to deal with that. I'll make him pay for being so rude and vulgar with you later, okay?" Damien said, rubbing her shoulder and arm. She belatedly noticed he'd swiped the cigarette from Trent, and was taking a puff from it himself.

"You look really handsome tonight," she said, before cringing at herself. Handsome? Really? "I mean... hot." She was no good at flirting, that much was for sure. And while he'd gotten more comfortable, she was still trying not to hyper fixate on how much her top was straining. Without the aid of that upper button, her breasts were really fighting to get free, but her other tops were in the wash, and all the clothes she'd brought from home were much too small for her now.

But instead of laughing at her stumbling attempts, Damien smiled unevenly, plucking the cigarette from his mouth.

"Thanks babe," he said in his dark, seductive voice. And he pointedly looked down at her ready-to-burst free cleavage. "You're lookin' incredibly hot tonight yourself," he said, as he let his hand transition from her arm... to her waist and hip, that strong hand squeezing the bare skin between her skirt and blouse.

"Want a puff?" He offered her the cigarette just as they rounded the corner, overlooking a bit central area from where the music came from. The floor was grating, and there were many little nooks along the sides. Many covered off with curtains, or makeshift walls of cardboard or plywood. But at the center were some old pieces of furniture that belonged to the school, situated around the practically ancient boombox. An old school TV was there, with a DVD player that some were watching.

A bunch of people were just hanging out, mostly goths like Damien. Lounging upon the sofa, the chairs, or a heap of cushions.

"Uhm, okay," she said, though she'd never smoked before in her life. But she'd decided that tonight was a night for experimenting and trying new things, and she wasn't willing to back down already. She accepted the smoke and tried to mimic how he held it, how he puffed it, but instantly she began to cough as she handed him the cigarette back. "It's strong," she said, having no idea that cigarettes didn't really have 'strengths'.

Someone snickered at her in the room, but not Damien. He smiled and took it back, caressing her hip and side.

"Yeah, takes a bit of getting used to," he said, as her eyes noticed in the slightly brighter light of the main hall that his pants were hanging so low, she could see a curious little trail of hair traveling down, just above his groin.

"Hey everyone, this here is Casey. And she's my personal guest. So everyone be nice to her, and don't be a Trent. Hear me?" Damien said, and most of them smiled and said: "Welcome Casey!" in a jokey kinda family greeting sorta way.

But even though it felt a little silly, it also felt nice. Really, really nice.

"Hi everyone," she said a bit shyly, before her gaze was drawn back to Damien. "So you just, like... hang out here?"

"Yeah. It's like our own little slice of heaven," he joked as he nodded towards one of the alcoves that was walled off with actual boards. "If you wanna ease into things, we can crash in my personal office. No need to throw you in on the communal couch on your first night," he said. "How's that sound? You and me chillin' for a while?"

"I'd like that a lot," she confessed, her heart racing once more. The idea of spending alone time with him... It wasn't even a dream come true, because her dreams were never so... wild. After all, she figured she'd go on dates with nice country boys who studied hard and maybe went on to be a veterinarian or something. Not a guy with a lip ring and some edgy tattoos.

"Perfect. I was hopin' you'd say that," Damien remarked, squeezing her side then heading on over towards his 'office'. He plucked up a bottle from the table at the center of the room as they went, then slid the door aside.

It was an old mesh sliding fence at one point, but the wood panels had been added in more recently. And inside? Well, it wasn't an office. Not in any traditional sense, not

46

like Mr. Alder's office. It was a dimly lit little nook, with a worn but nice-looking old sofa, a radio, table and a small TV.

"Make yourself comfortable," He urged her, as he put the bottle on the table, then slid the door shut behind them, shutting out so much of the loud, angry music that permeated the place, but keeping it as a backdrop. He tapped his cigarette into the ashtray, before perching it on the edge of it.

She went to the far side of the couch, smoothing out her skirt beneath her and crossing her legs daintily at her ankles.

"I'm really glad you were here. I would've probably run out if you hadn't spared me from Trent," Casey confessed as she looked up at him with an appreciative, slightly hungry stare.

"I wouldn't blame you," he said, pushing a hand into his pocket, which only caused his low-hanging pants to dip even more, and she suddenly felt a kinship risk with her own constant state of nearly spilling out of her clothes. "I'll make it up to you though, I promise," he said as he came over to the couch with her, and made no effort to space them out.

Damien sat right beside her, with one leg taking up the rest of the sofa as he put his arm around her. He took up the bottle, bit the cork and pulled it out before taking a swig.

"Wanna try some?" he offered, holding the bottle to her. "It's strong, so don't take a big mouthful, you'll overdo it," he cautioned kindly. And she could see that in the dim light, either he was wearing a bit of dark makeup, or it was just the lighting making it look like he was.

"Wine?" she asked, hesitating as she took the bottle from him.

"Yeah. Not the best, but it's hard to get any liquor up here," he told her cracking a smile. "You really do look good. Especially when you cut loose a little," he said, reaching to her red curls, lightly touching them.

She resisted the urge to tell him her button fell off, and instead gave him a bright, appreciative smile.

"You think so?" she asked before taking a small sip of the wine. It reminded her of the old prune juice her mom had from time to time, and she made a little bit of a face before taking another sip and handing him back the bottle.

He smiled at her approvingly, then took a much more generous swig of it himself, licking his lips.

"I really do think so. Even if we had the internet here, I'm not sure I could pick out a hotter chick with all the search engines in the world," he said, his eyes rarely leaving her. Whether it was staring at her tits, or appreciating her face and hair, or over all figure... Damien certainly didn't hesitate to leave her feeling appreciated. "I never thought you were the type to wanna come here. What made you decide to pay me a visit here, huh?"

"I don't know... you just seemed interesting," she answered honestly. There was a lot more she wanted to say, of course, but she was far too shy for that. Even with the welcome heat of her tiny sips of alcohol. She turned a little towards him, her emerald eyes finding his.

"Why did you invite me here? Aren't you and Dahlia together?"

Seven

"We're not a couple," Damien said right away. "We were just havin' some fun," he said with a shrug of his shoulder, as his school jacket—which seemed a size or two too big for him—slipped from his shoulder a bit. "I don't have a girl right now or anythin'. What about you?" he asked, eying her as he took the bottle back, having another sip and offering it back.

"I don't have a girl. Or a guy. I mean, I never really have... I've always just studied and..." she trailed off, taking another sip of the wine, already feeling a bit heady from it. "Sometimes there's just this heat that rises up in me and won't go away no matter how much I want it to, though. And Dahlia... it's just so easy for her."

Damien listened and nodded along slightly.

"You think? Maybe she just worked as hard at it as you did your books," he offered lightly. And when his hand came over, she thought it was for the wine. But instead, he squeezed her thigh, caressing it's smooth, creamy skin rather

49

openly, nudging her skirt a little higher as he did. "So, you heard me and Dahlia... saw me as I came out. And you thought... I could help you with that heat, huh?"

"I don't know," she laughed nervously, her pale skin flushing with embarrassment. "I don't want to presume anything. I just wanted to see what it was like. And you were so sweet, and your eyes were so nice..." she confessed, the alcohol goading her along a little. She looked down at his hand on her leg, and that throbbing between her legs became more incessant. "You don't have to do anything you don't want to," she said reluctantly.

He didn't laugh at her, but he grinned evenly, and squeezed her thigh.

"Wanna know a secret, Sunshine?" he said, leaning in, as his fingers sank into her soft inner thigh flesh. His voice husky and gravelly in her ear. "There aren't many things I can think of I wouldn't be happy to do with you. And that includes everything I ever did or wanted to do with Dahlia," he murmured, before licking her ear slowly, then lightly nipping her lobe in his teeth.

She whimpered, unable to hide the warmth of delight that was marking every bit of her pale skin. It was insane how much that one touch ignited her nerve endings and made her sex throb with need.

"I'm not doing anything wrong, right? Dahlia knows you're not together, and... I mean, of course she won't be mad. I asked her right after you left, so she must know you invited me, and she still told me."

"Hey, if you wanna break and go ask her before we do anything, you can. But..." he said softly, and her indecision regrettably resulted in his hand lifting from her thigh, so close to the source of the heat in her panties. He brushed some of her red curls back, tilted her head towards him with that strong, steady hand of his. "You know what your friend is up to, don't you?" he asked, brow furrowed a bit. "Like... I'm sure I'm not the only guy she's taken there, am I?" he asked, brow raised.

"Dahlia is amazing. I know," she said with a nod of her head. "I don't want to break. It was so hard working up my courage to come the first time," she confessed, her hand gingerly reached out for his, slowly guiding it back to her leg. "I don't want to leave."

"She is," he said. "But I think you're a little more amazing," he remarked, as his hand this time didn't stop at just squeezing her thigh. He leaned in, tilting his head as he moved to press his lips to hers. And instead of just fondling her thigh, two of his fingers curled up, and began to caress over her slit through her panties.

She let out a squeak of surprise as she melted back into the sofa, her mouth parting against his.

It all happened so fast, but he was firm and steady, his motions clearly practiced. She couldn't imagine touching herself, and more than that, she couldn't imagine being able to make herself feel the way he was making her feel.

Her arm slipped around his neck, her thick thighs parting for his hand.

Damien leaned into her deeper, his lips capturing her lower morsel, suckling it softly as his skilled fingers caressed that needy, soaking part of her. The panties were utterly soaked through after another torturous day without relief from her longings, but he didn't comment on it, he just kissed and suckled at her lips, and continued to send such tingling bliss throughout her whole body as he pressed in against her slit, then nudged at her sensitive clit above.

If she had realized how good it would feel, there would be no way that she would still be a virgin. It was as though all the pleasure in her entire life was just culminating in this one moment, gathering at the tip of his finger. He was working her body as if he were a skilled magician, and she squirmed eagerly against him.

She wasn't a skilled kisser. After all, this was her first kiss. But she tried to respond to his motions, mimicking him as her tongue danced with his.

Luckily Damien seemed patient, and didn't rush the moment. And soon she felt his tongue lightly probing into her mouth, caressing her own tongue. He took his time, but then his hand left her slit, sliding up beneath her skirt further, about ready to plunge inside her panties, when he paused...

"Fuck. You are so incredibly hot, babe," Damien husked to her, kissing her lips again, then again, as if he had trouble drawing himself away from them in the moment. "I just... I gotta check with you," he said, lighting caressing her pussy through her cotton panties as he looked her in the eye. "How far do you wanna go with this? Because... dammit," he said, as if cursing himself for being so nice about it, "I wanna go all the way with you. But I don't wanna push you too far if you're not ready."

"All the way?" she asked, not quite sure what he was getting at. She'd never looked up sex stuff before moving to this school, and she only had the vaguest concepts of such things. But the way he said it... the way he wanted it?

That delighted her to no end.

"What did you do with Dahlia?"

He looked at her with such a fiery intensity in his dark eyes, and he bit his lower lip a moment as he moaned lowly.

"Fuck. What did I do with her? I took this part of her here," he said, nudging his two fingers at the entrance of her slit, pushing those panties up with them just a bit. "And I did it..." he raised his hand to his face, licked his fingers clean of the honey on them, before taking hold of her fingers, and guiding them to the thick bulge in his pants, pressing her dainty grasp to that bulging cock beneath. "With this. You feel that?" he asked, as his dick throbbed and jumped beneath her hand.

She had some vague ideas about a man having a hardness, but she'd never felt it before. Not knowingly, at least. And once he put her hand there, her curiosity took over, and she began rubbing and squeezing him, trying to be slow and gentle about it, just in case she was going to hurt him.

"And that's what made her scream?"

He nodded his head, groaning lowly as he shut his eyes and took another swig from the wine bottle before placing it back on the table.

"Yeah, it was," he husked out, before undoing the top button of his pants, then unzipping his pants. He took hold of her wrist, then guided her fingers in under his briefs beneath, to feel the raw, fiery heat of his hard cock. That veiny beast throbbing, pulsating with need that vaguely reminded her of her own heated need between her legs. "And I can do the same for you if you want... if you're up for it. But we can start out smaller too, if you like," he husked, leaning in, kissing her slender neck, as his hand went back to her pussy, caressing it through her panties again.

"No," she said immediately. "I want to know what Dahlia felt. I want to feel that. To feel this..." she purred, her hand grasping his cock a bit awkwardly, "inside of me." Just the thought of it, the fantasy of it, was working her up to heights she never knew she could survive. She was being so reckless, but he felt so good, and he was so kind, and sexy...

Besides, Dahlia sounded like she really liked him. Even more than most of the others she'd had Casey stand guard for.

He had definitely made her moan and scream the loudest at least. And to feel that thick, pulsating, veiny girth in her hand... part of her instinctively felt why. But soon, he was pushing his fingers inside her own panties, and the raw touch of his hand on her sensitive little folds amped things up a lot more.

"Fuck I was hoping you'd say that," he rumbled, kissing her again, moving up her neck to her cheek, then her lips. He frenched her deeply, letting his tongue slide into her mouth, as his fingers... well, one of them followed suit, slowly stretching her tight little virgin slit open as they sat, touching each other's junk on the couch.

Her free arm wrapped around him as they became more and more entangled together on the couch, until she was practically sitting in his lap. She was naive, but she'd always been a quick learner, and she began paying attention to his own moans and sighs, and soon she was stroking his shaft in a much more practiced manner.

That thick, hot cock of his spurt some sticky pre onto her fingers, giving her a surprising reward as she got so into it though. And he leaned into her, kissing her more passionately as his own finger slipped in deeper, deeper, stretching out her slick pussy with the addition of a second digit. And she felt the curious strain of being stretched open wider than she was ever used to, as they touched.

"I'm... I'm sure it's obvious," she breathed between their kisses. "But I've never been with a man before. So, I'll need you to tell me what to do, okay? I want to make you feel good too," she said, opening a Pandora's Box she might one day regret. But through it all, her hips kept grinding, her hand continued stroking him, and she leaned back, her legs spreading to let him delve deeper into her valley.

His eyes opened, and he looked at her, swallowing heavily as his dick swelled in her grasp.

"Fuck," He rumbled, before lifting her up off his lap, then standing. He laid her back down, lengthwise over the couch. Then reached up in under her skirt. He hooked both hands into the sides of her panties, and peeled them off her entirely. All as she got the gorgeous view of his stunningly toned body, with the view of his thick, hard cock, and heavy balls protruding through the V-shaped opening of his pants.

"I'll take over. If you trust me," he husked, as he looked to the table, nudging things out of the way as he looked for something, his cock impatiently twitching and throbbing.

"Why wouldn't I trust you?" she asked with a curious tilt of her head. "You're the expert here. I'm just an eager student." She smiled widely as she looked at him, admiring his body with a lust filled gaze. "What are you looking for?"

"Condom," he muttered, knocking a stack of old magazines over in his search. "Unless..." he looked back to her, "is it okay if I go in raw?"

Eight

"I'll pull out if you want me to," Damien added on.

She furrowed her brows as she looked at him, then relaxed back into the sofa.

"I trust you," she said, as if clarifying her earlier answer.

His thick cock was jutting out so tantalizingly beneath his gorgeous body as he turned his attention back to her, then began to unbutton her top instead of search for protection.

She watched as the strained blouse began to pop open as he undid each of her buttons, revealing her overfilled bra, her nipples peaking out from the edge of it without him even having to touch them. "Sorry, I know they're big," she said, genuinely apologetic. Declan had managed to make her self conscious about *that* too.

Damien only momentarily looked confused by that apology, but he then reached in around behind her, and undid the clasp of her bra more easily than even she knew how.

"You don't have to apologize to me for anythin', babe,"

he reassured her, before sliding her bra off, to let her ample yet perky breasts free. Those two hard, strong hands of his went to her bare breasts then, cupping each. "Fuck, they **are** huge... perfect and huge," he clarified, as his thumbs caressed near to her areola, carefully squeezing and fondling her supple mounds of tit flesh as he loomed over her hard and eager. "The best pair of tits I've ever laid eyes on, let alone hands," he husked, before bending down, and placing a kiss on one teat, then sliding his tongue around the other.

Since her growth spurt, they'd been crazy sensitive, but she had no idea just how sensitive they could be. A thrill went through her, and her pussy began to pulse even quicker. She moaned with delight, the alcohol and the low din of the music making her forget that there was a crowd in the next room.

But then it occurred to her, she'd heard some light pants and moans coming from behind other curtains when she'd arrived. Nothing like the passionate sounds of Dahlia and Damien, but similar. So maybe it was okay. Maybe it was what was expected.

Damien took his time, fondling, caressing, exploring her breasts. He seemed so intensely enraptured with them as he kissed and licked. Until finally lightly swirled his tongue around one sensitive nipple, then gave it a brief suckle until she squealed. He pulled off her breasts, then pushed his pants and boxers down, until his round, tight ass was bare.

"Fuck I wanted to take my time with you even more, but I am losing my mind at your hotness, Sunshine," he groaned, leaning in and kissing her lips as his thick cock jabbed at her mound.

"I'm ready," she whispered against his mouth, and even though she wasn't experienced, she knew she was ready. She wanted whatever it was that happened next. To feel herself meld together with him, until she was gasping and moaning for more. Her arms wrapped around his neck as she stared up at his eyes with affection and warmth. "I want this, Damien, I promise."

He groaned and angled his hips, until the head of his cock was trailing along her slit. The tingling from their loins meeting sending sparks throughout her whole body.

"I want this too. So fuckin' badly," he husked, kissing her as he got down, spread her legs open wider, lifted one up, then pulled back, their lips parting. He shut his eyes, used his free hand to caress her cheek and cup her face as he began to prod the bulbous, glistening, purple crown of his manhood against her pussy. That tiny pink vulva stretching around his girth as he began to ease himself into her.

She was blissfully wet, the entire day having teased her to such a heightened state, but still, she was a virgin. And because of that, she was tight.

It made her moan as he kept up that firm, steady pace, until his swollen crown was lodged inside her. She looked down between them, her breasts parted in the centre, giving her a perfect view of his cock as he helped himself to her innocent pussy, raw and reckless.

Damien moaned and looked down too, the two of them staring at the lewd sight where her pussy and his cock began to become one. He groaned, running a hand down over his light treasure trail, to the base of his shaft, then along it to her slit.

"Fuck it's so much better raw," he grunted, as he let his

thumb tease her clit a moment, before he began to ease more of his girth into her. "How's that feel?" he grunted out.

"So good," she whimpered, and it was so intense, she felt like she was at the brink of tears.

Her body trembled, and she held onto him with her fingers sometimes roaming up his head, or down along his shoulders.

"God, I can't even tell you how good you feel," she breathed out.

"Oh, fuck babe," he said, pressing his forehead to hers, kissing her lips. "I haven't even really started..." he huffed out, the promise of his words—that what was to come, would be far more than this—was more than she could reconcile at that moment. But he rocked his hips a bit, slowly working his girth into her deeper, his pulsating shaft filling her up more and more with each new pump.

"But first..." he said, just as his cock hilted itself inside her, and she finally knew what it was like to feel... whole. "Before I start... do you want me to pull out?" he asked her, letting his dick rest inside her deeply, as he asked her that simple, direct question.

Of course, he had no idea of the depths of her religious upbringing. How naive it had left her. How the phrase 'pull out' in that moment didn't mean to her what it did to him. It didn't translate as: 'do you want me to pull out before I cum and risk knocking you up'. No. It only meant one thing to her: did she want his cock out of her at that moment.

And she really, certainly, truly did not want that.

"Of course not," she said, her legs beginning to wrap

around his hips. It was a bit more comfortable, at first, but then she realized there were other advantages. He seemed to have a lot easier time pushing in an extra inch with her in that position, after all, and that took her breath away.

So, her legs tightened around him, her dark stockings and high heeled Mary-Janes locked around his hips and thighs as she offered up her fertile depths to his hard, virile cock.

Damien's spine arched, his shoulders back as he moaned deep and loud. The intensity of her tight, virgin pussy squeezing around his shaft, her long, shapely legs urging him in extra deep... he was nearly overwhelmed. It was more exciting than any of the other girls he was with.

"Ohh fuck, babe... you feel so goddamn good," he grunted, one of his hands going to her chest, grasping a breast as he began to pump his hips. Easing her into it at first, with the slow slaps of their loins together.

He must've been around her age, but his experience was far and beyond anything her naive mind could've conjured up. It seemed to her that he knew just where to touch, just how to touch it, how deep to go, and how quickly. Of course, she was a pretty open book about what she liked, given the soft moans and whimpers, and the throatier coos that escaped whenever he pushed her past the point she thought she'd break.

Her pink nipples were so hard, and the one he was grasping ached under his touch. With every thrust they bounced hard atop her slender ribs, and she gripped the couch for support.

He squeezed her large breast, pinching her nipple between his thumb and hand. And it might've been too much for her in that moment, except his thrusting had amped up at about the same time. His hips crashing into her faster, harder. His balls slapping her thick, bubbly ass as he pounded down into her raw and hard. His rippling physique tensing up as the couch groaned beneath them.

"Ohh fuck you are so goddamn tight!" he groaned out, shivering all over. He shed his jacket, so he was almost fully nude over her, his toned body glistening in the dim light as he rolled with each pounding thrust.

"You feel so good," she cried out, unfamiliar pulses of energy travelling along her limbs. She twitched, and she had to tighten her legs around his hips, strengthen her grasp on the couch. She felt that if she didn't, she might just spasm off the sofa all together, even with him pounding into her like that.

She didn't know it, but that budding sensation in her clit was rapidly sending her reeling towards a pleasure she could never have fathomed.

With Dahlia, Damien had lasted far longer. Their tryst had been ages for poor Casey outside the door, listening and guarding. But without a condom, that tight, virginal squeeze of hers was wearing him down faster than he was used to.

"Fuck! Dammit you feel too fuckin' good," he rumbled, releasing her breast, to reach down, his thumb pressing upon her clit, helping press and prod it as he grunted and moaned loudly. That thick cock of his beginning to swell up even thicker, as his own release approached.

She knew less about what was happening in his body than even her own, but she knew she wanted it. The way his thumb touched her, combined with his even, hard thrusts... it was far too much for the innocent young woman to handle.

She screamed, not holding anything back as she clawed at the couch, her body thrashing as her very first orgasm ripped through her.

And the slightly older, more experienced Damien moaned loudly, thrusting into her deep and hard as he threw back his head and...

"F-Fuck!" he shouted, as he began to cum. That thick cock of his swelling, the bulbous plum-coloured crown erupting with thick, virile seed. So many long strands of that cum blasting into her unprotected depths, flooding her, filling her. There was so much of it, despite his earlier fuck with Dahlia. That tight virgin pussy of hers milking out every last spurt of seed he had as he bucked into her, groaning loudly, gasping out.

She didn't know about the risk of pregnancy or anything like that. In that moment, Casey knew nothing except pleasure, and her screams were slow to die down. He felt so good, and every throb of his cock sent another jolt down through her.

It wasn't until he stilled for a few moments that her legs began to soften around him, unlocking him from her.

He was panting still, his eyes opening a crack as he looked down at her. And he leaned in, kissing her slowly, sensually. In no rush to disentangle from her. He even gave her a few more pleasing rolls of his hips as his cum pooled deep within her, locked there.

"You felt so fuckin' amazing," he said finally in his gravelly voice.

"Did I perform well?" she asked, her emerald eyes lidded as she stared up at him.

"Yeah, you really did," he husked, reaching a hand up to cup her cheek, caressing it as he kissed her some more. "You really did great. I just wanna keep fuckin' you. Again, and again, and again..." he rumbled, before kissing her more deeply, his tongue delving into her mouth.

His praise softened her shoulders, and she melted into him again, passionately returning his kiss as his seed continued to gather within her depths. It just felt warm and wanted, and she held him against her like a lover.

"I'm so glad I came here tonight, Damien."

"So am I," he husked, caressing her cheek some more. "I really wanna do this again sometime. If you're down," he said, his dark eyes probing her gaze. "There's more I can show you. Lots more," he said.

"I'd like that," she confessed, her eyes crinkling with her smile. "And... I like it when you call me Sunshine. It's sweet."

He grinned at that.

"Sunshine it is then," he husked, kissing her lips once more, slow and sensually. He broke away then, giving her a deep, meaningful look. "Hey... how do you feel about being my—"

Nine

Even down in the bowels of the Pit, the clanging noise of the nighttime bell that let every student know it was time to get back to their dorms or else face punishment, was felt like a pang of anxiety itself.

The moment was shattered, and he pulled back from her.

"Aw fuck. Feels sooner every night," he muttered.

"I'm usually in bed by now," Casey said, sitting up before she squealed. "Oh my God, I made such a mess! I'm so sorry!" she said, standing up instinctively. Of course, that meant that seconds later his cum was dribbling down her inner thighs and staining her thigh-high stockings. "Oh God, it's never been this bad before."

"It's okay, Sunshine. Don't worry about it," he said, not showing her sign of urgency as he caressed her cheek and kissed her lips again. "Come back again as soon as you like," he said, his dark eyes glittering. "You're my favourite," he said warmly, before reaching down and lazily tugging up his trousers., unconcerned about the big mess that their loins were left in, compared to her.

She smiled at him as well, but then quickly began to get redressed. Hooking her bra was always a pain, and even more so when she had an audience, it seemed. Luckily, he was happy to help, and after she pushed as much of the breast flesh back into her cups, she tugged her blouse shut once more.

"Where are my panties?" she asked, glancing around.

"Shit. I dunno," Damien said, lifting a cushion, crouching down, peering under the table and couch. But it was so dark it was hard to see anything. "I thought I dropped 'em right on the sofa," he said.

"Heh, they're probably next to the... what was it? Condom?" she giggled, before the tension knit back in her shoulders. She was worried she'd be late. Caught in the halls after hours.

The horror.

"Well... I can pick them up tomorrow?" she asked more casually.

"Of course," he said, smiling at her, his head tilted as he rubbed her thigh, up in under her skirt, then squeezed her backside. "I like the idea of you coming back here without any panties on anyhow," he said with a grin, flashing her a wink. "It'll make it a whole lot easier to bend you over and show you another way of doin' it."

"Another way?" she asked, unable to hide her excitement as she nodded. "Okay. Uhm, I have an assignment to hand in after class, but I'll try to get by after that," she said with a smile. She leaned in, kissing him passionately before she pulled away. "I gotta get back. But... thanks for being my first, Damien, and not holding it against me. I appreciate it."

He kissed her back, then picked up his jacket, slinging it over his shoulder as he went to the door, and slid it open for her.

"Any time," he said, reaching in under her skirt and giving her ass a little squeeze. "And don't worry, you've still got a few minutes to get back," he reassured her, clearly not as bothered by it all as she was.

But she wasted little time in scurrying out that door, only pausing to give him a smile and a wave before rushing to the exit. She didn't even really take time to say goodbye to the lingering crowd, just shouting out a 'Good night' as she rushed past.

The journey out of the maintenance tunnels and up into the school was mostly brief, especially since others were going, and the door was held open for her. Though there was a bit of a holdup there, as it served as a kind of bottleneck.

But once she was up above ground again, it went smoother.

She wasn't used to making her way back to her room after the first chimes, so it was strange to see how many other students were also hurrying on back from across campus. But at a point, she got a curious feeling of being watched.

It was just as she was crossing the open campus, in the outdoor area between the main building and the girl's dorm, that she got that tingling feeling. And she peered back.

She was near the end of the crowd of girls, so there were

just a few behind her. But beyond them, she saw a dark, hooded figure looking her way, who then turned and vanished into the blackness of night.

It was curious, and if she weren't in a rush, that curiosity might've gotten the better of her.

But as it was, she felt like she was breaking the rules, even moving with a crowd, and knew that feeling wouldn't fade until she was back in her dorm room.

Besides, without her panties on, the breeze was titillating her way more than it should, and she was nearly praying for a strong gust that would lift her skirt and flash the entire school.

She couldn't give in to *that* particular desire.

Was that how it worked? She had hoped that doing it with Damien would make the urges go away.

Or was she?

She pondered that on her way back up to her room. But once she reached her floor, she saw Dahlia speaking with some other girls, looking rather animated. But then one of them pointed Casey's way, and the dark-haired girl turned, eyes widening.

"Casey!" she said, and the two then went into their joint room after the count was taken, shutting the door. "I got all panicked! I've never come back and you've not been here already," she said.

"I lost track of time, Dahlia, I'm sorry. I didn't mean to make you worry," Casey said honestly as she went to her small dresser and grabbed her night clothes. Luckily those were a little more shapeless when she'd first got them, so now they hugged her curves while still giving her enough room to breath. "Hey, you're not, like, dating Damien, right?"

"What?" Dahlia said, as she took out her earring and glanced over her shoulder at Casey. "No, of course not. Like, he's hot, and a great lay, but... no. I'm not really into 'dating' right now. I'm just having some fun and... doing things my own way," she added with a mischievous lilt to the end. "Why?"

Casey flushed from head to toe under the incredibly mild interrogation.

"I don't know. I mean, I *knew* you weren't into dating, but I just wanted to make sure because, well... He invited me to the Pit and I went and it was... nice. That's all," Casey said, but she was underselling it a lot. It was way more than nice.

She just didn't have any polite words for it.

"I thought that was why you asked about it earlier. I was—" she paused, then her eyes went a bit wider. "Wait... you seriously went? And you liked it?" she finished taking out her last earring and turned, leaning back against her little desk to look at Casey. "Oh my god... my bestie is growing up," she teased lightly, placing her hands over her heart before coming up and hugging Casey from behind.

Casey was already bright red, yet she couldn't help but giggle at Dahlia's exuberance.

"He took me to his 'office' and we just... you know. I just got tired of listening on the other side of the door and not knowing what I was missing out on."

Dahlia paused, her eyes wide as she looked to Casey.

"Wait... oh my god, you've got to tell me everything," she said, her jaw literally dropping.

Casey was feeling like she'd suddenly stepped in way over her head as she stared at her bestie.

"Dahlia! You're making me blush! You know more about guys than anyone else I know," she gushed. "I just... we went all the way."

If she thought Dahlia's jaw had dropped before, it doubly dropped then.

"All the way...? You didn't even start with like... blowjobs or handy-J's?" Dahlia asked, wide-eyed and stunned.

"What?" Casey asked, her brows furrowed in confusion. "No. Some guy named Trent asked me to suck his... you know... but Damien came up and told him to eff off."

Dahlia looked quite stunned, sizing up Casey as if she were a totally new person.

"I don't know what you did with my friend Casey, but... damn girl. I mean, I really think you should've come to me for advice first, and eased into things. Y'know, a handjob here," she simulated a jerk off motion, "a blowie there, but... damn. I'm proud of you," she said with a smile.

"I... I liked going all the way. It felt really good. But maybe next time I'll try the other things, see what I like best," Casey mused. "But... thanks, Dahlia. I am sorry I worried you, but it was worth it."

Dahlia stared at her a moment more, then gave her a hug before they retired for the evening.

The next day was back to class however, and despite the intensity of the previous day... the strange mundanity of class felt so odd.

Casey found herself in math class at the worst of it. The miserable Mr. Mullard, the only teacher who Casey truly despised, was in full force, trying to embarrass her. Calling her out for making a mistake—when she was sure the answer was right!

He even called her to the front to show her workings then, and it all worked out! He couldn't demonstrate the actual "error" he claimed she made, but stepped in, erased what she wrote then said:

"So, everyone try a little harder to not stumble into the same pitfall as Miss Casey here," he said snidely, as the bell rang and everyone was dismissed.

"That guy is such a jerk," Nadir said as they walked through the halls to their next class. "You were one-hundred percent right, Casey," he remarked.

"Thank you," she said, still frowning a bit as they walked. "I was really starting to second guess myself. But I think he just hates it when his students are smart. Guys like that should never have become a teacher," she sighed. "Hey, you didn't hear if Claud found that guy after, did you?"

"No. And I hope he doesn't either," Nadir said as they moved along through the crowd. "Declan was a tyrant, and it was about time someone toppled him. As cruel as he was to you, you certainly weren't the only one he terrorized. If only he'd go after a few more bullies and brutes around here, like that guy in black," Nadir said.

"Maybe it'll be a warning, and people will rein themselves or their friends in. At least for a while. You know, just in case the masked vigilante strikes again," Casey said, a little over the top. She was in good spirits, and even though she had changed into a new blouse, she still had the top few buttons undone, just like her busted top. It was starting to feel a little less... awkward as the day wore on.

"Well, let's hope. See ya Casey," Nadir said as they parted ways, their classes diverging.

After that came gym class for her, and today it was being held out in the field. Casey headed to the girl's locker room to get changed. Unfortunately, the only person she really knew in the class was Claud, but that did nothing to help her in the girl's locker room.

Especially when that catty Leslie was there.

"Hey there, Casey," she said in her nasally, mocking voice as she was at her own locker. "Surprised you even show up to gym anymore. I guess Mr. Grieg is the one teacher you haven't sucked off yet, huh?" she said, jealousy of her grades bubbling forth.

Casey made a face at her.

"Why would I need to do *that* when I could just do my school work?" Casey retorted, not quite the skilled master of cutting comebacks.

Truthfully, Casey didn't care a lot for gym after her growth spurt. She didn't even own a sports bra before, and her breasts made running or jumping a challenge. Dahlia showed her how to use a bandage to give herself some support, but it really wasn't the best solution.

Luckily today wasn't going to be anything like track. They were just out to take advantage of the nice weather, according to Mr. Grieg for some push-ups and stretching.

"You're just a dumb bimbo," said Leslie as she slammed her locker shut.

Ten

Leslie stormed out, leaving Casey's mouth parted in a silent protest. It wasn't until several moments had passed that Casey muttered, "I'm not a bimbo." She really hated when people had the wrong idea about her. She prided herself on being open and honest, but still, some of the other students could be so mean.

She grabbed her outfit out of the locker, and just like her normal clothes, the t-shirt and shorts had begun to look almost comical on her. Her white ringer tee had become a belly top, and her navy shorts looked more like panties than shorts. She couldn't say that she hadn't noticed that most of the guys in her class didn't have a problem with it, but the girls like Leslie definitely did.

She tied the bandage around her chest, not constricting herself so much as just trying to keep her tits more or less in place, and tugged on the white t-shirt overtop. Her legs were pale as she pulled on the shorts, some freckles on her thighs from where she'd burned once before.

Stepping into her white sneakers, she pulled her ringlets back into twin ponytails, and went out into the yard.

Come to think of it, Leslie never had a problem with her at all until she grew busty. That definitely meant it was jealousy, right?

But before she could dwell on it too much, Mr. Grieg, himself a large, muscular man with jutting veins on his forearms and sleek blonde hair, blew his whistle.

"Alright! Today we're going to do some push-ups, sit-ups and stretching. So, everyone pair off with a partner to help you, and find a spot around the field to get comfortable. Because you're gonna be aching by the end of it. Hop to it!" he said, before blowing his whistle again.

Casey immediately felt every guy look in her direction, but it was Claud who beat the crowd. Or more likely, intimidated them into standing down and out of his way.

"Hey Casey! C'mon, choose me! I'll be your partner!" he said, the big guy's workout shirt leaving his pecs and most of his body revealed, while his shorts were intensely tight. The two had a similar predicament in regards to the school's clothes. Only in very different manners.

And since he was one of the friendliest guys she knew, she was eager to team up with him. He always made exercising seem so easy and fun.

"Yea, alright, but you can't use me as a weight this time," she laughed as she pointed off to the side, where the grass was a bit overgrown and softer.

"Yeah sure," Claud said, grinning excitedly as he led the way. "How about here?" he said, pointing to a cluster of trees near the area she pointed out, giving a tiny bit of privacy. "Thanks for agreein' to be my partner. None of the guys like workin' with me. They say I try to show 'em up, but that ain't so! I'm just trying my best, all the time! At everything. Even the stuff I stink at, like math, or English, or... well any of the non-gym stuff," he remarked.

"You're not bad at it, you just have trouble putting your thoughts in an order the teachers understand," Casey said, her words filled with compassion. She gave him a warm smile as she settled in next to the trees. "I always try my best too. But gym's the hardest now, without the new uniforms."

"Yeah, tell me about it!" Claud said excitedly as they got down together on the grass. "At least the tight uniforms look really good on you. I mean... really really good. I just walk around lookin' silly all day. But you... wow," he said, as usual holding little back of his true thoughts and feelings. "Want me to hold your feet while you do some sit-ups?"

"You're so sweet," she said with a flush of warmth to her cheeks. "I feel just as silly as you do, I promise. I'm sure no one minds you goin' around like you do. And sit-ups? Yea, sure! Those are fun," she agreed with a smile. She took a moment to get comfortable on her back, her legs bent and slightly spread, her heels digging into the grass.

Claud knelt down at her feet, his strong hands pinning her sneakers to the ground.

"But truth be told, I don't mind so much not workin' with the other fellas. Not when I get to hang with you at least. You're the sweetest person on campus, by far! You remind me of my mother like that. Only you're a lot prettier. But then that's not saying much, you're prettier than everyone I know," he said.

As much as he showered her with compliments, Casey

knew at least, that Claud wasn't capable of false flattery. Whatever came out of his mouth, was the truth as he saw it. The man stunk at lying. Or even withholding the truth.

It was one of the reasons they got along.

She took a breath and then started the exercise, but every time she tried to be too serious about it, Claud's smiling face was there, threatening to make her laugh.

"There's lots of pretty girls here," she said in between sit-ups. "I can't believe you don't have like... five girlfriends already."

He gave a shrug of his broad shoulders as he smiled at her.

"I could say the same about you. Except probably... boyfriends, instead of girlfriends. Well, it could be both I guess. That'd be cool too. Or girlfriends. Whatever you like best. What do you like best? I mean, I like girls best. But I could see me goin' out with the right kinda guy too. Not that I know any here," he said, doing his usual over-sharing.

It just made her laugh harder, which made the sit-ups a lot more challenging. She stopped at the top of one, her arms resting on her knees as she smiled, red faced at him.

"Oh my God, Claud, I don't know. I know I like guys, though," she confessed in a whisper.

His eyes sparkled at her whispered confession, and he leaned closer to her, speaking lowly himself.

"How about me? Do you like me? I like you," he said in that deep, warm voice of his, so innocent and strong. "You wanna go out with me? I mean, not like... exclusive. I know you're like... the hottest girl on campus, so you don't wanna be tied down by one big dummy. But like... I would do my best to make you happy and stuff. We could do dates!

Though I'm not sure what you do for dates around here. I mean, we wouldn't even have to tell anyone we were dating, it could be our secret! Because I'm sure you don't want to get teased about it."

She hadn't honestly thought about it before that moment. Part of her just really believed that he would like... someone else. Maybe some other fitness girl, someone who would go to the gym with him all the time. But part of her had just been in denial about the fact that she might actually be attractive to men *she* found attractive.

Her peachy lips parted into an 'o' shape, and her cheeks burned red again.

"I'm... kinda new to the whole dating thing but..." she trailed off, nodding her head. "I think going on a date with you would be really fun."

"No that's okay, I mean I didn't figure. You'd probably like a guy like Nadir, who's smart and more even-tempered, I just figured I'd ask and al—" he paused, as it sank in that she was agreeing. His eyes slowly widening, followed by a broad grin on his chiseled face. "Crap, seriously?" he said, his large hands drifting up from her feet to her ankles, along her knee socks over her calves.

It sent a rush through her, and she felt the butterflies in her stomach begin to flutter.

"Sure, why not? We've always gotten along, and... I mean, obviously you're handsome and strong..."

His grin only grew bigger, and his large hands came to rest atop hers on her knees. He leaned in closer, his huge, lumbering form overshadowing her as she murmured.

"Seriously? Wow... hell this is the best news I've had all year!" he said before pulling one hand away to do a fist pump. "What would you like to do, huh? Maybe we could uh, no that won't work..." he squinted a bit, looking off trying to think of something.

"Picnic?" she suggested. "We could find a private place at the edge of campus or something... Get some sandwiches from the cafeteria?"

"Picnic?! That's brilliant! Aww gosh, Casey. You're so smart about everything. You're the perfect girl for me! It's brains meets brawn," he said, flexing in a silly show of his thick, bulging biceps and grinning cheesily at her after, before touching his hands to her cheeks then leaning in and kissing her forehead. "I'll go nab us some sandwiches from the cafeteria before lunch, and we can do it today!" he said, obviously excited.

Even more so when her eyes dipped lower and saw that his shorts were about ready to pop open.

"Lunch? Yea, that sounds perfect," she agreed, her gaze glued upon his package. It made her feel like she might vibrate out of her skin, and she had to lay back down on her shoulders just to distract herself from it. She bit her lower lip, her eyes rolling up in her head for a moment before she was able to meet his gaze again.

"Wanna do push-ups? I'll get on your back for some extra oomph!" she offered.

"Oh heck yeah! Now you're talkin', Casey! See? Another reason you're the perfect girl for me!" he declared excitedly, before springing up onto his feet, then bouncing back down onto his hands and toes. He was starting to exuberantly do a few push-ups before she even had a chance to get up.

She laughed as she less gracefully got to her feet. She

walked around him until she got to his ass, then carefully began taking a seat.

"Is this okay? Where do you want me? More up top or?"

Claud grunted a bit, as he went extra low in his push-up, though seemed to find no issue with her added weight at all.

"Wherever's most comfortable for you, Casey! But gosh your butt feels nice on me," he remarked lowly, as he kept up that insistent up and down, making her breasts jiggle and bounce with his motions.

"Oh my God, Claud, bc good," she laughed, her hand covering her lips as she did.

It just felt so... normal. So fun! She had been awoken to a whole new world of possibilities, and she was quickly finding that the curiosity that drove her to always be studying in school was being directed in a new way.

"Hey Claud, you've ever been with someone before?"

"What do you mean? Like... dating? Or just... foolin' around? Because I never really dated. But there were a couple girls that we did stuff and it was a lotta fun!" he said, grunting now and then as Casey felt herself rise and fall with that steady motion. "Well, I guess one of 'em wasn't really a girl, but I'm not supposed to talk about that. Made a promise."

"I just mean... can you teach me some stuff? About what you like?" she said, not prying into his secrets, and not bothered at all that he had some experience. That was what she was after!

"Oh, heck yeah! Sure! That'd be so cool! Imagine, Casey... me... teaching **you**!" he laughed deeply, as he picked up his pace, causing her to bounce around. And the poor bandage that was to hold her breasts in check finally lost its war just at the worst time.

She looked and saw Mr. Grieg there, standing beside one of the trees. Hands on his hips as he stared.

She gasped, her forearm going beneath her bust.

It suddenly felt like the innocent thing she'd been doing was very, very dirty, and the heat of shame coloured her cheeks.

She quickly looked away from Mr. Grieg, putting her hand on Claud's shoulder as she half turned.

"Try going slower! I'm gonna fall off..." she exclaimed, muttering after, "or out."

"Keep it decent, you two," Mr. Grieg said, shaking his head at them. "And come see me after class, Casey." He walked off, looking very much like the older version of Claud, with some graying streaks through his hair, looking more tanned.

"Crap, what'd we do?" Claud asked, as he continued doing push-ups, albeit more slowly.

"Almost bounced outta my shirt," Casey said with an embarrassed giggle. "It'll be okay, he probably just wants to tell me to get a new uniform, and I'll tell him I'm trying," she reassured Claud. "We'll be fine before our date, I'm certain."

"Aw man, you nearly spilled outta your top and I missed it?" Claud said, clearly not joking. "What rotten luck!"

Eleven

Casey reported to Mr. Grieg's office at the back of the gym, as ordered. The big guy had never been mean to her, or anyone that she'd seen. He genuinely seemed to enjoy his job, which was always a plus in a teacher.

"Oh, hey Casey, come on in," he said, looking a bit distracted. "How are things goin', huh?" he asked.

"Uhm, normally, I guess," she said, closing the door behind her before sitting in one of the chairs in his office. She'd gotten changed back into her pleated skirt and blouse, and crossed her legs daintily at the ankle. "Is everything okay? Claud just wanted to make the push-ups more challenging, we really didn't mean anything by it."

"That's good," he said, running a hand back through his hair, as he bent over, searching through his old cabinet. "He's not pressuring you into anything, is he? I mean, I know the guy, he's a good kid. And I know he'd never intentionally do somethin' like that, but I feel I gotta check. Professional duty and all," he said.

"Oh! Oh God, no. Claud is like... the nicest. He'd never make anyone do anything they don't want to. But that's really sweet of you to check," she said, her posture immediately relaxing upon realizing she wasn't going to me chastised. "He just likes making working out a bit more fun."

"Alright, good. Glad to hear it," he said, genuinely sounding relieved even as he searched for something he seemed to be struggling to find. "Crap, well... I was hoping I had an extra sports bra around here that might fit you better. Or at least a top. But no luck it seems. But," he said, sighing a little, offering her a roll of some kinda of strange white tape. "This might be the best I can do for you. It's body tape, so like... you can use it to cover... y'know, parts of yourself. That might get exposed, that you don't... want to. I dunno, it's the best I can come up with," he said with a shrug. "But you're welcome to be excused from class if you'd prefer too. Or do your exercises in private, with a partner of your choice if you want. I just wanna make sure you're comfortable. And don't worry, the tape doesn't hurt coming off."

"Tape?" she asked with a tilt of her head. "Yea, sure, I'll try it! I've been using a bandage, but... apparently that broke today, so..." She reached out for the tape, standing as she did so. "Thanks, Mr. Grieg. I'm still hoping that new uniforms will come soon, but everyone keeps telling me no such luck."

"Yeah, I'm not gettin' my hopes up," he said with a sigh, looking to her. And she realized he'd been trying to avoid doing that until then. "So just do the best you can in the meantime. And don't be hard on yourself if it doesn't work out, okay?" he said, his eyes darting to—and from—her cleavage real quickly. "You're not responsible for other people's actions. Keep that in mind."

"Yea... Thanks Mr. Grieg. I guess we all have to make some sacrifices so that everyone can be safe out there. I know we got off pretty lucky all things considered," she said with a soft smile. "I just really appreciate you lookin' out for me."

He cracked a smile at that.

"You're a bright, beautiful girl, Casey. You deserve all the best chances. So, uh... good luck. And if there's ever anything you need... well, I probably won't be able to fix it, if it's like the uniform problem, but... I'll do what I can," he said with a light laugh.

"Thanks," she said with a small laugh in return. "See you later this week! Have a good day!" she said, ready to excuse herself.

"Later Casey," he said as she headed off. "And please shut the door on your way out," he said, slumping into his chair with a big sigh.

She headed to her next class, but she couldn't help but find her thoughts drifting to Claud. She was so surprised he'd asked her out, but she was excited, and kept squirming in her seat as her teacher lectured.

It couldn't end soon enough for her! The next class dragged on, until finally she was heading out the door.

And soon, there came Claud, with a basket in hand. Looking like he hauled it out of some old-timey picture of what a picnic is.

"Hey Casey!" he called, waving one big hand her way, ushering her away from the cafeteria doors then off towards the exit.

She was eager to follow, and there was even a little skip in her high heeled step as she trailed after him.

"Wow, did you grab, like, half the cafeteria in that thing?" she teased, knowing full well how much he had to eat to keep up his strength.

He chuckled all the same, grinning brightly at her.

"I would've if they let me!" he said with another loud chuckle. He pushed open the door for her, standing there in his sleek black school pants that were tight at the thighs and groin, and only his workout top barely covering any of his stomach and nothing much else. "Hope everything went fine with Mr. Grieg and your last class," he said.

"Oh, yea, no trouble at all. I was worried about nothing, as usual," she confessed easily. "I'm really glad we're doing this... You've always been so great to me. And everyone, really, but I'm looking forward to spending some time with just you."

"Same," he said with a grin as they walked across the grass towards the wooded area behind the campus. He was moving fast, as usual, never one to skip leg day, but he tried not to overdo it and let her keep pace. "You're the only one who ever made me enjoy learnin'. Did I ever tell you how much I appreciated all your help with my assignments and study?" he asked, and boy did he ever tell her before.

"Of course, Claud," she said, lightly touching his muscular bicep. "You'd never be ungrateful. I know that much about you."

He smiled at her warmly, looking quite touched by that remark. He put his arm around her then, similar to how Damien had the night before. Not quite as confident, and his hand wasn't quite as low on her backside—in fact he stayed at her waist, just above her hip—but similar.

"You get me," he said sincerely, as they went in beyond the trees, walking along a light path until they very soon came to a small clearing in the woods, and Claud laid down the basket, then spread out an old blanket. "Can't believe we're finally doin' this."

"Was perfect timing, honestly," Casey said as she gently sat down upon the blanket. "I don't know if I would've been ready before now. At least, not to like... do anything. Experiment. Whatever. I would've probably even been too nervous to hold your hand."

Claud knelt down, and opened the picnic basket, looking to Casey with some surprise.

"So, like... you really wanna... do stuff? Experiment I mean... not just hold hands?" he remarked, and already, his cock began to bulge. His striking, muscular physique keeping him in tip top shape in all ways it seemed, as his libido was ready to jump at the slightest hint of sex talk.

"I don't think there's anyone better that I could learn with," Casey admitted. "Dahlia last night mentioned I should start with like... blowjobs or hand jobs but I don't really know what either of those are, and they sound like kind of a drag. Do you know?" she asked candidly.

Food seemed to have vanished from Claud's mind as he stared at Casey, swallowing and licking his lips. His trousers were tented so much, straining, that they seemed ready to burst from his throbbing manhood.

"Y-yeah, oh yeah... I know about them," he said, a smile slowly growing on his face. "I mean, I can show you... and if

85

you don't like it... we can do other stuff," he said, reaching over, placing one of his big, strong hands on her thigh.

"I don't mean to be so forward or anything... or make you uncomfortable," she said as her breathing caught in her chest. "I just know you're a safe guy, and that... that we get along well and everything."

"Oh, you haven't made me uncomfortable! I mean... you've definitely made me... somethin'. But it ain't uncomfortable," he said as he caressed her thigh, squeezed it and smiled. "Well... I guess we should eat first, but gosh... I can't think of anythin' else right now but... but showin' you how to do handjobs and blowjobs," he said excitedly.

"We could eat after?" Casey suggested with a soft tilt of her head. "After all, it'll be like workin' out. Working up an appetite, right?" She gave him a soft, innocent smile, even as they spoke of such lewd things so casually. The bright sun was bathing them in light, and though they'd found a somewhat secluded place, they were still in the outdoors.

"That's true!" he said, his eyes widening, before he excitedly began to unbuckle his belt. "Heck yeah! This is unbelievable! The most beautiful girl in school... and me!" he said with a bright smile. "Oh... you wanna start with a bit of a hand job? Then move onto a blow job?" he asked as he undid his trousers, and the garment seemed to groan with relief as his thick bulge erupted through the fly, still covered by his boxer-briefs.

She glanced around nervously, trying to make sure they didn't have an audience. Then she moved the basket strategically so it would block the most likely angle that people might see them by before shifting next to him.

"Well, would it make the most sense to start like that?"

she asked curiously. "You're the teacher, remember? You can set the lesson plan for the day."

Claud grinned at that.

"Imagine... me? The teacher?" he chuckled, before pushing his pants down lower, and his thick cock sprang out. That girth of his was impressive. While he wasn't as long as Damien's cock, he bulged thicker, and just as hard, with pre-cum glistening at its tip. "Alright, so, uh..." he said, reaching for her hand, guiding it to his manhood. "You wanna wrap your fingers around it like this..."

Twelve

Her skin was hot to the touch, but her limbs were malleable, and she seemed very studious as he guided her to his cock. She licked her lips as she gazed down at it, and there was a huge part of her that just wanted to go all the way again. To feel his weight atop hers, his powerful hips thrusting...

But this wasn't about that. This was about learning, and she redirected her focus as she wrapped her dainty fingers around his thick dick.

And Claud immediately groaned at that, his cock throbbing in her touch. He bit his lower lip, shivering as he squeezed her hand around his shaft.

"Oh wow... your hand is so soft and nice," he groaned, looking to her dainty digits wrapped around his girth, then to her face. "You can use two hands if it helps. But, uh... you basically just go like this," he said, guiding her hand up and down his shaft, moving the skin of that rigid organ as he grunted.

"It feels nice," she said, looking fascinated by how it

looked as the skin moved along with her strokes. "I can feel your veins pulse with blood... You're so thick." She added her other hand as he suggested, able to give him a lot more coverage like that, and then she smiled at him. "Does it feel nice for you too?"

"Ohh yeah, way better than my own hand," he said, tonguing his lower lip, pulling it into his mouth and moaning. He watched her hands move along his shaft, his broad chest heaving, his pecs twitching with excitement. "Way nicer than the other girls who did it too... your hands are so dainty and soft, Casey," he said, his voice heavier as she worked his shaft.

She practically radiated with joy at his compliments, and she shifted a little closer to him, so that she was straddling his calf with her thighs.

"So why do they call this a job?" she asked.

"I dunno," Claud said with a shrug of his broad shoulders. "I guess it can take a while. Um, Casey?" he asked, licking his lips again. "Would you mind if I, uh... asked you if you'd... um... open your top and take off your bra?" he said. "It'd help a lot," he said as his chest heaved, his dick throbbing in her hands.

She looked down at her exposed cleavage, pushed up between the opening of her button-down blouse, then at Claud.

"You want to see them?" she asked before she glanced over her shoulder. "Well, as long as you try to keep watch," she said, removing one of her hands from his cock. It didn't take a lot to undo the first button, given the immense strain it was under as it tried to contain her massive chest, and from there, she continued to unbutton herself until the top fell open to the sides.

"Okay, perfect," he said, but his watch soon ended, as his gaze was drawn back to her cleavage, staring at it as he grunted. A dollop of pre-cum shooting from his thick tip and onto her fingers as he grunted and shivered. "Oh wow, yeah... seeing such a beautiful pair, hnngh... that'll help a lot. You have no idea what they do to a guy," he said, staring at her breasts.

"Really?" she asked, fumbling with the hook at the back of the bra for a moment before it finally unclasped and bounced forward. She shrugged her arms out of the straps, still keeping her blouse on so that she'd look dressed from behind. It meant she had to switch out her hands on his cock, but quickly they found their way back to his hot shaft.

Her breasts were massive, but they were still firm, and her nipples were perky and stiff as they were exposed to the air.

"Mmmph... oh gosh, wow!" he said, reaching out to touch them, but stopping himself just short. "Is it okay if I touch them, Casey? Gosh, I wanna touch 'em so bad. I think about doing that every night. And in the locker room shower... and sometimes when I slip away to the bathroom during class," he confessed. "You've got such amazing breasts."

She blushed hard, her gaze dropping to his lap at his words. Her head bobbed in a nod, even though she couldn't get her eyes to meet his.

"You can touch them," she said softly. "I'd like that a lot, actually."

Claud grinned with excitement, that big, thick hand of his reaching for her chest. And despite his immense size and strength, he fondled her tits with some care. Gently caressing them, kneading the supple flesh.

"Ohh shoot... those feel even better than they look," He grunted, shivering. "How do you feel about the hand job so far, huh? You can keep going until I'm done. Or we can switch to the blowjob stuff now..." he said, hiding his enthusiasm to move onto a blowjob rather poorly.

"You set the lesson plan," she reminded him, flicking her emerald eyes up to his. He was so much bigger than her, so much stronger, yet he was so in control of himself. It was really quite admirable, and did quite a good job at helping her relax into things. "Just tell me what you want."

He gave her breast a light squeeze, then as a whole-body shiver ran through him, he nodded. He reached his other hand up, caressing her red ringlets, brushing his thumb against her ear.

"Here. It'll help if I guide you," he said, licking his lips as he carefully knit his fingers into her hair, grasping the back of her head to pull her gently down to his groin. "You'll wanna use your tongue a lot, swirl it around the tip. But, uh... you don't really blow. I dunno why they call it a blow job."

"So... more licking?" she asked as she inhaled the scent of his fresh arousal, that masculinity so hot as she neared it with her face. "No one's looking, right?" She didn't wait for the answer to either question before her tongue poked out between her full lips and began to gather up the leaking precum with it.

Claud was doing a very poor job of restraining himself

and watching out for prying eyes. He moaned deeply as her tongue lashed along his shaft, gathering up his sticky pre. That potent scent of musk all around his manhood was powerful, but not bad or overwhelming. He was a clean man, who showered regularly, after all.

"Mmm, yeah... yeah, like that. You lick a lot at first. Focusing on the tip, but... like also licking down around the shaft. Sometimes even the balls down bottom," he instructed, his hand guiding her along. "Though after doing that for a while... you stretch your mouth open and put the whole thing inside."

She took his instructions in, testing them as her tongue wandered downwards, tracing the veins with the tip of her wet muscle. He couldn't see her tits very well in her current position, but he felt them as they pushed into either side of his thigh. Her curls hid most of her face, but every so often, she'd glance up at him, looking for praise.

And she got it from him in abundance, as he kept one hand fondling her breast at the side, his other hand caressing her hair.

"Ohh wow, Casey... you're a natural at sucking cock," He grunted out, as more pre spurt onto her tongue. "Now... try pushing it into your mouth, see how far you can take it without gagging, okay?" he instructed.

It was a strange warning about gagging, one she didn't quite understand, but still, she was obedient. She wanted to learn, and he was a great instructor, she thought. So she began to stretch out her mouth, taking the fullness of his swollen crown between her lips before she descended.

And Claud let loose such a deep, loud moan as his thick, veiny shaft slid across her tongue towards the back of her throat. His strong hand guiding her down around his shaft as he grunted and twitched in her mouth.

"Ohh Casey... yeah, oh dang, you're so good at this," he grunted, as he began to guide her head up and down his shaft. "I... I think you got the hang of the basics of both now. What... what do you think?" he said, slow to stop pumping her lips up and down his shaft.

She didn't answer right away. She was still so curious, her tongue having less room to lick and tease, but it felt nice to just flick it back and forth along the shaft. To feel him filling her. She'd long forgotten about the risk of being caught, and wasn't worried at all that bent over as she was, with her legs spread, and her skirt lifted, she was flashing anyone who came by.

She'd lost one pair of panties, but she'd found another in the wash, luckily... but those were already slick and slipping between her vulva to outline her sex intimately.

She slowly rose up on his shaft, wiping her lower lip of drool.

"Is this where we go all the way?"

Claud's eyes immediately went wide at that.

"Yes," he said without a moment's pause or hesitation, the word just tumbling from his lips. "I don't have a condom or nothin' though. Not that I mind. I like it better without 'em," he said, licking his lips with excitement glinting in his eyes. He picked up her panties, and inhaled her scent with a soft 'ahhh' before continuing. "How you wanna do it? You wanna lay back and let me get on top?"

"What do you think is best?" she asked with a broad smile that equaled his own. If he was excited, she was no less so. That heat between her thighs had grown to an inferno, and her body was practically trembling with need.

"Um well... I've only done it a couple ways. With me on top, or, uh... you bend over. I guess, you'd get on your hands and knees, and I'd get behind you. I kinda like bein' on top best," he said with a smile, "it's sorta like doin' push-ups then. And I'm great at those."

She nodded at him, her white teeth peeking out from her peachy lips.

"Okay," she said with an eager breathlessness. "I think I'd like that a lot. Here," she said, squirming to the side so that she could slip her soaking wet panties down. She was so caught up in things, she was even forgetting to glance around and keep watch. It was as though the entire world had slipped away, leaving just the two of them.

Sure, it was about as private as things could get on campus, but still... anyone could come by at any time. There was even that path leading to the clearing! Which heavily indicated they weren't the only ones to come here.

But Claud was so beyond caring too, he just stared at her pink little pussy as she unveiled it, swallowing heavily as his dick jumped with excitement.

"Wow Casey... every part of you is so perfect and beautiful," he said in awe of her, leaning forward onto his two fists, as he got up over her, his broad, muscular form ready to pounce as his cock throbbed.

She still wore her Mary-Janes, stockings, skirt, and blouse, but her heavy breasts and slick pussy were readily revealed to him. She lay back, her legs spread, and her green eyes glittered at him.

"You're so handsome," she said to her gentle giant, her

hand lifting to graze across his jawline. "I'm glad you asked me out."

Claud smiled down at her, so warm and excited.

"I wish I'd had the guts to do it sooner," he said, as he put his hands on her knees, guiding her legs apart even more as he positioned himself over top of her. He then rested his weight on one hand, as he guided his thick shaft to her slick, glistening pussy. "Mmm, Casey... you're so wet. I love it," he grinned, beginning to press his dick into her slowly.

She mewled with desire as her head tilted back, her spine arching.

"Oh God, you're so thick," she whimpered, her recently deflowered pussy hungry for more. Her eyes fluttered open, and she stared up at him with desire and amazement clearly written on her face.

Thirteen

⟋⟍

S he wrapped her arms around his neck as her knees parted wider for his powerful hips.

"I've been told that before," he grunted, as he pushed more of his cock into her, "but I think you're just really tight and small Casey... Mmm gosh that feels so good," he grunted. And then one of his big hands grasped her breast, squeezing and fondling it as he put more force behind his hips, sheathing his cock inside her as he grunted and moaned, pressing the full length of his dick into her.

As he hilted in her, her legs wrapped around his ass, her stockings pressed against his skin. She loved the feeling of his weight atop hers, and she held him lovingly as he groped her.

"I like having my breasts touched," she said, becoming more certain of that fact as he played with her. "They're really sensitive, but... it's good."

Claud began to thrust into her firmly, not too fast or hard, but a nice, firm thrust into her with each pump of his hips. It made her tits jiggle, and he squeezed and fondled one of them more at her words.

"Gosh Casey... I'd play with these all day if you let me," he grunted out, as he pumped into her steadily, his pace rising gradually, as she watched his thick, muscular form over top of her rock. His pecs tensing up, that muscle trembling as he moaned.

It felt so good. It was different than with Damien, because she knew Claud, and so it felt a bit more casual. That was really hot too, in its own way. Knowing that she could ask him anything, and he'd teach her whatever she wanted to know...

And she had so many questions. So much she wanted to learn. Yet in that moment, all she could learn was how much she loved a man's hard cock thrusting into her womanhood.

"Oh God, Claud, that feels so good!"

"Ohh gosh Casey! So do you!" he groaned out, as he squeezed her breast a bit tighter, then began to pick up his pace even more. Those heavy balls of his slapping to her rear as he pounded. He wasn't as skilled as Damien, but he made up for it in exuberance, and his raw strength and thickness, his shaft pounding into her as he spurt more pre-cum.

She was still naive to the risk of pregnancy, blissfully unaware of how either of them could potentially knock her up if they came in her. She was still only vaguely aware of what a condom was, even, and she didn't think it was necessary. It seemed to her that it was almost like a sinful accessory that one used to thwart the Lord. She wouldn't be interested in something like that.

Her legs wrapped around him more tightly, driving his cock deeper into her as she moaned and panted, not holding back her pleasured cries.

"Ohh Casey... Casey, you're so hot and beautiful and tight," Claud grunted out, his big, muscular form heaving over top of her, his bulging muscles glinting a bit in the sun that shone directly over head. "I'm gonna cum... oh gosh I'm gonna cum soon!" he grunted out, his dick pumping into her faster, harder, his shaft swelling even thicker as his moment got nearer.

They hadn't even kissed, yet the moment felt so deeply intimate and perfect. She held onto him with such intense need, her grip not loosening at all at his warning. He was a strong man and could certainly pull away if he wanted, of course, but it was clear that she didn't want him to pull out. Not then, and not when he was about to cum.

She let out a few more breathy cries, panting to the rhythmic thrusts.

"Ohh! Here I come Casey," he grunted out, his muscles bulging, as he pounded into her. The slap of their flesh together drowning out the sound of a distant voice calling out. He was pounding away, thrusting into her fast and hard and a little more haphazardly as he neared his climax. And while she was unaware of the consequences... Claud seemed no less aware or concerned, at the very least. He let loose a loud roar of a moan, as he hilted his cock up inside her, then unleashed that thick, virile load of seed, flooding her depths.

She didn't cum, not without the aid of a more practiced lover, but she did feel *amazing*. It was a beautiful high to make a man experience such pleasure with her body, and she was quickly becoming addicted to it. Her nails dug until his muscular shoulders, her calves wrapped around his ass and upper thighs as she helped him empty himself deep within her.

But while she didn't find her ultimate release, Claud certainly did, his body pounding a couple more times as he spurt once, twice, then... his final strand of virile seed. He grunted at the end, though didn't struggle to hold himself up over her, even as he trembled with the intensity of it. While his other hand slowly released its tight grip on her breast.

"Oh wow, Casey... haven't had anythin' that intense since my first time," he moaned out, shivering, as a distant voice could be heard from the direction of the academy. Faint and totally inaudible at that moment.

Maybe Casey didn't want to hear it, or maybe the moment had just been so magical that it created an illusory dome around them that protected her from intrusion. Either way, he was the only thing that existed for her.

"You are wonderful," she said, lightening her grasp around his neck and instead stroking his jawline. "So handsome and strong."

Claud smiled down at her, looking touched by her kind words. And he leaned down slowly, his eyes shutting as he planted their first kiss on her lips. The strange nature of having it after they'd fucked lost on both of them, as they just savoured the moment.

"Claud! He struck again! Are you out here?!" called a voice in the distance, clearer this time, more distinct and definitely audible.

It sent a jolt through her, and she pulled away from their kiss with a gasp.

"Did you hear that?" she whispered urgently.

Claud looked none too pleased about the interruption, but as he made out the words on repetition, he seemed to jolt himself.

"Oh no," he said, before rising up, breaking out of the clasp her legs had on him. It left her pussy drooling his big load of pearly white seed, and also... sadly empty. "I let my guard down, and he did it again," Claud said, as he began to stuff his manhood back into his pants.

She shifted, pulling down her skirt before struggling to get her bra back on under the blouse.

"But it's the middle of the day! What masked crusader would take a risk of being caught?" she asked, not having a lot of luck with her bra. She was clearly going to have to take off her blouse in order to get it back on.

"Sorry Casey. I gotta go try and help catch this person," he said as he stood up, doing up his pants. "But..." he smiled at her, "I really enjoyed this. I wanna do it again. Lots! You're the best," he said, bending back down to one knee, kissing her on the lips passionately, then jolting up to rush off.

She didn't even have a chance to say anything other than an, "Okay, bye!" as she brought one arm through the sleeve, undressing her torso.

But in their haste, neither realized that her panties were still wrapped around one of Claud's large hands, from when he took them up and sniffed them earlier. Leaving her without anything down beneath her skirt.

But as she undressed, left to the quiet of the clearing, she heard someone giving a courteous cough.

"Sorry to disturb you," came a strange voice. "Um, I just wanted a word."

"Eek!"

She squealed, trying to cover her large breasts with her forearms, doing little more than covering the nipples. She was still sat on the blanket, drooling cum, and was very exposed.

"Who's there?"

"Just a friend," said the voice, as she saw a dark figure step out from the trees. It was the guy in the long coat, with the hood and mask. "I'll leave you be. I just wanted to thank you," they said. Their head was tilted down, and Casey couldn't see their eyes, making it look like they were politely averting their gaze.

Her body softened slightly, but she frowned.

"Claud just left... You'd be safer from him here for now. But they said you hurt someone else? Why?"

"It was Mr. Mullard. Do I need to say more than that?" said the masked stranger, standing there in that sleek black coat, with its curious straps. "And you're very sweet to be concerned for me. As much as Claud seems a nice guy, his head is in the wrong place here. But he'd also probably crush my head if he got a hold of it," said the stranger in that muffled, indistinguishable voice.

"He just thinks that everyone's as decent as he is, they just need a good talking to," she said, gazing curiously at the stranger. She had even temporarily forgotten about her state of undress, and her arms lowered from her chest for a moment before she realized.

"Do you go to school here?"

The figure shifted a bit, not seeming to like being asked direct questions. But their black, leather-gloved hand moved to one hip.

"I guess you could say that, yeah," they said. "But again. I wanted to thank you. I feel I owe you one. Or two. Is there anything you'd like?" they asked. "Someone who's been cruel to you, maybe? Or..." they trailed off, gesturing vaguely towards her.

Casey's brows furrowed in thought, the question further delaying her in getting dressed once more.

"I don't want anyone to get hurt because of me," she said earnestly. "And you really don't owe me anything. I mean, my shirt's ruined, but no one seems to mind."

Mentioning that, however, did remind her that she was currently topless, and she let out another little squeak as she raised her arms to cover her heavy chest again.

"I'm afraid shirts aren't really something I deal in," the masked figure said, moving a bit to the left. "Did you want a hand getting dressed?" they asked. "Not that it would really count as a favour to you... more to me if anyone, honestly."

"Oh. Oh! Uh... yea, actually. It's really hard for me to get the band on anymore. I got used to just pulling the bra over my head but that doesn't work anymore," she said, her posture softening again. She lifted up the dainty white bra that was clearly way too tiny for her, offering it to the stranger.

The hooded figure came in close with but a moment's hesitation. He knelt down, and took the bra from her.

"It would be my pleasure," they said, as they got behind

her, and then very carefully reached around, wrapping the cups around her ample breasts. "If you ever want something from me... you can leave a message for me in the hollowed out log over there," they said, gesturing towards it with a point before tugging the bra to her back, and sealing the clasps. They sealed the clasp shut, then reached back around, adjusting the cups a bit more. "How is that?"

"So much better," she said with a sigh. "I'm always missing a hook, or getting them on crooked. I usually have to get my roomie to help."

It was strange how normal it all felt, talking to this vagabond. But... he did take out her bully. And the mean ol' teacher...

"Wait! You hurt a *teacher*?" she asked, as if it was just dawning on her.

"Well... hurt is a strong word. I just... scared him really. Hopefully enough to put him in his place," said the stranger, still knelt behind her, those long arms still around her, their hands at her midsection. Their bare fingertips idly caressed her stomach, and she realized they had taken off their gloves to help with the bra.

"Part of me wishes we didn't keep meeting like this though. Because I would really love to be with you the same way Claud was."

Fourteen

∾

It sent a little shiver down her spine. It felt very, very sinful to be talking like this with a stranger, but... Damien was also pretty much a stranger as well. She'd just seen his face. How much of a difference did that make, she wondered.

"You would?" she asked with a curious tilt of her head, glancing over her shoulder at the masked person. "Why?"

Peering back like that, up close... she could see beneath the stranger's hood. But it didn't help. They wore a mask, and even their eyes were hidden by some dark goggles that might've been used for swimming, but now helped their identity stay secret.

"Why? Because you're simply the most beautiful girl I've ever beheld. And you have a good heart. Two things that are downright irresistible to me," they said before she felt one hand slide down along her taut tummy to the edge of her skirt, the other cupping her breast through her bra.

She let out a gasp and a whimper, still feeling so aroused. She never finished with Claud, and the stranger was capitalizing on that fact. She shimmied a little at the sensation of his hands on her, biting down on her lower lip in a worried way.

She felt the masked stranger nuzzle to the side of her head and neck, as their fingers curled, drawing her skirt up.

"I can help finish what Claud started too," they said, before she felt fingers curl into her cleavage, then more touch at her sensitive clit. This person clearly quite skilled with it, as they made her tingle and shiver with their masterful touch. "I can tell... you're still a bit... pent up," said the muffled, low voice.

"I am," she breathed out with such raw need. "It feels so... *wrong*." Yet that word was wrapped with such illicit, budding desire, and perhaps the fact that it felt so sinful made it even more exciting. "Claud could come back at any moment..."

"Then I guess we shouldn't waste a moment, should we?" they said, those masterful fingers teasing her slit as they spoke lowly into her ear. "Get on your hands and knees," they said, their voice so commanding, even distorted through their mask.

It felt like her lesson with Claud, but it was ramped up in intensity. He wasn't asking her. He was instructing her, and she responded very well to clear instructions. She shifted away from him as she rolled onto her hands and knees, her legs on either side of the stranger. She looked over her shoulder, her ringlets bouncing as she did.

"Like this?"

"That's right," they said, as they unzipped the bottom of their coat, revealing their belt buckle, then began to undo that. She could see a bulge there already, thick and large. And the masked stranger, caressed her ass with one hand, as they unzipped and then...

They were a he. That much was confirmed, as a thick, hard cock sprang out, ready to fuck. It was long and hard. Longer than Claud, but not as thick. About the size of Damien. But then she'd fucked Damien in a dark underground, so it was hard to compare to this ruddy shaft in the open daylight.

"I won't bother asking about a condom or whether I should pull out, since it seems Claud did neither," they said, before grasping their shaft, then pushed it into her cum-filled slit, causing more of that seed to squelch out as he moaned with a deep satisfaction.

She let out a squeal of delight, that feeling of fullness so welcome.

Her torso bucked forward, and she softened her elbows, finding that gave her a bit better support. She'd learned that in gym class when doing push-ups.

But she wasn't prepared for just how *deep* he was able to go in that position, and it made her toes curl inside her high heels. She bit down on her lower lip, just in case Claud abruptly returned and thought she was in danger, as her full ass pressed to the masked stranger's hips.

But true to his warning, there was no time to waste. And he was no gentle kitten.

Gripping her hips tightly, he began to thrust into her. He didn't do a slow build up like Claud or Damien had, he just thrust in hard and fast. Perhaps because he knew the previous guy already had her warmed up. But whatever the reason, the thick, hard slam of his dick up inside her was rough and firm. The wet slap of his balls against her clit adding to the noisy mess as he grunted.

"Ohh you are such a sweet girl," he grunted. "Mmmph, your pussy is so good," he said, punctuating it with a slap to her ass cheek.

It was so different and exciting, the intense pace, the melding of sharp pain and building pleasure at the smack of her ass. It sent a shockwave through her, and she gasped and shuddered at that powerful jolt.

Her pussy squeezed his dick as her orgasm rapidly began to build.

Whoever the stranger was, he was more like Damien than Claud in another respect: he seemed to have more experience pleasing a woman. His hips angled just right, so that his thick cock pounded in deliciously. And he reached a hand in under her, squeezing her breast, before trailing down towards her mound.

"You want me to cum in you, don't you?" he husked through his mask, panting.

She didn't know what he meant, not precisely, but she'd picked up on enough to get the gist of things. That mess between her legs wasn't all her own, and she didn't want him to stop or pull out. So her strawberry blonde hair bobbed as she nodded, her body beginning to tremble.

"I don't want you to stop!"

Her ass cheeks clapped to his groin, that bubbly round surface rippling with each pump into her. And he let his fingertips tease her clit ever so slightly amid that ravenous, rapid-fire pace of thrusts.

"Mm... I'm gonna fill you up... with my seed," he

grunted, shuddering. "Beg me to cum inside you," he commanded her, giving her ass another slap with his hand.

And even if she didn't fully understand... she was obedient. So sweetly obedient. Especially as he was working her body up into such a state. She felt even more desperate and needy than the day before when she'd never even been touched.

"Oh. Oh God! I want you to cum in me," she panted out, the jolts of electricity building at the apex of her sex.

She felt his dick twitch with excitement inside her at that. And he moaned out long and low. And his fingers slid down, masterfully swirling around her clit, working that little bundle of nerves.

"Cum with me like a good girl," he commanded, barely audible through his grunts and her moans and cries. And then he gasped, as his cock stiffened and... eruption. Thick, anonymous seed flooding her depths, mingling with Claud's inside her as he moaned and grunted wildly amid his thrusts.

It was his actions more than his words that sent her over the edge, even as obedient as she was. But as he was cumming in her, her pussy was tightening around his, milking him of every strand of cum he had in the throes of her own orgasm.

She'd been so good at keeping her voice down, but in that moment, she couldn't help but cry out, her arms weakening and failing her. She dropped down, her ass still posed up in the air as her limbs twitched and spasmed.

But her masked suitor just kept thrusting. Her pink little pussy pounded repeatedly as she came, with each new thrust firing a thick new burst of his virile seed. He moaned and grunted, then gave her ass another slap, before gripping her hip and pulling her back against him.

"Ohh you are the very best little girl," he husked as he shivered and moaned.

She liked that so, so much. His words sent a thrill of delight through her, the threat of an aftershock buzzing in her veins. She pushed back into him as he held her, filled with a sense of warmth and affection for a man she didn't even know the name of.

Or what he looked like.

It hardly seemed to matter when he was calling her the very best little girl, though.

"You think so?" she cooed affectionately.

"Mmhmm," he husked, shivering as he gave her a final push forward, causing that last spurt of seed to fire into her. He caressed her spine, then lovingly stroked her hair. "Now be an extra good girl... and tell me the name of someone who wronged you," he said, before slapping her ass again. "Tell me," he commanded.

That was so much harder, but she was too high on the orgasm and the compliments to be able to think so clearly anymore. It certainly had brought her walls crashing down, and earnestness broke through.

"Leslie's always mean to me, but I don't want her to get hurt. She's just jealous," Casey said, as if it weren't any big deal, despite the woman having sent her to the showers in tears more than once.

"It's okay. You're just being a good girl. Don't worry," he husked, caressing her hair, those lush red ringlets. He even rewarded her with a few more gentle thrusts. "We'll meet again soon, Casey. And you'll be a very good girl for me then too, won't you?" he said with a sigh, as he nudged his cock in extra deep.

"Yea," she breathed out lustfully as she looked over her shoulder at him. "Can I know who you are?"

He pulled out of her suddenly, leaving her slit so achingly empty—but for the copious amounts of pearly white cum that was now spilling out of her pussy. And she feared he might be upset at that question. But then he spoke in that approving voice.

"Come here. Turn around," he said, a hand in her hair still, as he guided her head towards his glistening hard cock.

She suddenly felt very grateful for Claud's lesson as her lips instinctively fell open. She looked up at the stranger curiously as she sat on hands and knees, seeming more like an obedient little puppy than anything else.

"Blow job? You can do that out of order?" she asked curiously.

He gave a light laugh, caressed her hair and said, "Yeah. You can. But think of it as more like... cleaning up the mess you made of me right now. Like a good girl. You're all about being a good girl, aren't you?" he remarked to her, as his hand guided her to her task.

He had successfully distracted from her question, and her tongue began to lick and suckle his flesh with such affection. She was feeling a little sleepy and dopey from her orgasm, but it seemed to make the blowjob a bit more dreamlike. It was beautiful, and new, and the taste of their pleasure mingled on his long shaft.

"Good girl," he reaffirmed again, caressing her hair, watching her lick and clean his shaft, his drained balls. "I'll leave a message for you sometime after this. It'll let you know when and where to meet me. And we can get to know each other a little better... maybe I'll even tell you who I am," he said with a sigh, his cock slowly softening, but giving a little twitch of life at her attention.

She'd of course never seen a softening cock, and her brows furrowed with confusion and concern. She cleaned him until there was nothing more to clean, then looked up at him.

"What happened?"

He pet her head again, then caressed her cheek.

"It means you did a very good job, and drained me dry. You're just such a great girl," he commended.

"Oh," she smiled, relaxing slightly as she sat back on her haunches, her gaze still trained on him. "I really liked that. It was a lot of fun."

"We'll do it again. I promise," he said, and though she couldn't see his face, she felt he was smiling. "Do you mind if I pay you a... surprise visit sometime?" he asked, as he stuffed his member back into his trousers, tidying up. But the way he said 'surprise visit' sounded so... naughty and tantalizing.

She was nodding eagerly before she was even able to think it through.

"Oh, I mean... No, I don't mind. That sounds exciting!" she said a bit too loudly. She giggled as she covered her mouth.

"Such a good girl," he commended again with a sigh, caressing her cheek. But then a rustle in the trees made him stiffen, and he stood back up, grasping his gloves from his pocket. "Until then, cutie!" he remarked before dashing off into the trees.

She turned and sat back on her ass, grabbing at her shirt to try to quickly put that back on. She presumed it was Claud returning, but she had no way of really knowing that, and her heart was already racing from the illicit tryst. It was making her a bit giddy and anxious, truth be told.

Whoever—or whatever it was—they didn't show up any time soon. She had enough time to put her top back on, before a familiar figure emerged.

"Casey?" said Nadir, pushing his glasses up his nose as he looked to her there in the clearing. "Everything okay?" he asked.

"Nadir!" she gasped, having been trying to find her panties to no end. "Yea, yea, I'm fine. Did Claud send you?"

"Yeah. He said he felt bad about abandoning you so suddenly," he said, before looking at the open basket full of food. "Oh hey, mind if I help myself?" he asked, crouching down.

"Go for it. I haven't had any at all. We were supposed to have lunch but then apparently that vigilante struck again?" she said as she grabbed a sandwich, taking a dainty bite. It was lettuce, bacon, tomato and turkey. One of her faves!

Nadir laughed.

"Yeah, you could say that. He struck... **big time**," her friend said with a curious emphasis. But he sat down on the blanket and began to eat casually.

"What happened?" Casey probed, hoping her friend didn't notice her dishevelled state... or the fact that she'd just been fucked by two men. And she was once more without her panties.

"You know Mr. Mullard? Yeah, real jerk. Well... he was heading back to his office during lunch, since he always eats alone. I don't even think the other teachers like him," Nadir said casually as he ate. "Well... he opened his door and..."

He let that hang. Tension filling the air.

"And...?" Casey prodded, squirming with the anticipation of it. She'd forgotten all about her sandwich, still held in her hand. She was both excited and fearful at what would come next in the story.

Nadir kept chewing, looking her in the eyes over the rim of his glasses, which had slid down his nose again.

"Boom. There was a bomb," he said.

Fifteen

The news had sounded so dire. It had Casey utterly at wits end! But once she got back to school, and found out that class had been suspended for more study in the afternoon, it gave her time to work on the grading, but her mind was elsewhere. Until Dahlia found her.

"Yeah, it was a bomb, but not like... a bomb-bomb," she said to Casey, laughing a bit. "It was like... a prank bomb," she said.

"Oh my *God*," she said with relief. "I got so scared when Nadir said that. I couldn't believe the vigilante would, like... use a real bomb. But you know Nadir. He loves a little drama." Casey looked at Dahlia, her expression softening towards her friend.

"Oh, and just so you know, I might be late again tonight. I have that assignment to hand into Mr. Alder."

Dahlia, leaning on her table at the library, tits out in that unabashed way, only grinned as she twirled a lock of her dark hair around her finger.

"Ooohhhh, you and Mr. Alder?" she said, a sparkle in her eye. "You've been lovesick about him since you got here," she said with a toothy smile.

Casey let out a sigh, part annoyance, part wistfulness, at Dahlia's reminder.

"I know. He's just so romantic. But he's also, you know, a professional. And probably married or something. But still, I'm looking forward to learning more about being a teacher, and I think he'd be willing to teach me that." Casey gave Dahlia an impish smile before she leaned in to whisper, "Claud taught me about the handjob and blowjob you were talking about."

Dahlia's eyes widened, and she mouthed 'oh my god.'

"Girl you are on your way to becoming a regular slut," she said with a playful slap of Casey's arm. "I'm so proud of you. And Claud's a hunk," she said, quite definitively at the end.

"He is. And like... big and strong," she said a bit dreamily. "But then he had to run off to find the vigilante so we never did get to finish our date."

"Oh," Dahlia said, shoulders slumping. "That's a bummer. Hate it when I get interrupted," she said with a grimace. But then she smiled again, shaking Casey's arm, "That's why I'm so grateful for my bestie who keeps watch for me!"

Casey giggled and nodded.

"I get it now, Dahlia. I really do." She stood up, wrapping her arms around her friend in a warm hug. "I think this will really help bring us closer together. I'm so glad we got assigned our room."

Dahlia hugged her back warmly, just as the bell chimed for the end of the day, and the beginning of supper.

"Oh, time to go eat. You're coming with me, yeah?" Dahlia said, smiling at her friend.

"Can't, I'm meeting Mr. Alder," she replied with a bright, eager smile. "I had to take a quick shower after lunch, but I'm like... totally out of panties. I lost my last pair today, I think," Casey sighed. "I don't know... maybe I can tease him a little bit. What do you think?" she asked before immediately flushing. "I mean, just to see..."

Dahlia looked at her friend, appearing more than a little amazed.

"Damn girl. I think you're gonna outdo me soon..." she said, looking wide-eyed and impressed. "You get it. Whatever it is that you want," she said, caressing Casey's arm. "I'll catch you later then. And... if you end up being late getting back..." she grinned a little, "I'll tell a fib about you being in the ladies' room. They wouldn't buy it for me, but for you? Oh yeah."

"You're the sweetest, Dahlia. Thank you," Casey said, leaning in to kiss her friend on the cheek. "See you tonight. And... wish me luck."

"Goodluck," Dahlia said, kissing her cheek back. "Oh, need any condoms?" she asked, brows raised curiously.

"Oh! Yea, what are those? No one ever seems to have them."

Dahlia's eyes went wide.

"Casey... you should definitely be making them wrap it up. Here," she said, reaching into her skirt and panties, taking out a plastic wrapper. "Don't tell anyone you got it though. The school doesn't allow them. They think it'll stop us from having sex," she said with a roll of her eyes.

Casey took it, looking it over before tossing it in her backpack.

"Oh. No wonder no one has them. So it's like... what is it?"

Dahlia looked a little concerned about her friend's ignorance on the subject, but the doors opened and a guy—Yuri, a handsome older student—called out, "Dahlia! C'mon!"

He got immediately shushed by the librarian, but Dahlia waved to him.

"It's to keep you safe," she said. "From disease—"

"C'mon!" called Yuri and another guy behind him.

"Oh crap, I gotta go! Yeah, just be safe," Dahlia said, blowing Casey a kiss as she headed off.

"Okay... have fun!" Casey said with a wave, her own heart beginning to thud with excitement, butterflies awakening in her stomach.

She was clean, her hair freshly styled, and she was wearing her vanilla lip-gloss, but she put on a little bit more just to be safe. She couldn't wait to see Mr. Alder and show him her work, and... she couldn't get the memory of him glancing at her cleavage out of her mind.

Maybe he wasn't *just* a romantic.

But as she went, she nearly stumbled into a very disgruntled—and purple—Mr. Mullard. The man was wearing a fresh suit, but his face and hair—and hands—were stained a deep, dark purple.

"Watch where you're going," he muttered lowly.

Which, for him, was a vast improvement on his usual yelling and insults.

She decided not to push it. He'd had a miserable enough day, so she just muttered, "Sorry, Mr. Mullard," dutifully as she passed.

She came to Mr. Alder's door at just about the perfect time to meet the handsome instructor carrying a cloth wrapped bundle back to his office.

"Well, what perfect timing, Ms. Casey. I think a jinx is in order," he said with a playful smile before unlocking his office door. "After you," he said, courteously, sweeping his arm towards the interior.

She stepped inwards, her high heels clicking on the linoleum floor. It was dark, but she remembered the layout pretty well, and he was a diligent man who liked everything in its place, which made it easy to avoid the furniture.

"A jinx?" she said with a little giggle. "Doesn't that mean one of us can't talk?"

"Oh no. We can't have that," he said as he came in, turned on the light—then adjusted the dimmer to make it a bit less bright—before shutting the door. "We will have to come to some accommodation," he remarked, putting the bundle onto the desk with a smile. "And I hope you're not shaken up after the incident today," he said, concern on his face.

"It was a pretty wild day," she said, though she wasn't *really* speaking about the ink-bomb. Well, she was, but in a roundabout way.

"Are you okay? I guess all the teachers must be a little worried."

Mr. Alder shrugged a little at that as he began to

unwrap the package, showing it was a neatly parceled meal, and didn't seem to be something from the cafeteria at all. He arranged the containers onto the table, the separate ramekins and dishes, all square or rectangular so they fit together into that neat package.

"Some are. But to be honest, everyone knew that Mr. Mullard kinda... invited students' wrath," he said diplomatically.

"Yea... he told me I had the wrong answer this morning. Got me up in front of everyone to prove my answer, couldn't find anything wrong, and still told the other students not to be stupid like me," Casey lamented as she delicately took a seat, folding her skirt under her rear as she did. She looked up from the meal to him, and smiled warmly. "I'm sure no one would want to hurt you, though. You're always fair."

"Oh shucks," he said teasingly at that, as he took out a bottle, uncorked it and poured up some sparkling water into two glasses. "But no, I don't think I've managed to make an enemy of many students in my time. And I don't think embarrassing students is good for inducing learning, personally," he said with a smile.

"It wasn't very nice," she agreed. "But the dinner looks... amazing. I don't think I've ever had a meal that looked this fancy before."

Mr. Alder stood there in his fancy suit, looking even better than usual, Casey thought. The blazer was black, but looked like it was made of some soft fabric. Beneath he had a paisley gold vest that glinted in the dim light, then with a red tufted silk ascot, instead of his usual tie.

"You think so? I made it myself," he said with a smile.

"It's not easy operating out of my cottage, but... I do hope you agree, I think it pays off," he said warmly with a smile. "Oh! That reminds me," he said, opening a desk drawer, and taking out a long, fancy gift box.

Casey's mouth dropped open in surprise, or perhaps confusion.

"What... you got me something?" she asked with a tilt of her head, her strawberry blonde hair curling to the side.

He was making this little grading session so special, and he looked so handsome, and the food all looked so delicious, it was making her feel a little out of her league. She wasn't even wearing *panties*!

"I told you I would have something for you," he said with his usual dashing smile. And he opened the box, revealing a bright red, silk scarf. "It's not exactly the same as a fitting top, but... I thought it might look lovely around your neck, and could be worn to make yourself more modest... if you like," he said with that charming half-smile of his.

She was *almost* disappointed at his suggestion, but it was too beautiful to give her more than a half-second's pause.

"I know you said you'd have something for me, but I thought perhaps a lend of a book. Not something so... exquisite and beautiful," she admitted, her green gaze drawn to his handsome face. He must be in his mid-thirties, she thought. Old enough to look masculine, but still with some youth and vibrance to his warm countenance.

"Mr. Alder, it's really beautiful."

"Would you like me to put it on you? See what you

think?" he asked, taking the silk scarf out, then placing the box back into the drawer.

"Okay. Should I go to the mirror again?" she asked, delicately standing. Her stockings had a slight sheen in the dim light, hugging the curve of her toned calves, before finding purchase in her softer, feminine thighs. With her skirt pulled up as much as it was, the hem ended just below the lace rim of her thigh-highs.

"That should do just nicely," he said, as he placed one of his nimble hands at the small of her back, guiding her to the mirror. He stood behind her there, so much taller than her as he gingerly gathered up her hair, then began to wrap the soft, smooth silk around her neck. "You're luckily a very lovely girl, so it'd be hard to go wrong with you, fashion-wise," he explained, as he situated the scarf meticulously, making it look like a collar, before he tied the scarf to one side. "Now... you can wear it a few ways. One of which is like this," he said, putting it to the side, thereby leaving her cleavage still showing. "Or, like this..." he said, tucking the loose ends down into her open shirt, in such a way that vaguely resembled his ascot, but hid her cleavage.

Of course, another side effect of that was Mr. Alder's hands were touching her breasts! Well, through the silk scarf and only momentarily, but still.

On a normal day, that would have been enough to fill her dreams for weeks, and she let out a soft coo of delight. A thrill ran down her spine, and she smiled at his reflection.

"What way do you like it best?" she asked, her voice coming out like honied syrup.

Mr. Alder smiled, and very smoothly pulled the scarf

back to her side. The silk serving as like a shiny red collar on her slender neck, with the billowy part over her shoulder.

"You have absolutely nothing to hide or be ashamed of, Ms. Casey," he said in his warm, affectionate voice.

Just being in his presence was an aphrodisiac for her. Her skin was flushed, her knees gave a little tremble, and she looked up at him with her emerald eyes.

"We match if I wear it the other way, though," she said with a soft trill of arousal beneath her sweet, syrupy voice. "Can you show me again how to tuck it in?"

"Of course," he said with a smile, his voice seeming to have changed, becoming a little deeper. His arms reached around her and over her shoulder, his long, slender fingers pushing the silk down into her shirt. The tips of his digits lightly pressing into her bust as he looked at her in the mirror. "Just... like... this. You got it?"

"I think so," she said with a ginger smile. "Though the material is so soft, I'm not sure how well it'd stay in place when I move around. I was in gym today and my top nearly flipped up while helping someone do push-ups." It's a detail she would've likely mentioned innocently enough, but today, she wasn't bringing it up innocuously. She wanted to see how he'd react to that.

Mr. Alder's smooth hands went to her shoulders, rubbing down along her arm then back up as he smiled at her.

"It's not too surprising. You're a... particularly gifted young lady, Ms. Casey. In many respects," he said warmly. "I hope it wasn't too embarrassing for you however."

"No. I thought Mr. Grieg was gonna chastise me, but he just gave me some tape to help. I don't think it'll be enough to wrap around me every day, but I guess I'll try to figure it out," she said with a shrug. "But everyone's been pretty understanding. Most of all you," she purred affectionately at her teacher.

"I'm glad to hear that," he said to her, squeezing her shoulders and smiling. "It's at times felt quite lonely out here, no longer free to head off to visit family, friends, or vacation. But you're a rare sunny spot on my days, Casey," he said, still smiling at her in the mirror.

"You don't have a sweet little wife in that cottage?" she finally got up the courage to ask, even though she really didn't want to know if the answer was yes. Even if her love was unrequited, it still brought her such joy and excitement every day.

"Alas... no," he said, bringing a hand up to her face, lightly brushing her red ringlets from her ear, to let the backs of his fingers lightly caress her lobe and neck. "I end my days in a warm, tidy... lonely cottage," he said.

"How?" The question wasn't really a rational one, she just really didn't understand. She looked at him with such tenderness, a desperate longing hidden in the recesses of her gaze. "I mean... you're so handsome and charming and... perfect."

He smiled a bit bashfully at that, looking down for a moment. But he leaned in and kissed the back of her hair, pausing a moment to inhale its scent.

"I guess I just... hadn't found the right woman before," he said lowly, in that lightly accented voice.

Her heart thudded in her chest and she nodded. It was the only explanation that made sense. That he would be looking for his soulmate.

And while she could never presume to be that, she hoped that maybe... she could be something else.

"It's hard to find your soulmate when the whole world is shut down, huh," she said, her voice lowered.

"Indeed," he said, smiling warmly. "But having you here with me today... it doesn't feel so hopeless," he remarked, brushing the backs of his fingers along her cheek. "And what does the beautiful and brilliant Ms. Casey hope to find in life, hm?"

"Oh. Ah," she replied, being a bit taken off guard by the question. She *hated* to lie, or even to fib. Especially with someone she respected so much.

"I think I'm still learning what I like. But I know I want you. I mean, to be like you. A teacher, someone who's so passionate and filled with love for his work..." she blurted out.

"And my students," he said, tilting his head and then slowly turning her around to face him. "Or at least one in particular," he remarked with that charmingly crooked smile on his handsome face. The aroma of his light cologne so delightful.

Her heart was beating so loudly she wasn't quite sure she heard him right.

Her lips parted as she silently worked through it, her gaze darting from his eyes to his mouth and back again.

"Wh-what do you mean?" she breathed out, barely a whisper.

He cupped her cheek, caressing it with his thumb, letting it stray close to her lower lip as he leaned in and kissed her forehead.

"You must think me a foul man," he said softly. "To

invite you here... to talk to you so," he remarked as his other hand trailed down her arm, then to her side. "But you are like a beautiful oasis, in the center of an endless desert, Casey... with glittering pools, verdant, lush foliage... and all I can think of anymore, is taking a dip."

Her breathing caught, and for a moment, she felt faint. Her knees threatened to give way, and she reached out to his chest, steadying herself upon him.

"I could never think you foul," she said, her first instinct to defend him at all costs. Even against his own guilty conscience. "You're... amazing. I've never been so happy as to have you invite me here..."

"Even if I told you that my motives were... less to do with the work than with spending time with you, sweet Casey?" he asked, his head dipping lower with time, drifting closer towards her own face as his head tilted to one side.

"I want you to spend time with me," she whimpered back. She'd started out fairly confident, flirtatious even, but she was quickly being swept up in the moment. Her mind was going fuzzy, her body trembling like an excited fawn. "This is all I wanted."

"This is all?" he asked, brow arched as he let his hand slid to her back, pulling her in closer, holding her tight as their mouths drifted closer together.

"I can want more," she whispered, her breasts pressing in against his ribs as he held her. She was learning, though, that without the safety of her panties, her arousal was becoming even more apparent, and it was making her squirm.

"And what could you want, my lovely Ms. Casey?" he

asked, his fingertips grasping some of her curly red hair, toying with it, as he caressed her cheek, and held her closely. "Because... I want but a little... though it's still too much. I should not even say," he remarked.

She'd been with other guys, but Mr. Alder was different. Not only was he a teacher, a real man, he was also her very first crush. The man she dreamed about on lonely nights, who had always seemed so untouchable. Yet here he was, caressing her, pushing his body against hers, making her pussy pulse with such undeniable need.

"I'd give you anything you asked for," she whimpered.

"Ohh Cascy..." he said, sighing softly as he kissed the very corner of her lips, ever so lightly. "Dangerous words. Such dangerous words... if only you knew how deep my desires run. How much I yearn to have you, every which way a man might imagine."

Sixteen

 ❧

It was stunning to have all her dreams come true in one moment, and her mouth parted with a sigh of delight.

"I mean it, Mr. Alder. Try me. I promise. I... you can see how much I want it, can't you?"

His hand sank a little lower, to the cusp of her bottom, his pinky finger caressing along the waist of her skirt and dipping lower for fleeting moments. He sighed in longing, nuzzled his nose to hers.

"Ohh Casey... it's more complicated than that. Even though I long to hear about what you want from me... and how deep that yearning goes too," he said.

"Why does it have to be more complicated? I won't tell anyone. I promise," she said, so sweetly. She looked up at him, her emerald eyes sparkling as her lower lip trembled. "Please, Mr. Alder. Tell me what you want."

He looked her in the eyes. His own gaze so intense, so deep. And then he closed the gap, and their lips met flush and together. His skillful kisses more intense than any before, as he thread his fingers through her hair to the back of her head, and let his tongue explore into her mouth.

She could have screamed with delight in that moment, but she restrained herself. Her arms were thrown around his neck as she pulled him closer, her kiss still amateurish, but filled with raw and undiluted passion.

And as she clung to his neck, his hand slid down onto her ass entirely, squeezing and cupping her bubbly round ass cheeks, feeling their supple flesh. And he lifted her up by it, as they made out passionately. His tongue caressing hers, their mouths mingling, his lean, hard body against her soft, feminine form. It all felt oh so perfect.

And the swell of his manhood, that incessant throb she was becoming so familiar with... exquisite.

She knew that he could feel that she wasn't wearing any panties, and more than anything, she hoped it eased his conscience. She didn't want him to feel guilty for giving her what she'd been wanting for so long. She just wanted to come together with him, to be one...

She held herself against him, her legs wrapping around his waist as her glossy lips pressed against his.

He lifted her, carrying her to the wall, pressing her back against it as his hand went up beneath her skirt. And that deep moan he gave, as his fingers felt along her smooth, bare flesh, felt her heated wetness eking from her fertile slit...

"Casey," he gasped her name in between smacks of their lips. "You want this to... don't you?" he asked, as his fingers moved in, and caressed her bare, glistening pussy.

She was so wet; it was impossible to deny just how much she wanted it.

"I thought I was being silly to hope that you might...

like me," Casey said, her voice filled with such raw emotion. "I've dreamed about you so many times... I tried not to, but I could never get you out of my head long."

He looked her in the eyes after plucking another kiss from her lips. Then brought his hand up from her pussy, to slowly suckle the honey from each fingertip in turn.

"You are exquisite, Casey... I have been unable to stop myself from fantasizing about having you. From the moment I met you, I knew you were special. That I would find my heart melting for you..." His hand went back down, undoing his belt, his pants. "I need you. I need to feel myself inside you..." he confessed.

Dahlia had given her a condom, told her about preventing diseases, but Mr. Alder was a perfect specimen, so it didn't even enter Casey's mind to suggest it, let alone disentangle herself to go get it from her bag. She was too wound up to think about anything other than the actual gift he was about to give her.

Eagerly, her fingers went to her blouse, letting the strained buttons pop free of their holes before tossing the shirt aside.

"You've done this before, haven't you?" he asked breathily, as his pants opened, and his thick cock sprang out. That purple crown brushing along her cunny, as he teased her, positioning himself slowly. All the while showering her with kisses.

"I wanted to learn, so I wouldn't embarrass myself in front of you," she confessed breathlessly. Her fingers went to her bra hook, letting it spring free, her large breasts bouncing as they were released. But her gaze was instantly drawn to his cock, fascinated by the sight of it as it touched her soaking wet pussy. Her skirt was flipped up in her lap, and she tugged up the pleated hem a little more so that she could get a better look.

But Mr. Alder smiled, and kissed her neck, down to her breast, showering it with sensual affections from his mouth as he continued to tease her pussy with his cock.

"You are an amazing woman, Casey... this makes everything so much easier. I was afraid I was corrupting you," he confessed, as the head of his cock nudged against her vulva, making it blossom around that plum-coloured tip. His mouth caught her nipple, and suckled it into his mouth at that moment.

She gasped, her hand going to her under bust and pushing it up to his hungry mouth, so he didn't have to arch down so hard. She offered herself up to him, her high heels digging into his calves as her hips instinctively began to wriggle forward.

"I want you to teach me what you like," she whimpered. "I want to be your perfect student."

"And I want to know everything about you, Casey. Everything you crave and desire," he said as he teasingly sunk an inch of his cock into her, stretching her little slit open, before rocking back. Then he pushed in again. Back and forth, easing just a bit more into her at times, drawing out the moment as he suckled her breast again before letting her teat fall from his mouth. "I want you to be mine for a long time..."

"Yours?" she breathed out, as happy as she'd ever been. Her cheeks were flushed with desire, and the hand that was holding her breast dropped down between them. She wrapped it around the root of his shaft, and began jerking him off, that crown of his still teasingly lodged within her pussy.

"Do you like that?" she asked curiously.

Mr. Alder's gentle rocking slowed, as his whole body trembled from the intensity of his rising desire. Her soft hand stroking his shaft, as the head of his cock was barely lodged within her. He had a long shaft, nicely thick, and he moaned lowly as he nodded.

"Oh yes…" he grunted, before licking her breast again, then kissing her neck. "Mmm, that feels so… so good… Ohh Casey," he moaned.

She got drunk on his praise, her back arching to give him any bit of access he wanted to her body. Never did she think that one day, she'd be sat on the edge of her teacher's desk, feeling his cock as he teased her.

"When you unbuttoned my blouse yesterday, I wished you had done more," she confessed.

He shuddered and moaned some more as he nodded, one hand cupping a breast, fondling it. His soft, expert hands caressing that large, but sensitive breast.

"So did I…" he confessed, as she kept stroking him. "You are so… exquisite. Beyond beautiful. It has only gotten harder and harder to resist you, Casey… my little teacher's pet," he husked, before giving her neck a light nip.

She moaned louder, that sensation so delightful for her, and her stroking hand stumbled in its rhythmic motion.

"But I'm glad you didn't, because now you don't have to feel bad about corrupting me," she whimpered, her hips rocking a bit more urgently as she teased the both of them. He was already in her bare, the only one of her suitors who never even mentioned a condom. So, she knew she had to be right about him. There was nothing for them to worry about.

"Mmm, oh god, Casey... there is still a lot for me to feel bad about," he said, squeezing her breast, kissing her lips, then beginning to rock his hips once more, pumping his shaft into her slowly, sensually letting his pace ramp up only slowly. "Like how I want to cum inside you... how I want to knock you up, and mark you as mine... even though I know it could be the ruin of us both..." he groaned.

"Knock me up?" she moaned in question. She'd heard Dahlia say something about that once. That a girl got knocked up and had to go home.

She didn't really know what it meant, but it sounded fun.

"As long as I don't have to leave school..." she said as she looked up at him with those innocent, green eyes. She started to remove her hand from between them as he started thrusting into her, allowing her soft thighs to press in against his firm hips. "If it's what you want, I mean..." she said, having no idea what she was agreeing to.

His eyes were heavily lidded when they met hers, and he moaned as he reached down to her knees, pressing her legs open wider. He nodded and licked his lips as he thrust into her deeper, until almost all of his shaft was sinking up into her.

"I do," he confessed breathily, as he picked up his pace, and finally, his cock hilted up in her, hitting her utmost depths to make her give a little squeal. "I want to see you knocked up by me... smiling at me from your seat in class... our little secret... our love unquenchable," he moaned.

She'd kept lots of secrets for Dahlia, but never any of

her own. It was sinful to keep secrets. Yet he made it sound so good! It was impossible for the naive young woman to resist that, and she held onto the edge of the desk. She leaned back, letting him fuck into her deeper as she gasped and panted.

"Then I want you to knock me up, Mr. Alder! I need it just as bad!"

He bent over her, one hand gripping the desk, the other squeezing one of her large, jiggling breasts. He moaned out loudly, as he picked up his pace, the meticulously laid out meal shoved aside a bit, the dishes rattling as he pounded into her fast and hard. Harder than any but the masked stranger had dared take her.

"Mmm, oh god Casey... you're so perfect. I want you to cum on my cock as I breed you," he rumbled, releasing her breast, to let one smooth hand slide down to her mound, his thumb working at her clit expertly.

"Breed me?" she gasped out, though it was impossible to tell for sure if it was a request or a question. Either way, her body was already quaking, and with his skilled touch, she wasn't going to last much longer. She panted out loudly, not holding anything back as she began to gasp and cry out.

"I want you to cum in me!" she squealed, repeating what the vigilante had commanded her to say.

"Ah, oh god, I'm gonna cum in you, Casey!" He gasped out, trembling as he pounded into her. Those large tits left to jiggle and bounce atop her chest as he hammered into her with wild abandon. "A-Ah! F-Fuck!" he gasped, as he shoved himself in one final time, thrusting up deep as his cock erupted. His virile seed flooding her fertile depths as he tensed up, feeling a firework of sensations behind his closed eyes as he came inside her quite intentionally.

It was that action, that final thrust, that made everything inside of her begin to sing. Her calves tightened around his hips, pulling him into her as she came. She might not have known the risk she was taking again for the fourth time in 24 hours, but she wanted it so bad. Her body wanted it so bad. Her pussy muscles grasped Mr. Alder's cock, milking him dry as they both cried out with glee.

He tried to shove in even deeper as his cock spurt thick, creamy seed into her. But there was no further to go, he just grunted and moaned, as he emptied all he had inside her, with that full, illicit intention of knocking her up. He shuddered and kissed her lips, passionately making out with her once more as he trembled atop her.

Until finally his load was emptied and he was panting.

"Oh god, Casey... that was... unbelievable," he gasped, kissing her lips repeatedly.

Her lips met his eagerly, no less blown away by the sex. She didn't want it to end, for them to be interrupted.

"Can we hide here for the night?" she asked so softly and sweetly.

"Mmm." He kissed her, lingering there for a moment. "We can stay for a couple more hours at least... but aren't you worried about getting in trouble for being a no-show at roll call?" He panted over her as he slowly lifted himself up, sliding his cock from her slit as he tugged out his kerchief, to cup her mound and prevent his seed from spilling out. "Press your thighs together tightly," he instructed her.

She followed his order obediently, clamping her soft thighs down on the kerchief, sealing his seed within her.

"I'm sure no one will think anything untoward about me," Casey said earnestly. "Dahlia said she'd tell them I was in the washroom if I was late tonight."

He smiled and rested back in his behind his desk, his cock still glistening with her honey and exposed as he caught his breath.

"She did? You're not going to tell her about us though, right?" he asked, licking his lips as he eyed her, with obvious hunger in his eyes as he swept his gaze over her form.

"I'll tell her you were a perfect gentleman and we got caught up talking about books. And I promise, I'll look suitably disappointed. She... knows how I feel about you. What I wanted," Casey confessed, her gaze dipping to his cock hungrily. "Should I clean you?"

Seventeen

⟨decorative flourish⟩

r. Alder looked from her to his cock, then a grin grew on his face.

"Of course," he said, taking up his glass, sipping some of the sparkling water. "God Casey, you are even better than I imagined," he said with a husky moan as he laid back, and relaxed, taking up some kind of finger food from a dish, to bite into.

"I want to be the best," she said as she carefully slid from the desk, not wanting to disturb the handkerchief as she moved.

She got onto her knees in front of him, her hand going to his hip as her other palm grasped around his shaft. She stared up at him with such awe and desire, and then her kittenish tongue poked out, beginning to gather up their fluids on it.

"Mmm…" he groaned as she began to clean his cock of their combined fluids, his free hand going to her thick, strawberry blonde hair, caressing it, luxuriating in it's rich, lustrous feel. "We'll stay late then… but we still have to creep back before the night's over... it'll be too suspicious if we're both not in our beds come morning," he said, his voice deeper than usual as he relished her attention.

"Okay," she whispered between luxuriating laps of her tongue along his shaft. "I love how you feel. This is more than I ever dreamed of." Her mouth went lower, finding his sac, beginning to clean that gently and diligently.

He looked down at her, knelt between his thighs, licking at his cock... talking about how this was more than she dreamed of. It was like a license for him to give into all his most depraved desires, as he caressed her hair.

"You are so stunningly perfect... I want to do this with you every day," he said, moaning softly, as his semi-turgid cock twitched from her attentions. "And when you graduate... I'll make you mine officially. You can move into my cottage with me. Do you like the sound of that, Casey?" he asked.

"I want to be yours," she agreed, a warmth flooding her face as her mouth continued to work his shaft, not ready to be finished cleaning him until his shaft softened. She was diligent in all things, and certainly no less so in this. She was eager for the opportunity to please him, to show him that she could be his soulmate.

But with her sensual attentions, and his utter enrapturement with her beauty, his cock never quite went down. Not even as they chatted and talked a while, with Mr. Alder snacking lightly. And in fact, before long his cock was fully thick and hard again.

"Mmm, look what a good girl you've been... you've gone and gotten me hard all over again, pet," he murred, caressing her hair.

It was strange, being a good girl in letting a cock go soft, and also in getting him hard again. But what Mr. Alder said superseded all else, and her plush lips quickly spread into a wide smile.

"Wanna breed me again?" she asked innocently, in a perky, chipper tone.

He smiled at her lewd little question, and groaned.

"More than anything," he said, his hands going to hers, helping her rise up. "Come here. Ever ridden a cock before, my pet?" he asked her, as he guided her to straddle over him. He brought one hand to keep the kerchief in place, until she was positioned over his shaft.

"No, but I want you to teach me," she said, her hand on his chest for balance. Her skirt was still on, shielding their view of her puffy, pink pussy, the tip of her high heels hooked in against the edge of the chair for balance.

"What do I do?"

Mr. Alder watched her, then took her skirt, undoing it at the side and tossing it to the floor so he could get a full, perfect view her tiny, tight pink slit, swallowing up his shaft as he guided her down around it.

"Mmm," he moaned, watching that tiny, young flower swallow up his cock, before his hands went to her hips. "You ride up... and down," he said, as he began to lift her body, then guide it back into place. "Like this... again and again. Until you've milked every last drop of cum from me... you understand, my sweet Casey?" he asked.

Her hands went around his neck to the back of his chair, getting herself a little more comfortable.

"Whatever you want, Mr. Alder. I'll do anything for you," she said, too naive to know what a dangerous promise that was to make. Still, she intended to keep it, and she began to ride his shaft, letting out a little gasp of pleasure as she got used to the new sensation. She was more in control, and she was learning that even a slight tilt of her hips could make her see a smattering of stars.

And while she took over on riding him, his smooth, nimble hand went to her breasts. The other remained on her hip and ass, helping her rise and fall, while he toyed with her bouncing, jiggling breasts. Fondling those perky mounds, luxuriating in their soft yet supple allure. He teasingly caressed her sensitive areolas and nipples as he moaned without restrain.

"God, Casey... this is even better than I dreamed," he groaned out, his cock twitching inside her as it shot off some more pre-cum.

"You dreamed of me?" she gasped, a slight dew appearing along her collarbones as she rode him. It highlighted her pale skin, the smattering of freckles on her sensitive flesh. She had a pleasant pinkishness to her, a youthful glow that was only accentuated by the intimate moment.

"You dreamed of me riding you like this?"

"Mmm," he nodded slowly, watching her body move so sensually as he guided her, unable to tear his eyes away from how her tits jiggled and bounced. "Constantly. You have no idea how many hours of sleep you cost me... keeping me awake at night, cock harder than steel because all I can think of is you... your gorgeous body, and how I wanted—no, needed—you, Casey."

"You should have told me," she said, her voice filled with regret. "I would have been happy to have had you teach me everything." Her fingers caressed the back of his neck as she leaned in, kissing his mouth, letting her tongue explore his. All the while, her hips kept rising up and coming back down, her round, firm ass slapping against his thighs.

He kissed her back, caressing her ass and breasts, then alternating between squeezing and fondling both while their tongues played. Until finally his lips broke from hers, and he spoke in such lusty tones.

"Mmm, you really would've jumped to help me, wouldn't you? Even then, you'd do whatever I asked? God I am so fortunate to have you as my student... as mine," he husked. "I wanna cum inside you every day if we can manage it... fuck Casey," he moaned, kissing her again, as this much longer fuck drew onwards into the night.

She didn't show any signs of tiring, not really. They weren't going at a fast speed, but taking their time, this time allowing themselves to luxuriate in the moment and experience it more fully.

"I want you every day," she whispered as she kissed down his jawline, towards his ear. "I've lost all my panties, too."

He grinned at that, tilting his head a bit as his cock pulsated and throbbed inside her.

"I could buy you more..." he said, leaning in and licking her earlobe. "Sexy panties and bras. Lingerie... what would you think of that, sweet pet?" he asked amid his deep moans.

"I'd like any gift you brought me, Mr. Alder."

She breathed her warm, sweet sighs against his chest as she rested there, her hips still rising and falling to take him into her hot pussy. It was so nice, almost romantic, if not for the wrongness of it all.

He kissed her again, squeezing her ass with both hands, as he helped her move as they went on longer and longer. There were no words for a long time, just them moaning and panting, oohing, ahhing. Until finally he kissed her neck, suckled her ear, and spoke into her ear.

"I have another gift for you... you want another big load of my seed, deep inside you, Casey?" he asked, groaning.

"I do," she cooed out, her words a bit slurred after the prolonged session, but it only made her sound more desperate for him. For his cum. For that risk that she was only too willing to take for him.

"Mmm, good girl..." he groaned, biting her earlobe as he helped her ride his shaft, with his two hands lifting her up, then pulling her down. He panted, moaned. The moment drawn out long, even after their rutting had already lasted for... two hours? It was hard for her to even wrap her head around it anymore. There was just his body, the sounds of his moans and pants, and then...

"Ohh, Casey..." he sighed out, as his cock thickened, then shot off another rich load of his cum into her.

It was no less intense the second time around, but it was different. More intimate in a way, like a mental orgasm of pride and pleasure mingling together. She'd gotten him off twice in one evening, and she celebrated with excited kisses over his cheek, jaw, down his neck, before finally returning to his lips.

"I love you, Mr. Alder. I'm so happy you want to make me yours."

He smiled and laughed softly, caressing her as his cock

finished firing off the last of what he had into her. He groaned and wrapped her up in his arms, squeezing her all around as he lavished kisses on her in return.

"Mm, you are mine. But until you graduate... we'll have to keep acting as if everything is normal. No changes in how we act or live, you understand?" he said to her, smiling as he then offered her some braised carrot from one of the dishes, that she'd so far still hadn't tried. It was cold now, but still delicious.

And that was how they spent the rest of the evening. Still entangled, touching each other, caressing, kissing. Talking about what they'd done, what they wanted to do, and far more. Until the hour was so severely late, she'd be lucky to get a couple hours sleep before class began.

She was still reluctant to leave, but he told her she had to be a good girl, so she got sloppily redressed, and grabbed her bag.

"Oh, right! I should give you the assignment you gave me," Casey said, taking out the file folder and setting it down on his desk. She didn't notice the condom had gotten stuck between one of the pages, too enamored with him to even chance looking away for a second. "I hope I did okay on them. Ever since you gave it to me, I've been... distracted, but I still tried my best," she promised.

Mr. Alder leaned over his desk and kissed her, not noticing the odd addition in that moment either.

"Mmm, I am absolutely certain you did great, Casey," he said, caressing her cheek. "Now be safe and quiet on your way back, hm?" he cautioned, smiling at her, then kissing her again.

"I will, I promise," she said, wrapping her arms around

him in a warm hug. "You're the best teacher a girl could hope for. But I'll pretend to be devastated that you turned me down. A true professional in every regard," she said, turning towards the door and giving him a brief flash of his handkerchief between her thighs.

He smiled and grinned at her, as she headed off into the night.

Everything was so deathly silent as she made her way back. It was unsettling in a way. Quite unnerving. And despite its stillness, she couldn't help but feel like she was being watched on her way.

But she made it back to the girl's dorms, and to her room. Finding Dahlia quite unconscious, snoring away as she was able to slip into bed.

She got changed into her nightgown, and even though she was exhausted, it was hard to fall asleep.

She was in love, and he was in love with her.

Sure, he never said that, but a school girl crush was anything but rational. She lay there for what felt like a long time, imagining what it would be like to belong to *him*.

Of course, she was unused to staying up so late, and operating on so little sleep. She was deep in slumber when finally Dahlia awoke. And even when her considerate friend tried to wake her, she didn't stir. So finally, Dahlia decided to let Casey sleep and tell everyone that her late-night delay to the bathroom, must've been the onset of sickness.

The thoughtful gesture, however, meant she was alone and unconscious when her window slid open, and a mysterious figure crept in.

Eighteen

The hooded figure moved silently into Casey's room, finding the girl deep in sleep.

Her curls fanned out around her face, her blankets having got slightly pushed down as she sought to get comfortable. The night dress she wore was fitted, snuggly wrapping around her voluptuous form as it inched up at the bottom.

She was lost to a world of pleasant, erotic dreams, and little half-moans escaped her lips as she slept.

The masked stranger sized her up, then took off his gloves. He touched her forehead, finding nothing off in her temperature, no sign of sickness. So, he knew the real reason she was still in bed: staying out late.

True to their discussion of a 'surprise', he then began to help himself to her. His hands sliding her nightdress up over her hip, revealing her panty-less bottom. That beautiful sight enough to make his cock throb and thicken.

Casey had fallen down a deep rabbit hole in her sexual awakening, one that she never could have anticipated. The

147

depths of debauchery and delights were extreme, yet her body had been denied for so long, it all too readily responded to the slight touch.

"Ah," she breathed out, shifting onto her side, faced away from the stranger.

The keen eyes of that anonymous man watched her shift, patiently waiting before he got down, bending his knees. He stared at her ass, before squeezing one cheek lightly, parting it from the other to stare at her pretty pink pussy. He then carefully reached in, lightly nudging at her vulva, to test for dampness and arousal.

And oh, she was *aroused*. That had been her near permanent state for months now, and finally giving in to her libido had done very little to quell that. In many ways, it simply ignited her needs, considering how enjoyable the act was.

At some point, the kerchief that Mr. Alder had given her had fallen from between her thighs, leaving her swollen, pink pussy slick.

And the anonymous masked vigilante took that as his free pass. He undid his pants, then took his cock in hand, giving it a few strokes to get it to full size, while his other hand caressed her ass.

Once that bulbous purple tip was fully hard, he guided it in. His one hand parting her ass cheeks again, as he slid his cock along her pussy folds, teasing them, as he watched her for some response.

It had been a long day. She'd been fucked by three men, on top of her classes, and stayed up way too late. That all made her a lot slower to respond than she might usually, and even though she moaned lewdly, her lashes still fluttered only lightly.

To her, it was all a beautiful, hot dream.

For him? It was a little more tangible, as he slowly sank inside her pussy, stretching her tight little hole open. He tried to be quiet, but a soft moan passed his lips as he sank into that wet, willing pussy, easing himself in so as to not startle her awake. He was just grateful that her ass had been so conveniently positioned towards the edge of the bed as he began to rock his hips slowly and gently.

She made it so easy for him to take her. She barely even stirred, except to shift and arch her back just a little more, giving him easier access to her depths. She was starting to come to, her breaths coming out faster as she began to moan more readily.

He might've stopped then, given her time to slip back into deep sleep. But he'd promised her a surprise, after all. And he kept rocking his hips gently, pumping into her, raw and unprotected. That thick, hard cock pulsating excitedly as it got to experience her tight, wet depths unimpeded, just the way nature intended.

Soft little moans escaping his lips as he helped himself to her, letting his hand caress her ass, while the other lifted her nightdress further. After all, he wanted a view of those gorgeous tits, that every guy on campus was drooling over.

"Ah," she gasped, the air feeling chilly without her coverings, though it didn't startle her awake. Not yet. Not even as her nipples stiffened, her breasts pressed together as she lay on her side.

Her hand went to try to find the hem of her nightgown and pull it down, but he kept it hooked on a finger so she couldn't tug it back into place. Not while she slumbered, at least.

Maybe that was the thing that started to pull her awake, made her moans sound more real.

It was the perfect soundtrack to fucking her tight pussy, and watching her tits jiggle lightly. His rock-hard cock eager to fuck her harder, faster, but holding back... just barely.

He groaned softly, as he let one hand caress a breast lightly, as his cock spurt pre-cum into her. And he felt himself building towards his release surprisingly early. He shuddered at that growing, fiery sensation, chalking it up to how fucking hot the situation was, that he was getting close to cumming so soon.

"Wh..." she murmured, her eyes beginning to flutter open against the dim morning light that filtered in through the curtain.

"A-Ah!" he gasped, as his pace suddenly quickened, his hips and groin smacking against her ass as he worked his cock into her. His hand squeezing her breast, letting his long fingers sink into that flesh. And he shuddered, moaned... and then...

"F-Fuck!" he gasped out, as he began to cum inside her. Thick long strands of pearly white seed flooding her depths as he shuddered and tensed.

She was still barely awake, even though her body tingled with delight at that illicit romp she was only just becoming aware of.

She wiped her eyes with her fists, her torso contorting slightly to look at him, her lips parting in surprise and confusion.

And he greeted her with a few more hard thrusts that

made her body reel a little, jabbing his virile seed deep into her as he grunted and groaned. That hand squeezing her breast as he panted out, moaning.

"Ohh f-fuck, Casey..." he groaned as his body trembled at the tail end of his climax.

"It's you," she murmured sleepily. "You know my name?" She couldn't remember him using it before, or introducing herself. Perhaps it was just the grogginess. "We went all the way?"

"Y-yeah," he said with a nod, squeezing her breast, giving a few final slow pumps into her as he tried to get every last drop of seed out of his balls. "I promised you a surprise after all," he said, grinning beneath his mask as he gave her ass a playful little slap.

Her expression softened and she looked at him with such affection. She clearly saw nothing wrong with his actions, and only seemed endeared by them.

"Oh. Well, I was mostly sleeping for it, but I was having a wonderful dream..."

"Mmm, I'd say I hope it was me in your dream too... but that might be wishful thinking," he remarked as he slowly caught his breath, caressing her flesh, admiring every perfect supple curve, every inch of pristine skin.

"I don't really remember the details. Just that it was so nice," she said, her torso twisted so she could look up at him. "I'm glad you came to visit," she said, before looking at Dahlia's bed and belatedly realizing her roommate wasn't there.

"Oh my God, what happened to Dahlia?"

He glanced to the other girl's empty bed then shrugged. "Already at class, I presume. I snuck in here to check on you, when I noticed you weren't at class. Seems your friend covered for you, so you could sleep in," he said, letting his finger tips trail around her clit ever so lightly teasing her.

"Oh my God! I'm late for class?!" she exclaimed, jerking upwards to sit, a frantic energy to her that was not even calmed by that desirable touch. She had never missed class before, and the panic ran deep.

Her sudden movement caused their bodies to disentangle, and his cock slipped from her pussy, leaving her drooling his freshly unloaded seed. He grunted and stepped back, reaching for some tissues at her bedside to tidy up.

"Yeah, you won't wanna miss gym class today," he said to her, touching his fingers to his lips then blowing her a kiss. "Anyhow, I just wanted to see if you're okay. And give you a gift. Or two," he said.

Her hand went to her forehead, and she was in too much of a tizzy to even remember that she'd told him that Leslie had been bullying her, or that it was the reason she shouldn't miss gym.

In fact, she almost looked on the brink of tears, quite the departure from the happy, dazed smile of finding him fucking her while she slept.

"I'm sorry, I don't mean to be rude. I'm really glad you came," she said, not even aware of the double entendre. "I just really didn't mean to oversleep. Oh, Casey, you've really done it this time," she said, hopping out of bed and rushing to her closet.

The masked stranger watched her a moment longer.

"Best wishes, beautiful. Hope you enjoy the day," he said as he finished tidying himself up as her back was turned.

"Yea, you too," she said, grabbing a blouse and skirt from the closet and throwing them on, somehow forgetting her bra in all her hurry. "I really don't mean to be rude, you know. I'm not mad at you," she explained.

But once she turned, she saw he was gone already. Her window sliding shut.

And when she glanced at the time, she realized she'd missed her first two periods entirely. Luckily one of them was with Mr. Alder, so he'd cover for her. But still... that was her favourite class!

That left her with time to get to... gym.

"Shoot, shoot, shoot," she said, rushing to put on her high heels, foregoing her stockings entirely. She grabbed her gym bag, and began to rush down the hall, her tits bouncing dangerously without her bra. She realized too late that she'd forgotten it, and decided she'd just have to go back for it during lunch period. There wasn't enough time!

With her rushing around, she did manage to get to gym class before everyone else had left the locker room. But she found a sneering Leslie looking at her all smug.

"Oh, look who's late, everyone," she said to the other girls, arms folded beneath her chest. "And looking a terrible mess at that," she said, seeming so smugly confident.

"Leave me alone, Leslie, I already feel bad enough," Casey pouted, rushing to a change room so she could at least get dressed in privacy. She was in too much of a rush to figure out the tape that Mr. Grieg had given her, so the voluptuous Casey had no choice but to wear her gym shorts and white, nearly see through top, with no bra, and no panties.

She pulled on her sneakers and tucked her bag into her locker before heading into the gym.

Except Leslie was hellbent on making her life a misery.

"Don't you talk to me that way!" said the angry girl, grabbing Casey by the shoulder to turn her around. That sudden jerking motion making her tits nearly spill out of her top. "You're gonna pay for talking to me like—" but then the angry girl kinda twitched, and she began to scratch at her own chest. Then more. Soon she was looking almost manic. "What the fuck?!" she said, her eyes looking panicked.

Casey was already almost at the brink of tears. She was *not* one for confrontation, and the other woman's sudden reaction only served to upset her more.

"I'm telling Mr. Grieg!" Casey shouted.

A big commotion broke out as Leslie began to freak, then pulled her own top off. Beneath, everyone saw her skin had broken out into a deep, dark red rash as she scratched at herself. But Leslie yelled:

"You did this!" her eyes watering with tears.

Everything was chaos.

Nineteen

❦

M r. Grieg came rushing in soon after that, finding Leslie peeling off her bra and shorts, her whole body beneath the garments covered in those rashes. Leslie adamantly blamed Casey, but not only did Mr. Grieg not buy that, everyone testified that Casey was late to class and got there after Leslie had dressed.

"Someone else must've put some kinda... itching powder or something in her clothes. Broke into her locker before class," Mr. Grieg said afterwards in his office with Casey. Leslie had been taken to the nurse. "So don't feel bad about anythin', Casey," he reassured her.

But Casey had been periodically bursting into tears, muttering, "I didn't do it. I would never!" She swiped them away, and looked at Mr. Grieg earnestly. "She was always mean to me. She was about to hit me, but then she started itching!" Casey rattled on, clearly upset by all of it.

Mr. Grieg, who had been constantly trying to reassure her throughout it all, even as he tried to manage the two girls, looked at her, wide-eyed with concern. He came around the desk, putting a hand on her shoulder.

"Casey, I know you never did anything," he reassured her, squeezing her shoulder. "You don't have to worry at all," he said, towering over her in his shorts and t-shirt, stretched over his muscular frame. "I'll report to the administrator that it was some prank by someone else. Everyone backs up your story."

She sniffled and nodded her head, the tears in her eyes making them look even wider and a more vibrant green.

"Thank you, Mr. Grieg," she said with a bit of a pout as she tried to collect herself. "She'll be okay, right? After a shower or something?"

"It's just a rash," he said, as if it were the most piddling thing ever. He didn't sound concerned at all. "The only part of her that was hurt, was her ego," he said, rubbing her shoulder. "The last person you need to be worried about right now is her, Casey," he said.

She sniffled and nodded once more.

"Okay," she said, exhaling. "I just hope that this doesn't make things worse. She's always been so mean to me, and if she thinks I did it, then who knows how she'll try to get back at me, you know?"

Mr. Grieg got down on one knee, so he was closer to Casey's eye level as she sat in the chair. He squeezed her shoulder and looked into her gaze.

"If she tries anythin' at all after this. Even so much as looks at you mean... tell me, and I'll have her transferred outta this class and into detention instead. You hear me?" he said, his broad, handsome face so much like Claud's. But more wizened, with his silvery strands, and the light wrinkles around his eyes.

She nodded again.

"Okay. I really don't wanna get her in trouble. But I guess she'd be getting herself into trouble," Casey said softly. It had been a rollercoaster of a day, and she took in a deep, steadying breath. "Thanks, Mr. Grieg. You're always so nice. It makes class a lot more fun."

He cracked a smile and nodded.

"That's right. You can only be responsible for yourself and your own actions. Not Leslie's, or anyone else's," he said warmly. Though his gaze did dip to her chest. "I, uh... been having trouble still, with your, uh...?"

She didn't quite pick up on what he was saying until a brief pause, then her lips parted into an 'o'.

"Ah, I... I couldn't figure out the tape thing in time for class. I'll spend some time practicing this weekend, I promise," she said with a bit of a blush. "I just don't think the one roll will last long."

"Hey, it's okay. No need to worry," he said with a smile. "Take it easy on yourself. And if you ever got a problem... you can come to me. Whether it's Leslie related or..." he glanced at her chest again, her top practically see-through. "Whatever."

Without the bra, it was even more revealing, the white fabric clinging to her sumptuous curves.

It sent a shiver down her back, which in turn made her nipples perk up at the visual attention.

"Sorry I look like such a mess today. I wasn't feeling so well, and was in a hurry to get here."

"Hey no! No, you look great. Really you do! And like... if you want help with the tape, or need more... just ask," he said, licking his thick lips. "I know it can't be easy for a... gifted girl like you here. And that's all that thing with Leslie is about. Her being jealous. Wishing she had your body," he said.

Casey's gaze dipped down to the hands she had clasped in her lap, nervously scratching her nails along her palms.

"I know. But I didn't ask for this. It just kind of... happened all of a sudden." Casey's eyes met his again, a soft flush in her cheeks. "And I know it's kind of weird, but... I really don't have any idea about how to use the tape."

"I can show you," he said immediately, then gave a bit of an awkward laugh. "I mean, if you want sometime," he shrugged his broad shoulders. "Just to help you out."

"That'd save me a lot of trouble and... probably embarrassment," she confessed. And no longer was she too naive to notice his excitement, that eagerness that he was working to confine. She wasn't quite sure how she felt about it, but her pussy throbbed with need, despite how many times she'd been fucked lately.

Her eyes even picked up on the growth in his shorts, as that bulge grew bigger, despite his best efforts to not think about it.

"Great," he said, his enthusiasm edged with nervousness as he realized... now he would have to go through with it. He stood up, then went to the blinds, shutting them before he went and got some more of the body tape from a drawer. "So, uh... the way it works for girls, I think," he began to demonstrate, showing how the tape would wrap around. "So it sticks to your, uh... your breasts, and... then around here," it wasn't the best demonstration, especially not with his nervousness.

It was almost cute, watching him struggle, and poorly try to instruct her in a way that didn't really make a lot of sense.

"Can you just... show me?" she asked with a tilt of her head. "I can turn my back to take my top off if that makes you more comfortable."

"Uh, sure... yeah. Okay," he said, scratching the side of his head a bit as he pondered it, but found himself wrapped up in it too deep to stop. "If you're comfortable with that, go right ahead, Casey."

"Yea, it's fine," she said as she stood and turned. She grabbed the hem of her top and pulled it up over her head, folding it on the edge of the desk.

She felt that familiar rush as she turned back to face Mr. Grieg, wearing only her sneakers and gym shorts, her heavy breasts rising with her deeper breaths. "Will you do it for me? I'll learn better that way."

She watched as this older man's eyes—older than even Mr. Alder—went right for her breasts, her stiff, pink nipple visible thanks to her turn. He just nodded slowly, as he came up behind her, pulling some tape off as he swallowed.

"Yeah, uh... so," he touched his big, thick hand to her side, tracing it along beneath her arm to her breast. "Right along here..." he said, that strong touch so much like Claud's, but more mature.

She lifted her arm slightly to give him access to your youthful body, looking at his hand quite studiously.

"Ohh, okay, so it is kind of like the bandage I was using. But I guess I just wouldn't need as much?"

"Right yeah. Though... you'll still probably need a lot, I mean... you're very large," he said, as his fingers slid along the underside of her breast, caressing that smooth flesh, lifting her heavy tit. "Oh gosh, you are huge. I hope it'll be enough," he said, swallowing as her supple yet soft bounty sank into his hand.

"Yea, I know," she said with a sigh. "I was, like, completely flat when I got here, then I actually started eating good food, and it's like five years of puberty caught up with me all at once. It wouldn't be so bad, but the pandemic... well. It just feels even more obvious than it would if I had clothes that fit me."

She didn't pull away from his touch, or chastise him for lifting her tit. She just stood there, curiously.

"Do you mind? My touching I mean," he said, as he put down the tape for a moment, then brought his other hand to cup both breasts at once. "They're even the same size and weight... huh," he said, sounding impressed. "Even Claud's mother never had a pair this big," he said casually.

"I don't mind," she said in that sing-song tone, all the earlier unpleasantness with Leslie melting away. "Wait, are you Claud's dad?"

"Uh yeah," he said, with a light chuckle, his two hands still fondling her breasts carefully for such a powerful man. "Don't spread it around... not that I don't think it's pretty obvious. We kinda look alike, don't you think?" he said, as his thick, hard bulge bumped into her backside.

"Yea, I thought you looked alike, but I just figured it was all the muscles, you know," she said innocently enough. Even if he *was* being rather distracting. She frowned thoughtfully, looking down at her tits as he manipulated them from beneath. She knew it was inappropriate, or at least, a part of her did. But she just found it interesting how her body could so easily make men do inappropriate things with her.

It felt really powerful.

"Yeah," he chuckled lowly, his cock throbbing against her ass as they brushed together. "He takes after his old man in a lotta ways," he said, as his fingers brushed against her nipples. "Oh, uh... sorry about that," he said, before slowly beginning to withdrawal his hands. "I should, uh... put that tape on I guess, huh?"

"Yea," she smiled, her nipples instantly stiffening against the rough pads of his fingers. "Is that how you learned this, then? From your wife?"

"Yeah," he remarked, as he took up the tape, tearing some off. "You remind me a bit of her in some ways. But she was big into gymnastics, until she developed too much for it. Then she got into track and bodybuilding, same as me. And Claud," he remarked, as he gently began to apply the tape along her side, then around her breast.

"Aww, that's sweet," Casey said earnestly, her gaze following his motions so that she could repeat it on her own later. "So yesterday... you wanted to make sure Claud wasn't being out of line, not just because you're the teacher but his dad? It takes a lot to even be willing to ask." She was a bit awed by it, with that additional piece of the puzzle falling into place.

"Yeah, I, uh... I just wanted to make sure he was being good to you. I know my boy has a good heart," he said, as he kept applying that tape with care, caressing her breasts through it as he smoothly attached it. "But... but you're a really beautiful girl. I wanted to make sure he wasn't tempted to do..."

He trailed off.

"He's always very sweet, Mr. Grieg, I promise. Just like you."

She beamed a smile at him, looking so much more like herself in that moment, so bubbly and full of life.

"And... you're not doing anything wrong either. I asked for your help, remember?"

He laughed at that a little.

"I guess you're right, but... if anyone else found out I was doin' this, I'd be fired... and heck, that's not even includin' the stuff on my mind—" he groaned a bit. "I shouldn't have said that, sorry, Casey."

"It's okay, Mr. Grieg. It's only natural," she said with a shrug of her shoulders. "And I won't tell. It's no one's business but our own, anyways. And besides, you're helping me."

He pulled in a deep breath, then swallowed as his cock throbbed against her backside.

"You're too sweet, Casey. Makes me worry for you. But if you ever want anythin', come see me," he says, as he moves to her other breast, doing his best to replicate the same placement. "Gotta try and keep you even here. Wouldn't want these perfect tits to be all askew, huh?" he said.

She let out a soft giggle.

"Yea. It'd be better with nothing than have me crooked," she said lightly. "And you don't have to worry about me. I mean, sometimes people tease me, but... I'm making lots of friends lately."

"Oh, I bet... if I weren't your teacher, I'd wanna be your friend too. Real bad," he said, emphasis on 'real' as he caressed the side of her left breast, applying that tape. "Almost done here now. Hopefully this helps a bit, especially if... you can find a bra to go with it," he said.

"Yea... I kind of forgot mine today. It was a rushy morning," she said apologetically. "You're so gentle, though. I really appreciate you taking the time to show me. I would have wasted so much more than I needed to."

"Think nothin' of it, Casey. I'm here to help," he said, as he slid the last piece of tape into place. "Annnd... there. I think we're pretty much done," he said with a broad smile, and a raging hardon that wouldn't stop pulsating wildly.

She turned to face him again, looking down at her breasts, then up at his face.

"Wow, it feels a lot better. Lighter," she said, reaching out for her top and quickly tugging it on over her head. "What do you think?" she asked, bouncing in place a few times, so that her breasts jiggled but didn't hit against her ribs quite so hard.

Mr. Grieg stared, licking his lips as he viewed her tits bouncing around.

"I think that's a big improvement," he said, his dick pulsating wildly. "And here... take some more of the tape," he gave her the remainder of that roll. "There's not much left to the period, so feel free to head off and get ready for your next class if you like, Casey. Or do as you feel like," he said.

"Okay," she said, immediately wrapping her arms around him in a hug. "Thank you, Mr. Grieg. This made me feel a lot better." Her slippery gym shorts pressed against his clothed bulge, her feminine mons giving him a teasing grind before she pulled away and accepted the body tape. "I'll head out and test how well the tape works."

Mr. Grieg groaned as they'd hugged, his cock going wild with excitement for her.

Twenty

But he let her go and swallowed anxiously as he nodded.

"Have a good one, Casey," he said with a faint, conflicted smile.

She headed to the door, giving him one last, beaming smile over her shoulder before opening up the door and heading back to join the rest of her classmates.

Claud was there to greet her immediately, abandoning what he was working on to come to her.

"Casey! I heard what happened in the locker room. You okay? Do you think it was the Black Mask?" he asked, eyes wide. And looking at him then, after finding out Mr. Grieg was his father, she got a whole new appreciation for what a handsome man Claud promised to become later in life.

"I'm okay," Casey said with a genuine smile. "Mr. Grieg helped me kind of calm down. And... I don't know." It was her first real lie, and it felt so uncomfortable. But she knew how Claud felt about the vigilante, and she didn't want to add more fuel to that fire.

"Mr. Grieg said it's just a rash so should clear up soon, anyways."

Claud nodded, then smiled.

"I'm just happy you're okay," he said, reaching out and touching her arm with his big, strong hand. And it struck her how similar that was to his father's.

But as his hand wandered lowered, and he looked like he was gonna fondle her backside, his father's booming voice broke the silence. And soon everyone was back to sports, before the bell rang and lunch began.

After getting changed, Casey set out to find Dahlia. Her raven-haired friend was nowhere to be seen in the lunch room. But she found a girl they both knew, Lydia, and she told Casey that Dahlia took off after her last class, looked like she was headed to the Pit.

"Oh, okay, great!" Casey said. She grabbed a sandwich to go, eager to go talk to her roomie. After all, she'd covered for her, and Casey didn't want to give her the impression that anything had happened between her and Mr. Alder. She'd never be able to forgive herself if that rumour started getting around.

As she went down to the secret hideaway beneath the school, she found the familiar little hatch and crept through. The tunnel seemed a bit less scary since she figured it out the first time. But still it was quiet and dark as she moved along.

She got to the final door, pushed it open and came on in.

The music was loud as ever, as she pushed on through. And she heard some talk and laughter through it. When she got to the main room, she found Dahlia lounging on the center sofa, sat beside the dreamy Damien, the two talking, while others were around smoking and eating.

"Hey! My girl Casey!" said Dahlia with a bright smile, waving her on over.

"Sunshine," said Damien, his face warming up with a glow.

She'd eaten her sandwich on the walk, but hadn't yet had time to go back to the dorm room and grab her forgotten bra. She smiled at the two of them, giving a friendly wave.

"Hey! I just wanted to let you know I'm feeling better, and thanks for letting me sleep in, Dahlia."

"Don't worry about it girl. I know you were up late... having fun," she said with a playful little sway of her head, smirking. "You'll have to tell me all about it later, sweetie," she said with a grin.

"Oh?" Damien said, brow raised. "My little Sunshine is branching out, is she?" he asked, sipping from a beer.

Casey let out a singular laugh, her skin beginning to glow as she tried to work the lie out of her chest, and make it sound natural.

"Not a kind of fun you'd like," she said to Dahlia. "We were literally grading papers all night." She had practiced it a few times on the walk back from his office, and so she prayed Dahlia bought it.

Dahlia gave her a scrutinizing look, that said she didn't quite buy it. But Damien put his cigarette in the corner of his mouth then pat the couch beside him.

"Come join us," he said, "we've still got all lunch before you gotta run. Or we could all slip into my office together," he remarked with a confident smile.

That made her blush a whole lot brighter, and she nervously shifted from side to side, glancing at Dahlia.

"Uhm, okay, I can stay for a bit. I have to get to our room before lunch is over, though. I forgot something."

She went to the sofa, tucking her skirt under her ass as she joined them.

Damien's arm went around Casey immediately, as Dahlia gave the man a playful shove in the chest.

"Perv. You'd just love to have both of us at once, wouldn't you?" she said, teasingly.

"I mean... of course," he said, putting down his beer then putting his other arm around Dahlia. She took the cigarette from that hand and puffed as he spoke. "The two most beautiful girls on campus are always invited to hang with me," he said, but his eyes were on Casey, smiling at her.

Casey licked her lips, looking between them nervously.

"If I'm a third wheel, I can go," Casey offered, though she didn't yet budge from her seat. While Damien's eyes were on her, she was staring at her friend. Dahlia was always the more confident one, and Casey looked up to her.

It only felt natural to seek out her guidance in times of discomfort.

"No, you are not," Dahlia said as she puffed at that cigarette. Casey had never known her friend to smoke really, but she did so like a pro then. "We're just friends," she said.

"Good friends," Damien remarked with wry amusement.

"Not that good. I still charged you to fuck," Dahlia retorted, and he laughed.

She listened to their banter, tilting her head to the side.

Her brows furrowed at Dahlia's claim of charging him, not understanding why.

"Wait, you make him pay?"

"Yeah," Dahlia said matter-of-factly, shrugging her shoulders. "I make 'em all pay," she said with a cocky little smile on her face, that was devilishly playful. "Why give it up for free when I can make some bucks on the side?" she said with a sinister laugh.

Damien chuckled along at that, rubbing Casey's arm, leaning into her and kissing her red curls.

She let out a soft giggle of delight, but she was still puzzled by Dahlia. It made a certain sense, but then... she wouldn't want to hurt anyone's feelings by charging. Especially not Damien. He was so good, and clearly experienced. She had just as much fun as he did.

Maybe more.

"But you can't even buy anything anymore..."

Dahlia shrugged again as she puffed on that cigarette.

"Save it for after graduation. Besides," she said with an impish grin as she looked over at her friend, "I like it when they pay. Makes it more fun for me."

"And she's worth it," Damien said. "You would be too. Though if you're thinkin' of charging me, I should warn you she drained my account last time," he said, squeezing Casey to his side.

This was a whole lot of new information for her!

But she curled up against Damien, putting her head on his shoulder so that she could still see Dahlia.

"You know so much," she cooed to her friend. "And I never even was brave enough to ask you about it. About what happened when I stood watch."

"I just thought you knew," Dahlia said matter-of-factly, as she ashed the cigarette, then put it to Damien's lips to give him a puff before taking it right back. "You really had no idea? I mean, I even gave you a cut a few times," she said.

Damien listened quietly, as he let his hand roam along Casey's side, fondling her breast briefly, before wandering down to her hip.

She let him explore her, passive, but quite enjoying the tender affections.

"I just figured that was a thank you gift," Casey said, letting out a little, "Oh..." A lot of things were starting to make sense to her. Whole new worlds were opening up, ones she never even imagined existing before.

"You must have, like, a lot of savings..."

"Yea, I want my own place after this. No more dorms," she said, before smiling over at Casey. "Not that I mind rooming with you. You're welcome to come join me once I get out of here. I'm going to be a dancer for a bit, earn some cash. We could have our own apartment," she said cheekily. "Get up to all manner of mischief together."

Damien's big hand slid down to her thigh, then back up, in under her skirt. That strong grasp, with its manly rings, squeezing her ass cheek, feeling her up as he let the girls speak. He nuzzled to Casey's hair, kissing her softly there as that hand of his sank into her fleshy backside, squeezing, kneading.

He'd been her first. And still, one of the best she'd been with. An equal, at least, to the so-called 'Black Mask' and Mr. Alder. But with the special privilege of having introduced her to the entire world of pleasure and excitement that was sex.

170

It made her feel a certain connection with him, one that he may or may not have shared.

She rocked onto her side, her hand on his chest as she gave him access to her bare ass.

"Our own apartment together?" she asked, and she felt a little rush of excitement. She never thought a lot about what she'd do after graduation, outside of becoming a teacher, of course. All the other stuff seemed like a far-off concern that didn't impact her yet.

She was smart, but she certainly wasn't wise about the way of the world.

"Oh, Damien, did you find my panties after?"

"Uh, yeah, I did," he said, as his hand fondled her rear, then... two of his fingers slid between her ass cheeks, and he began to finger her slit. Those long, nimble digits penetrating her pussy, and expertly teasing her. "They're back in my office," he said.

"God Casey, you're worse than me," Dahlia said with a grin. "I rarely lose my panties anymore."

"We were in a rush, the bell was going off," she said with a pout, though Damien's actions made her gasp and flush hard. It felt wrong, doing that out in the open, right next to her friend. Her hand grasped his thigh as she tried to push herself up a little bit more, though that only succeeded in driving his fingers deeper into her.

She moaned, then instantly flushed.

"Damien!"

Dahlia arched a brow at the two of them, then peered over and saw his hand. She didn't look scandalized or anything, she just... grinned in amusement.

"Hey, don't let me stop you..." she said licking her

lower lip and putting out the cigarette butt in the ashtray—which was really just a soda can cut off. "I mean... if you want, we can all go in there and have a lunch quickie. I won't even charge you two," she said saucily.

"Damn. That's a bargain. The Black Dahlia never gives it up for free," Damien said, looking to Casey, as his fingers kept pumping into her, his thumb teasing her clit. "What do you say, Sunshine?"

It was hard to say anything. It was hard to even think. Her eyes were rolling back in her head, and every time she squirmed to escape the pleasure, his fingers were right there. He worked her up into such a tizzy so quickly, and she was staring between the two of them in some bewilderment.

But she never turned down Dahlia, and with Damien's approval, it was impossible for her to say anything else.

"Okay."

Damien grinned, then slowly plucked his fingers from Casey's slit. He brought one to his mouth and slowly suckled it clean, before offering another to Dahlia. And she watched her best friend, teasingly lick at that digit, teasing it like it were a cock, before wrapping her lips around it, tasting her honey... then sliding her mouth up and down it as if she were giving head.

"Mm, let's go then," Damien said, as he got up, arm around two girls as he led them both back to his 'office'. Her neatly folded pair of panties were in the corner, as he pulled the door shut.

It all felt like some kind of waking dream, an experience Casey never could have imagined before. It was as though she were looking at Dahlia in an entirely new light, and seeing her as the beautiful Goddess she really was. Confident, powerful, in control... It was so much about what Casey wanted to be, though she never would have been able to admit it to herself, even a week ago.

Casey looked between her and Damien, her breath held in her chest as she waited to find out what was next.

Dahlia began things, by reaching up beneath her skirt, and seductively hooking her thumb into her panties. The way she so casually—and effortlessly!—pulled them down, Casey had to admit, her friend was still leagues ahead of her in seduction, despite not being as busty.

But Damien leaned to Casey, and kissed her lips first and foremost, as his other hand began to undo his shirt. That strong hand of his, gripping her backside as he moaned, then husked, "We'll take it nice and easy."

Twenty-One

"Okay," she murmured in return, that racing heart of hers impossible to ignore. She was nervous, but so excited, just like she had been when she lost her virginity. It was scary, but in that good way, that made her thighs slick with arousal.

She kissed Damien back, a bit more confidently, her arms lightly tossed around his neck.

The way Damien sensually made out with her, she felt like the center of his universe in that moment, despite there being three of them. His tongue so exquisitely caressing hers, she barely even heard his pants being unzipped. And it was only after Dahlia had freed his cock, and was cradling his balls in her hand, that she became aware that her friend was licking his shaft, getting it harder and harder with each moment.

All while Damien's hand fondled her ass, and his fingers teased her bare slit.

Casey rocked onto her high heel's toes, her legs parting as he caressed her wet pussy lips, eager to feel him inside of her once more. Her head was spinning, trying to take everything in, but it was too much. Too exciting!

She could barely pay attention to her friend, but her hand reached down, tenderly, carefully stroking Dahlia's hair.

Dahlia grinned as her tongue curled and teased the growing tip of Damien's cock, her eyes glinting up at Casey. But her dear friend Dahlia took hold of her wrist, bringing her soft hand to Damien's balls, and showing her how to gently caress them, to roll those cum-laden nuts along her dainty digits.

Damien gave a deep, lusty groan at the feel of Dahlia's lips and tongue, and Casey's lips and hand on him. And he reached to Casey's top, undoing the buttons there, to reveal her breasts and grope them.

There was an extra special lust, knowing now that Dahlia didn't do anything for free. Not until now. Not until it was for her.

She felt such affection swell for her best friend, and the guidance she was giving. She wanted to do a good job, so she repeated the motions, just like Dahlia showed her, as she leaned slightly away from Damien's chest to give him access to the straining buttons on her blouse.

Beneath was still the tape that Mr. Grieg had helped her put on, giving her heavy breasts more lift and support, even without the aid of the blouse.

But if Damien noticed, he didn't complain as he fondled her breasts. His strong, tattooed hand so good at toying with her tits as they made out.

"Our boy Damien here, is a very large man," Dahlia remarked as she took out a condom, tore it with her teeth, then placed the rubbery thing at the head of his cock. "You picked well for your first time, Casey," she remarked, before deftly rolling that thing down over his shaft, diligent and safe with her carnal escapades, unlike Casey.

"How you girls wanna do this?" asked Damien, his voice husky and lust-laden, as he looked into Casey's eyes.

It distracted her from her curiosity about the condom, and trying to puzzle out how she felt about that new look to his cock. Her green eyes sparkled with forbidden delight as she considered his words.

It was still hard for her to express herself, even though she had *so* much she wanted. Much of it she didn't even know how to talk about, though. Not yet.

She gazed at Dahlia in thought.

She bit her lower lip, before she forced herself to whisper, "Dahlia, can I touch your breasts?"

Dahlia lit up with surprise, but then smiled wryly as she rose up, her hands going to her chest, undoing the buttons of her blouse.

"Since you asked so nicely," she said, as she popped each one open with such seductive care. Until her own large pair of breasts—close to the size of Casey's, but not quite a match—began to spill out. Dahlia undid the front clasp of her bra then, and her soft-pink coloured nipples were visible to be seen. "But you gotta let me touch yours in return, Casey..." she teased, as Damien watched the two, cock throbbing.

"I'd like that," Casey said, her voice so soft and sweet as she smiled at her friend.

Then, she looked to Damien.

"Uhm, maybe we can go to the couch, and I can bend

over the side?" she asked, her voice quivering a little bit with nerves and excitement. She thought that if she did that, it would be similar to what the masked stranger did, except she'd be standing, instead of on her hands and knees. She wasn't sure it would work, but...

"That okay with you?" Damien asked Dahlia.

"Of course. My bestie deserves to be the center of attention," Dahlia said to Casey, caressing her friend's cheek before letting that hand go to one of her large breasts. "Damn girl, you really did blossom," she said, as she then guided Casey over to the sofa, with Damien behind her, helping get Casey in exactly the right position as his cock throbbed.

It wasn't a very spacious area, but the three of them were horny enough to make it work and ignore the little discomforts. Dahlia laid back on the sofa, Casey leaned over her, her heavy breasts swaying in front of Dahlia's face as she lightly fondled them.

And while Casey took a little longer to gather her nerves, her dainty fingers briefly grazed along the cusp of Dahlia's breast.

"You're so beautiful," Casey said earnestly, bent at the waist, her legs parted, her pussy lips presenting towards Damien.

"So are you," her friend said back to her with a sweet, sincere smile. The two girls fondled each other's breasts, as Dahlia then leaned up to place a soft kiss at the corner of Casey's lips, easing her into it as Damien gripped Casey's ass. That big cock of his, wrapped in that condom, beginning to stretch her pussy open as he groaned, sinking into her.

The new sensation of a dick wrapped in a condom was strange to her, as she'd only ever done it raw before.

"Mmm," he moaned, as he squeezed both ass cheeks and sank up inside her slit fully hilting himself there.

It felt as if he had a little more girth than before, stretching her open. But she wasn't quite sold on the whole condom business.

Still, Dahlia had encouraged it, so Casey figured she'd give it a try.

She moaned as the head of his cock pressed into her depths, and then dipped her head lower, her tongue delicately finding the edge of Dahlia's areola. She tasted her, teasing the tip around the circle as her breathing began to grow heavier.

Dahlia caressed her strawberry blonde hair in reward, encouraging her to lick and tease, as her own dainty hand fondled Casey's breast. But it all got a lot harder once Damien began to pump into her, that hard, throbbing cock beginning to thrust into her, making her ass cheeks quake as he took her from behind. Those masculine moans added to the air with Dahlia's, as the three of them touched and fucked.

"Mmm, fuck you two are so intensely hot," Damien moaned out, watching them.

It felt so dirty to explore her friend's body with an audience, but Casey was quickly learning that the shame she felt was nearly equal to the pleasure she received. She liked things filthy, despite her sweet and demure behaviour.

Casey's gaze went to Dahlia's as her hand gripped her friend's breast, holding it in place as she began to suckle her tit more eagerly.

Dahlia moaned from her attentions, and in turn, worked harder to please Casey. Her own soft little feminine digits lightly pinching and teasing Casey's nipples, the two girls getting into it. While Dahlia guided one of Casey's hands down to feel her smooth slit, Dahlia's pussy glistening wet, just like Casey's own.

While behind them both, Damien did more than just watch. His stunningly gorgeous, tattooed male form, thrusting into Casey at a building pace. Each pound of his dick up in her, making her body tremble. Though something about it did not feel as deeply satisfying as when his dick was raw inside her.

It was mildly upsetting. It felt... fake, somehow. As if she were having sex with a mannequin.

Her hand left Dahlia's breast, holding her in place with just her suckling mouth, as it went behind her. She found Damien's shaft, and wrapped her fingers around it, trying to work that bit of latex free from him.

She was becoming more skilled at multitasking, though, and as she suckled and stroked, she also toyed with Dahlia's slit. Two fingers went on either side of her inner lips, gliding along the sensitive flesh until they met at the apex. She touched her friend as Damien had, finding that bundle of nerves and coaxing her clit from beneath its hood.

It took Damien just a moment to realize what Casey was trying to do, and he grinned as he helped. Pausing his thrusting, he let Casey slide the condom off his cock, then thrust back into her raw. The dark-haired man looked intensely satisfied as he gave a deep, lewd moan. Casey wasn't the only one enjoying the raw sensation of their loins touching intensely, and that made her feel all the more validated for doing it.

And Dahlia—dutiful Dahlia—was too wrapped up in fondling her friend's breast, and moaning from Casey fingering her to notice. The three of them writhing and moaning together as they worked in tandem.

It was sinful, but Casey really didn't know how much of a risk she was taking, letting all those men raw dog her. It just felt so much better, and she craved it intensely.

As he fucked her again, the way nature intended, her groans and moans grew as her licking and suckling became more intense. She switched to the other breast as she kept teasing Dahlia's slit. She wasn't an expert—yet—but she was learning quickly, and she adjusted her pressure and tempo to Dahlia's squirms and moans.

Dahlia was far more experienced with all of this than her, even with fingering. And she occasionally helped guide her friend in how to finger her properly. Their breasts heaving, bodies writhing together, as they moaned and kissed.

"Oh god... that's so fuckin' good, Casey. Right there," Dahlia panted out as she mewled.

While behind her, Casey got to experience that same cock that had taken her virginity, pounding her with such strong, fast, masterful thrusts. It felt exquisite, and she'd never felt so surrounded by desire and affection as their bodies pounded, slapped, and melded together. Three into one.

It was all so intense, Casey's legs were quivering, her knees threatening to give out, but she wouldn't let them. She was too intensely focused on milking every ounce of pleasure that she could out of her friend, to make her as happy as Casey felt in that moment.

So when Dahlia said right there, she didn't change anything, not the tempo, not the pressure, not the intensity. She just kept up the same motion, with only a few slip ups, with Damien pounding into her wet pussy so forcefully.

She had to relinquish Dahlia's breast to gasp for air, but then she dove back down, hungry for more.

It was hard to keep track of everything, especially with Damien thrusting into her so hard and fast from behind. And finally, it jolted her forward, off Dahlia's breasts entirely. But instead of being disappointed, or pushing her back, Dahlia's lips just found hers, and the two friends made out and groped each other's chests, as Damien pounded away.

"I'm gonna cum..." Dahlia gasped, trembling as Casey's fingers kept up that motion even with all the jostling.

It was like music to her ears. Just like hearing someone call her a good girl, knowing that she was bringing her friend to the brink of pleasure was an aphrodisiac in and of itself. Her tongue swirled around Dahlia's as their panted breaths were exchanged.

"Mmm fuck! You feel so good, Sunshine," Damien moaned behind her, giving her ass a squeeze, then a light slap as he picked up his pace. He was still holding out, thrusting into her ravenously as the two girls kissed.

And then, Dahlia's lips broke from Casey's, as she threw back her head and squealed. The young woman gasping, panting, squealing and then...

Casey felt that gush of hot, warm honey around her fingers, as Dahlia held her hand to her tightly. Dahlia's whole body trembling, her legs twitching, toes curling as she came.

Casey squealed in return. It was so beautiful, so amazing, and her green eyes watched with rapt attention as her friend's body released every ounce of stress and tension. Casey's smile grew wide, her eyes twinkling with delight as she drank it all in.

And in reward for Damien, her pussy tightened around him, her back arching to take him in deeper as the schoolgirl moaned with glee.

The deep, rich moan that elicited from him was like audible bliss for her. And he rewarded her further with a deep, harder, faster thrusting. As he groaned out, moaning, "Ohh fuck you're gonna make me cum, Casey...!"

And Dahlia slid one hand in through Casey's thick curls then, gasping then kissing her friend deeply. And soon Casey felt Dahlia's fingers sliding down, teasing her clit as Damien pounded himself towards his own climax.

Casey might not have been the one to orgasm, but she was still lost in that heady pleasure, as if Dahlia's ecstasy had become her own. They made out as Dahlia's skillful fingers manipulated her, promising her that blissful ending before long.

It was all so exquisite, so intense, and it felt so right, the three of them together. Dahlia and Damien were misfits, but Casey was starting to feel like she might be more of a rebel than she ever thought possible.

Especially as she began to cum on that hard, raw dick.

And despite her best friend looking out for her, that raw, hard dick began to cum inside her too. Thick streams of pearly white seed flooding her depths. Virile cum adding to the tally of men who had blown their loads inside her, filling her up, seeking to sew their seed in her womb.

Damien was moaning lowly, Dahlia mewling, and Casey squealing as they came. Their lewd sounds permeating the air, reverberating around that tiny, enclosed space as they sought to please one another.

Casey really hadn't intended to spend her entire lunchbreak there, she just wanted to clear the air with Dahlia about why she was late coming home.

But she could not have imagined a more perfect way to prep herself for the afternoon.

Twenty-Two

Her trembling knees finally gave out, and she had to buck forward, landing on the sofa as her ass arched into the air, taking the last of Damien's seed in nice and deep.

Damien's cock slipped from her as she sank forward though, leaving her puffy pink pussy drooling his seat as he panted. While Dahlia smiled and kissed Casey's lips.

"That was really nice," Dahlia said. "I've never done a three way with a girl before... or been with a girl at all," she confessed, looking at her friend with adoring sparkles in her eyes. "You were fabulous, Casey."

Casey kissed her back with such affection, her hand going to her cheek and caressing her soft skin.

"You're really pretty, Dahlia. It's no wonder everyone would pay you for this," she replied sincerely, even though she was feeling that momentary disappointment at no longer having a cock inside of her.

Dahlia giggled at that—something she never did. But she kissed Casey back fondly.

"No charge for my bestie," Dahlia said with a playful flutter of her long, thick lashes. "I should be getting going though. I was supposed to meet someone, so I owe them an apology at least," Dahlia said, beginning to wriggle out from under Casey.

Damien helped, by pulling Casey back onto his dick, all that cum and honey softly squelching around his shaft as he groaned.

"Thanks for the great time, Dahlia," Damien said, as the girl got up, the two giving each other a quick peck of a kiss as she did her bra back up.

"I'll see you later tonight," Casey said as she pushed in against Damien, squirming with delight as he pressed his hot cock against her body. It was so welcome, and she began to wrap his arms around her waist.

"Ta ta!" Dahlia said, wriggling her fingers in a wave as she tugged her panties back, on then began to button her blouse only after she was back out in the common area. It got her a few cat calls, but she didn't seem to care at all.

That left Damien and Casey alone together again, his arms around her as he kissed her shoulder, her neck. His cock having stuffed and sealed his cum back up inside her.

"God that was so hot," he husked into her ear, before nibbling her lobe.

"Yea," she breathed out, stroking the back of his hands with the tips of her fingers. She felt so relaxed, so calm and powerful in that moment, unlike any other time. Making her experienced friend cum was a high she was gonna ride for the rest of the day, at least.

"I don't like the condom, though, it feels weird. Sorry I made you take it off."

Damien laughed at that softly after tugging her lobe carefully. He kissed her neck repeatedly in between words.

"You really don't have to apologize. That was the hottest maneuver I've ever seen a woman do. And besides," he husked, squeezing her in his arms tightly. "I love it way more without the condom on too," he husked, kissing her repeatedly. "I wanna only ever do you without it. You're the only girl I do raw. But I wanna do you like that a lot."

She let out a soft, sweet sigh, luxuriating in the after-glow of the moment. It had been so intense, but now she was just feeling warm and loving, stroking his arms and hands affectionately.

"I'm glad I came down here today. Again. You always make me glad I came."

He moaned and gave her pussy a few teasing pumps as he kissed her. His voice extra low and growly as he spoke seductively in her ear.

"If you were my girl, I'd make you cum every day," he said. Just as the awful chiming of the end-of-lunch bells sounded. And she realized she was being pulled away to another afternoon of classes, with little time left to get her clothes on.

"Darn it, darn it, darn it," she pouted. "Why does time always seem to go so fast down here?" she asked as she slowly slipped from his lap, feeling his cum drip down her inner thighs, staining her stockings.

Damien sighed as his cock was left glistening and messy, and he began to button up his shirt.

"Damn. Never enough time with my Sunshine," Damien said with that handsome, half-smile of his. So charmingly crooked and mischievous looking, even when he was being so wholesomely loving. "But you're always welcome to come see me, babe. I'd tie you down and keep you for myself all the time, if I could," he said.

"Tie me down?" she asked, not even bothering to look at him as she started to button her shirt asymmetrically, having missed a button somewhere along the way.

"Yeah. Ropes. Chains. Hold you here to be my girl. And fuck you silly, several times a day," he said with that mischievous glint in his eyes as he looked her over, then stuffed his still glistening cock into his underwear, trying to do his pants back up around that bulge with some strain.

She gasped a little, looking equal parts scandalized and curious. But there wasn't time for questions, she had to get to class!

"I'll see you again later, okay?" she said as she practically skipped to the door, feeling his slickness gloss her inner thighs.

Afternoon classes were suddenly much less interesting than they'd been in the past. Casey could only keep thinking of all the fun she could have with men and their cocks. With Mr. Alder. Damien. And the rest.

At the end of the day, she was heading towards Mr. Alder's office, when Nadir stopped her.

"Hey. Casey!" he called out, coming up to her. "Mr. Alder asked me to pass a note to you," he said, offering up a sealed envelope to the girl. "You okay? You weren't at class this morning," her friend inquired.

"Yea, I just wasn't feeling great," she said, the lie becoming more natural to her the more she said it. "I think I'm coming around, must have just been a little bug or something. Did I miss anything in class?" she asked, accepting the envelope.

The envelope was thick and creamy to the touch, a quality paper. But with Nadir rambling off about the work she missed, her attention was divided.

"So nothing that should be a problem for you," he finished. His eyes flitted over her from behind his glasses. "You coming to the cafeteria for supper then?" he asked.

"Uhm," she said, reluctantly remembering Mr. Alder's reminder to act naturally, and she nodded her head. "Of course, where else would I be going?" She gave a forced smile, annoyed that she'd be missing out on her favourite teacher all day, but... it was what he told her to do.

Nadir did an even more in-depth covering of the classes she missed with him as he led the way to the cafeteria.

The room was so crowded and noisy, such a change from the private meal she'd shared with Mr. Alder the night before. But she soon found herself sat at a table with him, and Dahlia came along to join after.

"Hey you two," Dahlia said, as they all began to eat.

Dahlia was acting normal, so Casey did the same, though it was hard to hide the fact that she flushed as she first caught sight of the woman.

Casey turned eagerly to her food, hungrily eating the delicious, fresh vegetables, potatoes, and meat that was on her plate. She'd been really working up an appetite with all her fucking, and she was quite ravenous that evening.

It didn't take her long to finish, and she waited for Nadir to interrupt his speech to take a bite before announcing, "I think I'm going to grab a shower then turn in early tonight. I'm still not feeling one hundred percent. Thanks for getting me caught up, Nadir, you're the best!"

"See ya, Casey," he said, pushing his glasses up his nose.

"Later hun," Dahlia said with a little prim wave, and a wink. As if they shared some naughty secret. But then... they did, didn't they?"

That left her to walk off by herself, back to the dorms. But once she was out the door, into the cool evening air, she smelled smoke on the air. Then heard a voice from the shadows in the cleft in brick wall.

"Well look who it is," said the masculine voice.

She let out a little squeak of surprise as she turned around.

She soon saw the familiar face of Trent, still wearing his dark eye and lip makeup, a cigarette in his hand as he had the other in his pocket.

"Come with me," he said very sternly, jerking his head off to the side.

Casey frowned a little bit, looking at him. She was excited to go read the letter from Mr. Alder, but... what did he want?

She tilted her head.

"Why?" she asked in that soft, sweet voice. "I'm just heading back to my room and I don't wanna get in trouble."

"Come with me then. And you won't. Get in trouble, that is," he said, sounding quite serious. "Now are you gonna come with me? Or do you want me tellin' everyone about what I saw you doin' last night, huh?" he said, tonguing the seam of his lower lip, looking so dark and malicious in that moment.

Her brows furrowed, her frown deepening, as her heart started racing.

She didn't even bother asking more questions. She would do *anything* to keep Mr. Alder from getting in trouble, and she took a step towards him. Her arms folded a bit defensively beneath her chest, but otherwise... she was ready to follow.

Trent grinned at that sign of obedience, then led her off around the building. The light was dim by then, and he took her off towards that private clearing in the woods. The same place she'd first fucked Claud and the Black Mask.

He didn't say anything until they were there, under the moonlight. The only other source of light his cigarette.

"Take your top off," he told her, looking at her sternly in the dim light. "You owe me after so rudely turning down my offer last time. Then getting me in trouble and kicked outta the Pit."

Casey pouted a little bit at the accusation, her arms still folded beneath her large bust.

"I didn't get you kicked out! And I didn't even know, like... what a dick was, really," she protested. She was still wearing her backpack, the letter daintily tucked inside a textbook, and it felt like it was burning a hole in there. She wanted to read it so badly, but... if Trent really saw her last night...

She sighed as she set the backpack down on the ground, leaning it against a tree trunk.

"Hey," he said, taking another drag on his cigarette, exhaling a puff of smoke. "If you're really sorry for it all... then now's your chance to make it up to me, huh? So... take your top off. And get on your knees. Unless you'd rather lean up against that tree, huh?" he said, stepping closer to her.

"I never said I was sorry," she huffed, her green eyes shaded by her long lashes as they narrowed at him. "I didn't do anything wrong." But she paused, taking in a deep breath, her voice lowering. "What did you see last night?"

He flicked his cigarette into the grass.

"Y'know, if you wanna play fuckin' games instead of making it up to me? I'll just go tell a teacher. Or better yet, the administrator," he said with a grin as he turned and began to slowly walk off.

"Hey!" she said, stomping her high heel in the dirt. "You're not playing fair, Trent! I deserve to know what you saw if you're going to try to get me to take my top off for you!"

"See ya! Gotta go tell the administrator that you were out whorin' around in the dark of night," he said, sounding so cocky and certain of himself.

"Stop it! I was not! I don't even know what that word *means* Trent! I only went all the way for the first time, like, the night we met!"

He spun around, looking at her intensely.

"And now you gotta go all the way with me or else I'm tellin' everyone," he said, his jaw set firmly as he stood there in the dark, shrouded by the trees, and out of the moon's glow in the clearing. "So, what is it?"

She stomped her feet in frustration, her mind all worked into a tizzy.

But she was *not* going to let anyone betray her secrets. No way. She might not be happy about it, but her fingers went to her blouse, only then realizing how lopsided it had been all day.

"You know, this isn't very nice, Trent! I didn't do anything wrong."

He grinned smugly and emerged from the shadows, moving back towards her. His eyes zeroing in on her tits as she began to open her top.

"Hey, you know what will be nice? You sucking my dick, right before I shove it up in your pretty little cunt. That'll be real nice for the both of us now, won't it?" he said, as he reached out to touch his fingers to her breast.

Even though she was still pouting, her skin prickled with excitement at his touch. She finished unbuttoning the blouse, trying to be careful as she flicked it to her backpack, letting it land on top.

"Fine, but you gotta swear not to tell anyone anything, okay?" she said, her emerald gaze going to his.

"Fine," he said with a ton of annoyance. "But I'm going in raw, and I ain't pullin' out. No negotiations," he said firmly. "Now on your knees and take out my dick. You've got some suckin' to do before I fuck you."

Twenty-Three

Her breathing caught in her throat at his order, and even though her thick lower lip still pouted, she got down on her knees, just as he said. The grass was soft and slightly damp in the evening air, sending a little shiver down through her as her hands went to the front of his pants. Just like all the other students, he was wearing a uniform, though he'd dyed his an inky black which faded into the darkness around them.

"You have to tell me what you like, though, okay? I'm not going to have you say I didn't do what I was told to get out of keeping a secret."

He laughed dryly at that, then reached down to caress her curly hair as she fished out his cock. It was semi-hard, and jumped excitedly at her soft touch.

"Damn, you are more of a freak than I thought," he said, then brushing the backs of his knuckles along her cheek. "Alright, you got it. I want you to tease my dick with your tongue, get it good and hard, bob up and down on it a while... then I'm gonna rail your pussy."

"Okay," she huffed, but up close with his cock, she was having a lot harder time even pretending to be upset. She was quickly becoming addicted, and the way her mouth watered...

She swallowed it back as she began stroking his dick, firmly, in her soft palm. Then she brought her mouth forward, her tongue poking out between her lips, giving him a soft swirl, just off the tip of her tongue, gathering up a bead of precum into her mouth.

Trent wasn't as big as the other guys she'd been with, and even as his dick began to throb and swell in her hands, she didn't think he'd equal up to Damien's length, or Claud's girth. But it was a nice, hefty cock in her hand, and she was learning to appreciate just how much she enjoyed having that in her grasp.

"Mmm, that's real good. Fuck, and you say you were just a virgin that day we met in the tunnels? Damn," he said with a light laugh, as he continued to caress his knuckles over her cheek, then ran his fingers through her hair, pulling her in against his cock tighter.

Her words were muffled on his cock as he pushed her down it, his shaft filling her mouth as her tongue swished along the underside. Her eyes fluttered closed, and she started to feel herself lose a little bit of control, her natural and learned instincts beginning to take over.

She moaned slightly around his cock as she took him in deeper, his hand helping her set the tempo that she obediently followed.

And Trent showed no hesitation in guiding her along, keeping up that fast pace, thrusting the head of his cock to the back of her throat as he moaned and groaned. His balls began to pounce off her chin at that pace, and he grunted, spurting pre-cum into her mouth as he finally pulled her off his cock, panting.

"Go stand up by that tree. Bend over and lean against it," he commanded her.

She didn't show the same reluctance that she had earlier as she got to her feet. She was into the zone, then, and her pussy was wet and ready. She wanted cock, and it didn't matter whose it was. Just as long as she could fill that aching longing within her core.

She turned and went to the tree, bending forward as she lifted up the back hem of her skirt, resting it on her lower back. Her hands reached out, finding the tree, and holding herself steady as her legs parted.

"Fuck," he said, surprised with her casual eagerness to do the act, despite his blackmail. He came up behind her, cock in hand as he gave her ass a rough slap then a grope. "I can see us enjoying this every night, huh?" he said, as he unceremoniously thrust his cock into her up to the hilt, wasting no time as he moaned, then began to pump into her.

She was so wet that despite how tight she was, her eager body offered little resistance to him. But at his words, she let out a weak cry of protest, quickly swept away with a slutty moan. It was so wrong, but it didn't matter. She was a full-blown addict then, willing to take any cock that might be offered to her. The thought of Mr. Alder's letter faded away to a dim memory, her mind emptying.

There was just the hard, fast pound of Trent's cock, thrusting in deep and raw. Their bodies slapping together, each thrust making her thick, round ass cheeks quake, her breasts made to jiggle and sway. And though he made no special effort to give her pleasure, the smack of his balls against her clit was nice in and of itself. That filling, wholesome feeling of having a dick inside her making her moan and mewl as he huffed and panted.

"Mmm... no fuckin' wonder Damien wants you all to himself. Fuck, he's never claimed a girl in all the time he's been here, and yet you've got him obsessed with this pussy of yours. I don't even blame him for kickin' me out now," he said, giving her ass another slap. "Bros before hoes don't count when the pussy's this good," he groaned, spurting pre into her.

It was bawdy talk to her, something she mostly understood through context, not the individual words themselves. And it brought a flush to her cheeks to know that Damien really liked her. It made her heart skip a beat, and she mewled out her pleasure.

Her hands were steady on the tree, even though her knees trembled, and she arched her back a little more so that he could hit her a bit deeper.

"Mmm... f-fuck," he gasped, panting as he hammered into her as deeply as he could. He wasn't as big, or as skilled as the other men she was with, but he was hard, rough and ravenous for her. And he reached up, knitting his fingers into her hair and tugging on it as his dick swelled, throbbing. "Beg me to cum in you... beg me to use you, slut," he commanded.

What else could she do?

She wanted him to keep her secret, of course, but also... how could she resist a direct order? It just felt so much better when she gave in, and those words quickly tumbled from her pouty lips.

"Cum in me... use me... Trent..." she huffed out between moans.

And that made him give a deep, long groan as his cock throbbed inside her.

"Ohh fuck... I'll use you slut, don't you fuckin' worry," he groaned out as his rapid thrusting made her ass cheeks sting. And he tugged on her hair a bit more, causing her to squeal as he worked his way towards his climax. "F-Fuck!" he gasped, as his cock erupted. His seed flooding her, the same as all the men before, only this time he'd extorted the privilege from her.

He hadn't lasted as long as the other guys, it'd been a quickie. But the sting of his rough fucking lingered as he jabbed his dick in, milking every last spurt out into her.

Her scalp prickled as he tugged her hair, though even that wasn't unpleasant. It was different... wrong... but delightful, in its own way. She gasped and gulped, bucking forward at the now familiar sensation of a man finishing in her.

He grunted and trembled as the last of his seed spilled into her. Then he relinquished her hair at last as he gasped. He slid that hand down her side, slapped her ass hard as he then pulled out of her.

"Fuck... you did good," he said, panting for breath as his dick dangled, glistening in the moonlight.

The compliment made her smile, despite herself.

"Thank you," she murmured as she looked over her shoulder at him. Her gaze flit between his eyes and his cock, drinking him in lewdly. "So, you're not gonna tell about whatever you think you saw?"

He pushed a hand back through his long hair, nodding his head.

"That's right. As long as you keep draining my dick dry," he added on with a dark grin. "Now come lick it clean real quick, and thank me for that big load of cum," he commanded her.

That wasn't the answer she was hoping for, and she pouted as she turned about.

"I just want you to know you got it all wrong anyways. I wasn't out doing anything wrong last night," she said, even as she obediently got to her knees. Her tongue flicked along his shaft, cleaning him as she spoke. "It's all just a big misunderstanding."

"Yeah, yeah," he said, as he watched her lick his cock, cleaning away the mixture of her own honey, and his creamy white cum. "Just do what I tell ya and don't complain. You like doing that anyhow, don't ya slut?" he asked her with a grin. And as she cleaned his cock, she was reminded of the hollow log behind him, that the Black Mask had told her she could use to contact him.

She didn't want to unleash him on anyone else, but... she also didn't want to have to fuck Trent every night and ignore her beloved Mr. Alder. She couldn't be beholden to anyone else. At least... not Trent.

But she wouldn't let him catch on to the deviousness of her potential ploy.

"Yes, Trent," she muttered obediently as she finished cleaning him up. "How's... how's that? And... Thank you."

"Good work," he said as he looked at his cock, softening

and glistening with honey. He stuffed it back into his pants. "Alright. Show up here every night right after supper. To pay your dues," he said with a grin as he turned and began to leave. "Don't be late. Or I might start gettin' loose lips," he said with a chuckle.

She didn't find it as funny, her lower lip pouting out. But she nodded and said, "Okay," to his back.

She was going to have to be a lot more careful, but... she thought she had been. She remembered feeling like there were eyes on her, but she had chalked that up to paranoia or excitement or nerves. Either way, it seemed that her instincts were right, and it wasn't just the masked vigilante keeping tabs on her.

She went to her bag, grabbing her shirt and beginning to button it up while she waited for Trent to disappear into the darkness.

It didn't take long, because Trent had been in no rush to linger around once he was done, unlike the other guys she'd been with. Another point against him. Not that she wanted him to, mind you. She was happy he was gone, leaving her alone to tidy up and do her business.

She got herself straightened out, then took a pencil and notebook from her bag. It was dark out, but her eyes had mostly adjusted, at least enough to write a brief letter.

"Dear Masked Vigilante,

Trent the goth is threatening to tell lies about me. Could you convince him not to?

XO"

She didn't sign it, just in case anyone else found it, and then folded it up into a complex square. She tucked it inside the log, hesitating just a moment.

She really didn't want anyone else to get hurt, but...

She stood up, putting her pencil and notepad away, throwing her backpack over her shoulder and beginning to walk briskly towards her room.

Luckily things with Trent hadn't taken too long. So, she got back to her room, the dorms still relatively quiet before the flood of students at the sound of the final bell. Shutting her bedroom door, she laid her bag down, then sat on the bed, opening up the letter from Mr. Alder.

The beautiful paper was matched by his elegant handwriting.

"Dear Casey,

Sorry you were held up so sick. You were greatly missed in class today.

I'm going to be heading to town right after class to pick up a few things in the shops, before they all close. We won't be able to meet for studies afterwards.

But we should make up for it when we can. If you're able, you can come visit me at my cottage. But come by the back, along the trees. Knock on the rear window if you're able.

We shouldn't linger long, but... I do miss you.

Yours,

Aurelius Alder"

Casey's heart raced as her fingertips traced over the elegant lettering. The butterflies in her stomach came to flight once more.

There were only a couple of hours left before lights out, but just being able to see him again, even if only for a moment, made her heart race. She *had* to go. She wanted to tidy herself up a bit first, though, so that she could be clean for her lover, and she raced to the showers. She pulled her hair up in a high ponytail, quickly undressing. She'd lost so many articles of clothing that it was quite easy, though taking off the tape for the first time proved to be a little bit of a learning curve.

Still, as Mr. Grieg promised, it didn't hurt coming off, though it did curl and stick to itself, so she had to throw it out.

Naked, she stepped into the warm shower, and began to soap her body down, careful not to get her curly hair wet.

She didn't linger too long in there, even though the hot, steamy water felt so nice on her pale skin. But she was a woman on a mission, and she let the soap glide over her soft skin as she found herself fantasizing about her teacher. About how he missed her when she wasn't in class, and had written her such a beautiful letter.

It made her feel so special, and after the quickest shower ever, she stepped out, and within minutes, she was dressed, lotioned, and ready for her 'date'.

The jaunt across the campus wasn't too long, the main problem was trying to avoid being seen. Students weren't really allowed in the section where the teacher's homes were. She followed Mr. Alder's advice, and crept in along the woods.

His cottage was right where she knew it to be though, and that helped at least. And she found the back window, tapping on it lightly.

There was a moment of strained silence, where she worried she had the wrong building. But then the window opened, and Mr. Alder's smiling face was there.

Twenty-Four

"Casey," he said, before reaching out, to take her hands. "Here, let me help you in," he said.

Walking in her high heels was normally a breeze for her, since she was so used to it, but walking through the woods was a bit more of a challenge, and helping herself in through the window even more of one. It was hardly graceful, but with his help, she found herself standing in Mr. Alder's home!

It was her dream come true.

But luckily Mr. Alder did all the hard work of lifting her up. And when her feet touched the floor of his study, he smiled brightly and put his arms around her.

"So glad you could make it," he said, before leaning down, his head tilted as he kissed her lips softly, sensually. The moment lingering as he held her tightly.

Her posture softened, melting into him as her arms were thrown around his neck with such loving passion.

"I missed you today. I'm sorry we can't stay together long, but I couldn't stand the idea of not seeing you, even if it is for just a moment," she sighed out, her inner romantic teased to the surface.

Mr. Alder smiled at her so warmly, his hands caressing her back, and down over the swell of her bottom.

"It was hard not seeing you in my class this morning. The first time that's ever happened. But don't worry, I didn't dock you any marks for attendance. And I informed the other teachers that you had a legitimate medical reason," he assured her. "I'll have to endeavour to be more responsible in the future, and not keep you up so late."

"I was the one that wanted to stay," she said with a wistful sigh. "Just like I know I'm going to want to stay again tonight. But I don't want to put you at any risk," she said, Trent having done quite a lot to remind her of the potential troubles of their tryst.

Mr. Alder smiled and kissed her softly again.

"We're taking a lot of risks regardless. But... I'll do what I can for you at every step," he said, squeezing her against him, so she could feel his cock twitch with excitement. "I have another gift for you..." he said, a charming smile quirking the corner of his lips.

Her green eyes lit up as she stared at his handsome face.

"You really got me something?" she asked. She hadn't even thought to hope when he was going to the stores that it might be for her. Her mother was a poor woman, and even special occasions didn't call for gifts.

Her austere religious upbringing didn't allow for such frivolous—or 'decadent' as her mother would say—things.

"I did," he said, as he disentangled from her, and took her hand. "Come with me," he bid her, leading her out of his neatly appointed office, with the big desk, the curious ancient art on the walls, the book shelves. Then down the hall to his bedroom. The centerpiece was a large four poster canopy bed, of some old make, with richly appointed furniture; it was a beautiful room. And he pulled back the canopy, revealing a little gift bag.

"I hope you like them," he said with a smile.

"Oh Mr. Alder, I'm sure anything you got me will become a treasured keepsake," she promised, hesitating only a moment before she walked forward, taking the bag delicately in her hands. "I've never had a man buy me a gift before. You're going to quickly spoil me, two in as many days."

Her fingers popped in the top of the bag, delicately unwrapping the tissue paper.

Mr. Alder's hand trailed along her spine, that light touch somehow making her tingle all over as he caressed her so delicately. He had more of an effect on her than some men who were far more assertive.

"I think I got your size right..." he remarked. "But if not, I'll try again."

She reached in the bag, her fingers grazing elegant, intricate material. She removed it from the bag, setting the bra and panties on the bed to get a better look at them.

The red material was vibrant, and would nicely compliment her hair, but the lingerie was simply... beautiful. Scandalous, and beautiful. There were delicate slits where her nipples and areola would be, with a matching slit for her pussy in the panties, and the patterned lace was clearly done by someone with great skill.

"You... you bought this for me?" she asked, turning and

tilting her head at him. She'd taken her hair down after the shower, and it tickled the nape of her neck.

"Yes," he said with a smile, his hands moving to her hips as he caressed her sides. "I thought you would look utterly ravishing in them... and like I said, if the size isn't just right, I can go try again," he said, his handsome face alight with warmth. "Did you want to try them on before you go?"

"Yes," she smiled immediately. "And I'm sure it'll fit better than my old bra, at the *very* least," she giggled. "Will you help me?" Her fingers began working the buttons through the holes on her blouse, the shirt popping open with each one. She didn't reapply the tape after her shower, so her bare breasts were released into the open air, her nipples hardening instantly.

"Of course," he said, as his large hands went to her blouse, helping undo those buttons, and peel away her top. "God Casey," he said, gazing at her full breasts in the moody lighting of his bedroom, those hands moving in to cup and cradle each heavy mound in his palm. "Every time I see these... I feel weak in the knees," he confessed, fondling them.

His sweet words made her melt, and she turned her head to smile up at him.

"I wish we had more time together. I don't think there's anything I'd like more than making you weak in the knees for days at a time," she purred. Her fingers found the button and zipper on her skirt, letting it fan out around her hips and feet.

"Or maybe if I was, like, in art class, posing as a model for you to draw for hours, so you'd always be able to have a picture of me."

"Ohh Casey..." he said with a shiver of delight, tonguing the seam of his lower lip. "Someday I will have to take you up on that..." he said with a hint of a grin. But his wide eyes scanned over her whole body, desire lighting a flame in his gaze. "You have to put it on before I lose control of myself," he said with a cheeky smile, as he took up the bra, then put it behind her. The clasps of this one were conveniently at the front, and though it was a much better fit than her old bra, it was still some work to squeeze her ample breasts into those cups.

It made her flesh swell out of the sides and the gaps, though in a much more erotic way. Her nipples poked through the slits, and the fabric teased her sensitive flesh, making it dimple with excitement.

She looked down at herself, but it was of course hard to tell from that angle how it looked, so she instead watched his reaction.

And she wasn't disappointed. The fire of desire in his eyes only grew higher, and he licked his lips hungrily as he caressed her supple tits through the delicate red lace.

"Exquisite," he said, almost breathless with awe as he fondled her tits, his fingers grazing her stiff pink nipples as they poked through the open slits. "How does it feel?" he asked.

"A bit weird, but in a really nice way. I think it'd be too distracting for class," she confessed, her voice a bit headier and filled with arousal. "It... there's a lot of sensation."

"You may be right there... I'm not sure I could concentrate at all if I saw you sitting in class... wearing this," he said with a bit of a grin. "Of course... none of that stops me from wanting you to do it anyhow," he admitted, then glanced to the panties. "Try those now."

"You'd want me to wear it? Like our secret?" she asked as she grabbed the panties. The sides were very thin and elastic, filigreed with lace, and she began to pull them up over her stockinged thighs. She wanted to be careful with them, because they were so beautiful, and when she tugged them up all the way, they pushed her plush lips together, making them pout between her thighs.

"Gods, Casey... how can I not?" he said, as he reached a hand down, two of his fingers parting, caressing along those panties, grazing her pouting vulva just a bit. He moaned lewdly, then let his fingers directly caress her there. "I am madly obsessed with you..." he confessed, using his other hand to caress her cheek, then kissed her forehead. "How do they feel?"

"They feel really good when you're touching me," she breathed out, looking up at him with such longing as he touched her. She shivered as he drew out her moisture from between her lips, her body so eager for him. More than any other, she felt a deep longing for his body. "How much time do we have before I have to head back? Can you hear the bell out here?"

"Less than an hour. Probably close to a half an hour," he said, as his index finger parted her folds and dipped between, fingering her slightly as he looked into her emerald eyes. "And yes... you can hear it here. Although more faintly," he said, letting his other hand squeeze her breast, fondling it through that bra.

"Will that be enough time for... what you want?" she asked seductively, her thick thighs pressing around his hand, keeping him in place so that she could lightly grind against him the way she wanted to. Her nipple was so stiff, the fabric doing a lot to excite her already sensitive nerves, and his hand...

Well, his body was like magic for her.

He could ask her to do anything, and she'd be only too thrilled to obey.

"Gods Casey... you are more enticing than Aphrodite herself," he said, as his hands fondled, caressed and fingered her. His lips kissing her. "If we're quick... we can do... something. Not everything I want but... enough time for me to cum inside you, nice and deep..." he said, as his finger pushed up into her further, to punctuate his statement. "That is, if you haven't changed your mind about me knocking you up..."

"I want everything you want," she promised, leaning into another kiss, her warm tongue toying along the seam of his lips. "I want you to knock me up, Mr. Alder, I promise," she swore, still not having any understanding that being knocked up, having him breed her, was the same as getting her pregnant. Her mother had 'protected' her from such sinful knowledge, but it only made her more prone to agreeing to things she didn't fully understand.

"Good," he said with a relieved smile, as he took his hands from her, suckling his glistening fingertips. He took his time, savouring her flavour, suckling them clean before speaking again. "Bend over my bed. Reach back and tug your ass cheeks apart... and beg me to cum in you," he instructed her, as he then began to undo his belt and pants, eagerly working to unveil his thick bulge.

She wanted to linger, to watch as he pulled out his hefty

masculinity, but when he gave an order, she was only too eager to obey. She turned her back on him, setting aside the giftbag and wrapping tissue, so that she could spread out a little bit. Her ass was lifted into the air, her legs spread as her hands went to her behind. The panties covered part of her ass with its intricate filigree, but it made the wanton slit all the more prominent. Especially as she pulled her cheeks wide, her pussy peaking out between her thighs.

"I want you to cum in me, Mr. Alder. I won't be able to sleep without it!"

She was able to see that thick, long shaft of his spring out, hard and ready from over her shoulder. And he groaned as he looked at her, offering herself to him so wantonly. He licked his lips and came to her, caressing her other ass cheek as he bent his knees. Because despite her high heels, he was still much taller than her. And he had to get down to line up his dick with her pussy annnnd...

"Mmm, Casey..." he moaned, as the head of his shaft stretched her puffy, pristine pussy open wide, and he sank in deep. "Ohh that feels better than anything else I have ever experienced... you are a goddess," he groaned out, his cock pulsating within her.

He made her feel like no other man could. There was just something about him being her first crush, the older man who was so smart and eloquent. Him calling her a goddess meant *everything* to her, and if she was wet before, those words brought forth a hidden spring from inside her.

She moaned, her hands squeezing her ass cheeks, keeping herself on offer for him.

"You feel so perfect," she moaned, her pussy squeezing pleasantly around his shaft.

"Ohh fuck Casey... I wish I could take all night to savour your body. And shower it with my appreciation," he said, groaning as he pulled his hips back, sliding that thick cock out of her pussy, before pumping it in again. "But I have to be quick if you're not to get in more trouble..." he moaned, as he began to quickly build up to a fast pace, making her thick ass cheeks quake with each thrust.

She had forgotten about their hurry, about all the responsibilities she knew she had, just moments ago. She was trying so hard to be a good girl, but when he was fucking her, the only type of obedience she cared about was being obedient to him. She was in love, or at least, what passed as love for a naive school girl.

And the way her body was fast working itself into an orgasm was enough to further convince her of the truth of the magnitude of her emotions.

"I want you to breed me!"

Twenty-Five

"**O**h, fuck Casey... I will," he promised amid his moans as he slid his hands from her ass to her hips and waist, gripping her firmly as he pounded into her faster, harder. That dick of his hammering deep into her, as he worked to relieve himself of his day's load of cum. The urgent need with which he ravaged her evident, as the slaps of their body hitting together filled the room, their pants and moans loud and uninhibited in that private place. Her crush's bedroom... so posh and beautiful.

They had fucked not even a full day before, but his erection was hard and strong for her, and it sent her buckling forwards. Her breasts pressed against his luxurious comforter, her nipples teased by the fabric as the lewd bra pushed her areola out, encouraging the sensation. She squealed and moaned, not holding an ounce of her pleasure back as she felt the beginning jolts of orgasmic bliss begin to shoot through her nerve endings.

Mr. Alder was working towards his own orgasm, as his

lean but strong body hammered relentlessly into her. And he huffed, grunted. One hand reached around her to squeeze and fondle her breast, his fingers pinching her nipple, tugging it a bit as he grunted and trembled.

"Ohh fuck... fuck, I'm gonna cum soon, Casey... fuck," he panted out, as the distant chiming of the bell sounded in the distance.

It was lost to her in the moment, just a hazy memory of panic that couldn't reach her brain. It was as if everything outside of the room, outside of their bodies, were put on hold. Her pussy tightened around him as he teased her sensitive nipple, her clit sending out pleasurable pulses as she began to gasp.

"I'm... I'm going to cum... too..." she whimpered.

And with the tone of the bell chiming, the two of them pounded away, the fire of Mr. Alder's release traveling up his shaft, He groaned deeply, then bucked into her wildly. He tossed back his head as his hand slipped from her tit, to her waist. And he gripped her tightly as he moaned loudly, thick rivulets of cum blasting from his cock into her depths as he trembled and moaned.

"Take it, Casey! Take it," he grunted out.

It was such a monumental risk, one that was more clearly expressed than with any other man. Sure, they'd talked about condoms and finishing in her, but they never talked about breeding her or knocking her up. Mr. Alder did, and Casey wanted it just as bad as him.

She just didn't know what it *was*.

She lost her ability to speak as she screamed out, her pussy tightening and spasming around his dick as their orgasms crashed into one another.

And while she may not have understood what she'd agreed to fully, her body did. It milked and siphoned as much virile cum from Mr. Alder's mature cock as it could. And it pumped into her depths, filling her up and risking changing her whole life... Of course, that boat may have long sailed, with how many men she'd taken in her pussy lately.

"F-Fuck! Oh gods, Casey..." he grunted, as he dumped every last strand of his seed into her, panting and moaning, groping her body as he wound down, emptying his last few spurts.

It felt so good to be taken by him, and she gasped and panted as she came down from that explosive high.

She wanted nothing more than to curl up in his bed with him, fall asleep, and wake up in the morning with his arms around her.

But she knew that couldn't happen.

She let out a moan as she turned to give him a sleepy smile.

"I love you," she murmured, though she quickly glanced towards the window. "Oh! Wait, was that the bell?"

Mr. Alder was catching his breath as he nodded.

"Yeah, it was," he said, slowly withdrawing his cock from her slit, leaving her stuffed full of his seed as he helped lift her up from her position and turn her to face him. He gave her mouth a kiss, slow and sensual, but didn't linger too long. "I like you a lot, Casey. I want you to be mine... forever. No matter how wrong it is," he said.

It wasn't *love*, but it was more than enough for her in that moment. Something to keep her feelings in overdrive as she kissed him back with such enthusiastic desire.

"One day. One day soon. We'll find a way, I'm certain of it," she said, sounding more self assured than she ever had before.

They had their touching moment, and he kissed her again.

"Alright. You should really go now," he said warmly, before bending down, and picking up her skirt to put it back around her waist. "You shouldn't need to worry about the new panties staining. The sales lady said they are resistant to that, and clean up very easily."

"Oh! Neat," she said with a bright smile, clearly impressed with his thoughtfulness. She grabbed her blouse, buttoning it up as he helped with the skirt, the two of them working efficiently to get her ready to depart. "I'm really glad I was able to get away tonight," she said gently.

"Same," he said with a warm smile, as he did her top back up for her. "We'll find ways of having... special moments together, whenever we can. Don't you worry," he said, brushing the backs of his fingers over her cheek, smiling at her adoringly. "But seriously... as wrong as it may be, as... problematic as I may be behaving, I do lo—"

But then the final warning chime went off, and he muttered, "Shit". He brought her to the window again, and lifted her up. "Be careful on your way back. Don't trip and hurt yourself, Casey," he cautioned.

"I'll be careful," she said, though really, she was more worried about Trent or someone seeing her. Her school outfit really wasn't the best for stealth, and she considered that she should ask for a black jacket or something one day. But he'd already gotten her so much, and been so kind to her, so she didn't want to overburden him.

She put her feet on the ground, her face looking up at him adoringly.

"See you in class tomorrow," she whispered.

He pressed his lips to hers in one final goodbye gesture.

"Until then," he said with a bright smile, as she was left to head off through the night.

This time, at least, she didn't feel any eyes upon her. Though if that meant anything, she wasn't sure.

She got back to the dorms just in time to see Dahlia talking with the inspector.

"She's just in the—" Dahlia was stressing, before seeing her coming over the other woman's shoulder. "There she is! See? You really suspect a good lil' girl like Casey would be up to something?" Dahlia said, shaking her head at the other woman, a hand on her hip petulantly.

The older woman sighed and ticked Casey's name off on the list as Dahlia ushered her into their room and shut the door.

"That was close, she was being a bit bitchy tonight," Dahlia said with a grin, looking over her friend.

"Thanks for covering for me," Casey said with a sigh, her heart racing. She *hated* being in trouble, and that was way too close for comfort. "I won't keep putting you in that situation, I promise." It wasn't a promise that would be easy to keep, but... she had to. She knew that eventually, she wouldn't be thought of as such a good girl with the inspectors if she kept up as she did.

"Don't worry about it, Casey," Dahlia dismissed easily with a wave of her hand as she went to her side of the room. "You covered for me plenty, remember?" she said with a smile. "There's just one thing you could do..." she said, with a tone of seriousness to her voice. Almost sounded like Casey was in trouble.

It made the skin on the back of her neck tingle.

"What do you need, Dahlia?" she asked, equally as serious.

Dahlia sat back on her bed, her skirt lifting up as she brought one knee to her chest, wrapping her arms around it. She looked to Casey seriously.

"Tell me who it is you're seeing. Because I know you are, and I know it isn't just some other student..." she said, with an impish little smile growing on her face. "No point in fibbing to me anymore, Casey..."

Casey screwed up her face, trying to fight the urge to blush.

"What makes you think that?" Casey blustered.

Dahlia grimaced.

"Don't play coy with me," she taunted, wagging an index finger at her. "Fine. You're making me guess," she said, cheeks dimpled, looking amused as she peered around the room, pondering.

"Oh come on! I've just been, you know... seeing random people. Trying to find out what I like! Just like you!"

Dahlia shot her a look that said she didn't buy that for a second.

"I bet it's a teacher..." she said, narrowing her eyes. "But why you think I won't keep that secret for you is... a bit insulting frankly," she said, tilting her head and staring at Casey accusatorily.

Casey folded her arms under her breasts defensively.

"Because you're wrong! And like..." she said, trying to think quickly on her feet. It was a new territory to her, lying. But she'd do it in a heartbeat to protect Mr. Alder's reputation. It wasn't that she didn't trust Dahlia. It was just that he didn't want anyone to know, so that was her priority. "It's just that I don't really know who it is, okay?"

Dahlia had been studying her skeptically, and then suddenly... she looked confused. Her brows furrowed and she asked.

"What the hell do you mean, you don't know who it is?" she asked.

Casey let out a huff.

"Okay, but like, you can't make fun of me, okay?" She stared at her friend seriously as Dahlia nodded. "Fine. So. You know how that guy, like, broke Declan's leg?"

Dahlia arched a brow at her even higher.

"That one they're calling the Black Mask or something?" Dahlia asked.

"Well, he ran into me the other night, and... then we ran into each other a few more times," Casey said cryptically. "But... he always wears the mask, so..."

Dahlia stared at her friend a while, in shock.

"Wow..." she finally said, looking genuinely surprised. "Really not the answer I was expecting... I mean, you're fine fucking a guy you have no idea the identity of? I mean... he could be anyone! He could be..." she struggled for examples. "Nadir. Trent. Or even... I dunno, Mr. Alder."

Twenty-Six

Casey let out a nervous laugh at that, shrugging her shoulders a little.

"I don't know, it's kind of exciting. And... I know it's wrong, but I also kind of like it, so maybe I'm just wrong in the head. But I don't think he's a bad guy, whoever he is. He just has a messed-up sense of justice."

Dahlia took a moment to think on that, then shook her head.

"Wow Casey. I think you've surpassed me now. Completely," she said before giving a laugh. "But I mean... yeah, I get it. Hope he's good," she said with a slight hint of a smirk.

"He is... And he knows what he likes, so that makes it a lot easier for me. I don't have to, like, guess with him. And he did say that I might be able to see him one day soon if I'm good. But you're not gonna tell, right? Like, Claud is out to beat him up, and some of the others are mad about it too, and the teacher's I'm sure would have a fit if they knew I knew him."

"Casey," she said with a roll of her eyes, "I told you. Your secrets are safe with me." She stood up, her skirt flouncing as she reached out to grasp Casey's hand firmly. "Your secrets are my secrets. And mine are yours. That's what being besties is all about," she said with a warm smile. "Nobody'll ever find out through me. Not that I can do much with the info anyhow. It's not as if you told me his identity," she said with a laugh.

"It's not as if I know it," Casey giggled in return. "Ulg, it feels so dirty when I say it aloud. I really am becoming a slut. Like I'm making up for all those lost years of just... wishing for something I didn't even know existed."

Dahlia laughed, practically giggled as they held hands.

"It's okay. Being a slut is fun," she said with a shrug of her shoulders and a twinkle in her eyes. "And besides, we're both sluts here. So... we're in it together," she said with a playful wink.

Casey let out a deep breath she didn't realize she'd been holding.

It felt good to tell someone, even if it wasn't the truth that Dahlia had been after. No, Mr. Alder would be her little secret. And she was pretty sure that the Black Mask wasn't Trent. Or Mr. Alder. And probably not Nadir, considering he'd been the one to scare him off that time.

It piqued Casey's curiosity.

Tomorrow, she'd try to figure out that little mystery.

Though nothing got simpler the next day.

Everything seemed so normal at first. And she went to her class with Mr. Alder, and exchanged little glances. The fact she was wearing those special little garments made her more excited than she thought safe.

But it was too good to stop.

Then came lunch period. And everything was going so normally, until...

A scream filled the lunch room, and dishes crashed to the ground. Everyone came to look, and Casey was no exception.

There, she saw Trent freaking out, face streaming with tears, eyes red, mouth open as he struggled to drink water, but stumbled around. People began to laugh, and...

It soon became clear the Black Mask had struck again.

By the end of the day, the full story was out: Trent's food had been laced with pepper spray, the stuff used by police and for self-defence, made from terrible ghost peppers. And he'd gotten a hefty dose of it. Seemed the Black Mask had filled a meatball with a round capsule of it, and it burst in his face.

But it got worse for Trent then, as while he was taken to the office, the administrator went to get his things from the locker to help him. Only to discover contraband. Not just drugs, but a knife, and other things. He was going to be expelled.

The school was in a furor from it all, and things were locked down tight. Nobody was allowed outside the dorms that evening, and Casey was stuck with Dahlia and the other girls. And the next day was the same. Rumours spread, that the administration was pissed off about the out-of-control pranks, and the contraband.

Something serious was going to be done about it.

And so, with her having found no time to see Mr. Alder again since, or have any fun at all besides chatting with Dahlia, they were called into the assembly hall one day.

The stern looking administrator, with his hawkish nose and severe glare from behind his glasses, stood behind two strangers.

"The series of pranks and assaults has gone wildly out of control. And for that reason, we have brought in two outside experts. To my right here, we have Mr. Mordule. An expert in school administration and discipline," and the tall, intimidating brute of a man gave a stern nod. He wore round glasses and had a cold stare. "He will be helping us deal with the break down in discipline," the school administrator, Mr. Steros said.

"And beside him, we have Dr. Ramlein," he explained. "He is an expert in youth psychology. And he will be meeting with everyone affected by the ongoing events here. And will be available to any of you that feel you could use some time with a therapist as well. Make use of him, because he's exactly what some of you need. I'll let Dr. Ramlein speak now," Mr. Steros said, stepping aside.

The charming, bearded doctor stepped to the podium. Looking warm and kind.

"I know this all probably seems rather drastic and severe," he said, his voice deep but friendly. "But know that we have your interest at heart. And I'm going to be speaking with many of you, one on one. To see if there is anything we can figure out together. To make it better. And rest assured, everything you tell me will be kept in strict confidence; that is, our secret," he remarked before stepping aside.

Mr. Steros looked none too happy about that last part, but he spoke on.

"Classes will resume as regular today. If you get a summons to see Dr. Ramlein, head to his office in Building

C. The old club house, for student's clubs, has been repurposed for his needs in the time being. And if you just wish to speak with him, you can go there in between classes to request a session," he said, before announcing. "Dismissed!"

And with that, Casey was filing out of the auditorium with all the others, making her way towards gym class, as usual.

She knew that, at some point, she was going to be called on. After all, she'd been with Leslie when she started itching so terribly.

And she was feeling really guilty about Trent. Sure, she knew that she didn't put the knife in his locker, but what if the Black Mask had? She hated how relieved she was that her secret was safe, and all it cost was a guy's future.

It made her a little bit gloomy as she headed into the gym, and began to get changed. She always went to the stalls, liking the additional privacy, and it felt nice to strip out of the lacy underthings. She was feeling super sensitive and overwhelmed with how horny she was. It had been a long few days without dick, and she was starting to climb the walls.

She tucked her usual outfit away, putting on the tape like Mr. Grieg had showed her before getting changed into her short-shorts and ringer top. She pulled her hair up into a ponytail before walking back into the gymnasium, glancing around for Claud.

The fact that he wasn't there did nothing to help her mood.

"Everyone pair off for some two-legged racing!" Mr. Grieg called after his whistle. "Let's take it light today, huh?" he remarked with a bright smile on his broad, handsome face.

Of course, everyone began to quickly pair off with friends, and Casey knew that boded ill for her. But before she could even get alarmed, Mr. Grieg came to her.

"Come to my office for a bit, Casey. Got somethin' for ya," he said as he led the way on inside.

It took her by surprise, but she wasn't going to argue. She wasn't really looking forward to pairing up with a stranger, and Mr. Grieg had been so nice to her. Even if it was just an excuse to get out of the exercise, she was willing to take it.

"Oh, of course, sure," Casey said, trotting behind him.

The office was familiar to her now, she'd been in there enough times. And he shut the door behind her.

"How are you holdin' up Ms. Casey? With all the changes and everything, I mean," he asked with a friendly smile, taking a seat behind his desk.

"I don't know, it's been weird, I guess. But it's not that different than when I lived at home. Less chores, I guess," she said as she took a seat opposite from him. "I've mostly just been trying to get ahead on my assignments. And doing those uh... low impact exercises you taught us."

He nodded and smiled, always seeming a little off his game when talking in private about personal things, but never failing to be kindly.

"So, you might've noticed, Claud wasn't there for today's classes," he began, taking a pause as he leaned back in his chair, the thing creaking with his weight. "He's been called in to speak with the new..." he waved a hand in the air, trying to think of a good word, "visitors."

"Oh," Casey said with a frown. "Because he was with Declan that night? Claud was only trying to do the right thing, you know. He doesn't think violence is the answer."

"Oh, I know," Mr. Grieg said with a wave of his hand and a kind smile. "They're just talkin' to him. Claud's happy to do it too. Thinks he's doing something important," he said with a soft chuckle. "And how about you? I, uh... I hope it hasn't been weighing on you? I know it's been happening around all of you, but you're a sensitive girl."

Casey's gaze dipped to her hands and she shrugged her shoulders.

"I don't know. Like, the people being..." she trailed off before settling upon, "targeted. They haven't always been the nicest people, you know? And everyone just lets them get away with it because it's too much of a hassle to find a way to get them to be better. But I think it'll just make them nastier afterwards. I don't know," Casey trailed off, unable to fully hide her guilty conscience.

Hopefully he just saw it as her being overly empathetic.

"I get what yer sayin'," Mr. Grieg said, pushing his thick hand back through his hair. "It's not really your burden to bear anyhow, Ms. Casey," he said with a smile. "You're the sweetest most innocent girl on campus. And I know that for a fact. So... uh, don't feel bad about this, and don't worry." He took out a slip of paper, then handed it to her. "They wanna talk to you. But it's just outta concern for you. So, I wouldn't fret," he said.

"About Leslie, I guess?" she asked, taking the piece of paper and looking at it. "They just seem so intimidating. Especially that Mr. Mordule one."

The paper was just a permission slip to be wandering the halls, so she didn't get in trouble.

"Mr. Mordule, uh... yeah," Mr. Grieg said, scratching his head. "He might have a few questions. But I assume they mostly want you to see the therapist, make sure everything is alright," he said as he stood up and rounded the desk. He sat on the corner of it, near her, resting a hand on her shoulder. "You don't have to be there until after this class, but I figured you might want some time to wind down and think."

"Thanks, Mr. Grieg. Mostly I just didn't wanna have my leg tied to a stranger's," she said with a little giggle, folding up the note and putting it back on the desk. "How have you been lately, anyways? I know how much you enjoy teaching."

"Oh yeah, I've been fine," he said with a shrug of his broad shoulders. "Been focusing more on my own workouts. Making sure to not skip leg day," he said with a chuckle. And his eyes swept over her, lingering at her chest for just a moment. "It's always nice to be teachin' though. I won't deny that."

It gave her a momentary tingle up her spine, to see his gaze drawn to her chest.

Ever since she lost her virginity, her desires were off the hook, and she hadn't even touched a dick in days. It was brutal!

"Well, you're really good at it. I never thought I'd like gym. Mother always said that only men and lesbians like sports."

Mr. Grieg's eyes shot up at that.

"Well, that's not quite... true. But I'm glad you've come

to enjoy it, Ms. Casey," he said with a smile, his strong hand rubbing her slender young shoulder a while, so strong and soothing. "And, uh... how is the tape holding up for you?" he asked, pointing to her chest, then licking his lips without even realizing it.

Casey just had such a strong effect on men. Without even trying to.

"Oh! Real good," she said with a lilt of arousal to her voice that she didn't mean to include. It was just... he *was* handsome. Just like Claud, only older, a bit more...

She didn't have the word for it. But she did know that him being older was pretty exciting, and that he likely had lots he could teach her. That was his job, after all.

Her gaze went down in her lap for a moment, drifting off thoughtfully, before her small, shy voice piped up. "Do you want to check my work?"

"Check your..." he trailed off, as it began to sink in what she meant. And her large, muscular teacher was suddenly struck by a conundrum. Because he wanted to be responsible and tell her, *'I trust you did it fine.'* But...

"I mean... I guess I'd better," he said, scratching the back of his neck as his dick throbbed in his gym shorts. "Just to make sure."

She smiled at his acquiescence, and brought her soft hand to the top of his that still rest on her shoulder.

"I really don't mind showing you, Mr. Grieg. You seemed so appreciative last time."

He laughed a bit anxiously, feeling her dainty little hand on top of his.

"I mean... I did. But, it's probably... I mean, appropriateness and all..." he murmured softly before clearing his throat. "My wife's been gone a long time. And... maybe I'm just... weak now..." he said, licking his lips as his gaze went back to her chest, as if drawn magnetically.

"I know. It's a lonely time. And I must remind you of her. I mean, at least, my breasts," she said as she daintily stood up, looking at him seriously. "There's nothing wrong with needing relief, Mr. Grieg. I understand what that does to a person's mind. It's like... a rubber band that gets pulled too taut. You either release it, or it snaps."

Twenty-Seven

Mr. Grieg's eyes widened at her declaration as he watched her stand up so sure of herself. He couldn't help but admire her more then, licking his lips as he stared at her stunning hourglass figure.

"You really sound so... so confident, Casey," he said as his dick made a blatantly obvious tent in his shorts that she wouldn't have missed even in her most oblivious days. "I... I really don't want to do anything... that might be off to you..." he said. "Are you sure?"

"I don't think this is off," Casey said, her brow furrowing a little bit. "You're my teacher. I'm just asking you to teach me a slightly different exercise, that's all. Something men and women do behind closed doors." She looked up at him, her innocent, green eyes glimmering with deviousness. "I want you to teach me something new."

Mr. Grieg's brows rose at that, as his dick twitched. He unfurled his arms from around his chest and looked at her curiously.

"Well... what have you done...? So far, I mean," he asked, clearing his throat as he sized her up.

Casey smiled patiently at him, her heart beginning to thud more loudly, quieting everything outside of the two of them.

"I was actually thinking... you really like my breasts. Maybe you could play with them for a bit? Teach me more about what... I can do with them?" she asked with a tilt of her head.

And before the words had even been fully formed in his head, he was saying them out loud to her.

"Ever done a tit job?" he asked, before looking a bit embarrassed. But his cock was eager for that, and showed no hesitation, unlike him.

She glanced down at it, her pussy slickening at the sight of that wanton, hard throb.

It had been too long...

She looked back at him, her smile brightening her entire face.

"I haven't! Ah, I hope it's just as fun as the other jobs I've done," she purred, squirming a bit excitedly. Her fingers went in under her gym top, lifting it up and tossing it aside, revealing her massive tits with the stiff, pink nipples atop them. She wore the tape as he instructed, and it kept them lifted up and pressed together, as if she were wearing a pushup bra.

And like that, Mr. Grieg's last inhibitions were killed off, and he stood up, towering so big and tall as he tugged his shorts down. That thick, hard shaft that sprang out almost a mirror image of Claud's. Only a little darker at the tip, and his pubic hair neatly trimmed.

"Alright then! Well, uh... I'll sit on the edge of the desk here, and the thing is," He began, instructing his student on how to do a tit job. "You gotta squeeze your tits to either side of your dick, like this..." he said, reaching out, his large hands fondling those two breasts, as he guided her into place, placing those warm, supple mounds to either side of his cock as that shaft excitedly twitched, spurting some pre as he groaned.

It was exciting for her, too. She *loved* learning, and she had a feeling that learning this would be something she'd happily use for years. She wondered if Mr. Alder had ever received a tit job... Perhaps she'd try it on him later.

Her nipples were hard as her heavy breasts rested on his powerful thighs, her hand squeezing the outer cusp of her tits as he showed her.

"Like this?"

"Y-yeah," he groaned, his cock throbbing up between her two large breasts. "Just a bit... tighter here," he said, showing her just how perfectly firm to hold her tits to his cock, as he then began to guide her up and down his length. "There you go..." he sighed, as if he'd not had the touch of a woman in so agonizingly long. "How's that?" he asked.

"It feels..." she trailed off, trying to think of the right word. Her legs straightened, helping her lift her torso before she bent back down, massaging his entire length with her tits. But then, with how gifted she was, she was really just having to focus on her hands, since her breasts were spilling over to cover the head of his cock when she lifted up.

"It feels right," she settled upon with a smile.

"Ohh gosh, you're a natural," he grunted, as he leaned

back on one hand on his desk, watching her jerk his dick off with her breasts. He moaned and shuddered, savouring it loudly, despite the fact they were just in his office in the middle of the day. "Not only are you beautiful, you just know how to use our body so well, Casey..." he groaned. "There's... there's another trick some girls do too," he suggested.

She perked up at that.

"I wanna learn everything," she said very sincerely, the sweet woman keen on the idea. "I wanna know how to do everything in the *best* way."

"Well," he began, unable to hide his grin as he shivered in delight at her attention to his needy, throbbing cock. "A lotta girls... also use their mouth on the tip as they jerk the shaft with their tits," he said amid his moans. "That way... when I cum... it's in your mouth too, instead of all over your face and... face and tits," he said as his thick, dark purple crown spurt some more pre excitedly.

She considered that with a growing smile.

She was enjoying 'corrupting' her teacher, teasing him and getting him so worked up. And she'd never had a man finish in her mouth before. It was an exciting prospect that stoked her curiosity, despite her untouched pussy throbbing in her shorts.

She shifted position, trying to angle herself just so, and looked down at the head of his shaft.

"Are you close, Mr. Grieg?" she asked before diving town, her tongue eagerly circling about the helm, just as his son had taught her.

Some people thought of Mr. Grieg and Claud as not too bright, but they had their own special skills. And lately

Casey was discovering she loved learning all about those. And to hear Mr. Grieg moan deep and loud as her mouth wrapped around the fat tip of his cock, she felt well rewarded.

"Oh shh—oh gosh!" he grunted, shivering, as his one hand went into her red ringlets, caressing her hair as his dick pulsated wildly. That thick cock straining. "It won't take much longer like this Casey, ohh dang you're good..." he panted out.

It didn't take long for her to find the right tempo, and she was pleased to find that moving her torso instead of just her tits did wonders to help her give him head at the same time. It made it all so much more fluid, and her pussy tingled with delight.

She kept licking him, every few strokes taking his full crown in her lips like a lollipop and suckling on it before rising back up.

And she was rewarded with Mr. Grieg's loud moans, the taste of his salty, potent seed on her tongue. That flavour of cum being something she'd started to truly appreciate the more she fucked and sucked.

"Ohh fuck," he swore, and she realized she'd never heard the man say anything worse than darn. "I'm gonna cum, Casey!" he warned, shivering as his cock swelled even thicker, and tensed up so hard. Until the abrupt eruption of the man's long pent-up seed came.

Thick gouts of cum flooding her mouth. More than any other guy she'd been with managed to unload, and it was all flowing into her warm, wet mouth with little warning.

It was a struggle to swallow it all down. Just the intensity and the shock combined to make her gasp and desperately try to lick and suck as he came. She missed more than one spurt, and desperately tried to make up for it, as if he'd be disappointed to see her tits and chin decorated in his cum.

But Mr. Grieg was too busy savouring the pleasure of the moment, his cock painting her mouth white, and adding a few thick strokes of that creamy seed to her face and tits too. He groaned and looked at her, as he shuddered with the last few spurts.

"Ohh heck... wow Casey," he said, licking his lips as he stared at her tits and face. "That was the best tit job I've ever had," he said with a groan.

She was beaming beneath his cum, her pink tongue eagerly cleaning his tip, then what she could of her massive tits.

She knew she'd need a mirror to get it all, but she felt such pride and joy in that moment. She'd learned something new and passed the test with flying colours.

She practically glowed as she looked up at him.

"You really mean it, Mr. Grieg?"

He ran a big hand back through his hair, looking blown away as he watched her 'tidy up'.

"Ohh yes. I really do," he said, his broad chest heaving. "You're like... amazingly good at that, wow. And heck, I needed that so bad," he said, smiling as he licked his lips. "What did you, uh, think of it?"

"I really liked it," she cheerfully replied, not seeming to think that there was anything wrong with what they just did. It was so natural to her, debauchery. It had quickly become her driving force. "And it was interesting to try to catch it all at the end, though I clearly need more practice with that."

"I, uh... wouldn't feel too bad," he said to her, sitting up straight. "I was a bit pent up. I haven't unloaded in... gosh, ages. I guess I just kinda got out of the habit of jerking off. It never really scratched that itch, y'know?" he said with a sigh and a smile. "But you really did."

She stood up, letting her breasts go and licking her finger clean of a dollop that had been splattered there.

"I know it must be hard on the teachers here, especially if their partners aren't around. And the signals out here, well... you know how it is. It really feels like we're living in a world of our own now. I don't think it's fair," she confessed.

"Well, I know I'm grateful there's someone like you around, Casey. Not, uh... not that I expect you have to keep doing that," he said, scratching the back of his neck again as he sat there, dick still out and glistening with her saliva. "Though that'd be great," he said, as the bell chimed for the changing of class.

"Oh shoot, I have to go see Mr... uh. Mr. Ramlein," she said as she grabbed her shirt. "Is there anything on my face?" she asked, and sure enough, there was a strand of cum lancing her cheek.

Mr. Grieg snapped his shorts back up over his slowly softening dick, then stood up. He scooped up that strand of cum from her skin, then held it in front of her face.

"Just this," he said with a smile.

She smiled as she licked his finger, the dichotomy of her innocent smile and the wanton act quite appealing.

"Thanks, Mr. Grieg." She pulled her gym shirt on over

her head, and grabbed the pass to get her out of her next class. "I'll see you tomorrow, okay? And don't worry, I won't tell anyone what you taught me today."

"Oh, uh... good," he said with a hand on his chest and a sigh of relief. He smiled to her, "See ya Casey. Goodluck," he remarked with a wave.

That left her to go get changed and head off to the old club building. It was a longer trek, but thanks to Leslie not being there to give her a hard time, she was able to get changed, and out of her tape and workout clothes, and back into her lingerie and uniform.

As she walked across the campus' grassy field, she saw Claud coming out of the doors, a look of surprise on his face as he saw her, followed by a smile.

"Casey! I missed ya today. They called me in," he said, jerking a thumb back, as his dick reacted with a throb. "I was really lookin' forward to class today," he said with a sigh.

"Yea, we were supposed to do three legged races, but Mr. Grieg let me skip it since you weren't there," Casey said with an earnest smile. He really was a sweetheart, just like his dad. "I have to go talk to them next. What were they like? Scary?" she asked, her gaze drawn to that hardon.

He was thick like his dad, so even in his formal school trousers that dick was obvious. Especially since nothing was made in a size big enough for him.

"Eh, it was fine. Mr. Mordule wants to find that Black Mask creep, so I was all gung-ho to help. But it seems he wants to do it himself mostly," he remarked, sounding disappointed. "I didn't really spend much time with the other guy. I guess he figures I don't need therapy," he remarked with a smile.

"You wanna, uh...?" he grinned at her.

It was hard to tear her gaze away from his throbbing bulge. She'd just gotten his dad off, sure, but she was still pent up and needing release just as bad.

Even if she hadn't gone without sex for a percentage as long as Mr. Grieg had.

It just *felt* like an eternity.

Twenty-Eight

"I can't, I guess I'm the appointment right after you," she said with a frown.

"Aww dang," Claud said, before touching her hand, then smiling. "Ah well. We'll find time to get together again soon," he said with a big grin. "Alright, good luck with the two of 'em I guess. I'll see ya later, Casey!"

And with that she was left to walk into that building alone. The main hall was long, its woodwork old and fancily inlaid, the same as the main building. She wasn't sure where to go, when suddenly the severe looking Mr. Mordule said, "You're Miss Casey, right?" and gestured her to come into his office and sit down on the tiny, austere chair.

She'd been hoping to see the therapist, Mr. Ramlein, first. He seemed a lot more friendly. Mr. Mordule just made her feel like she was in trouble for something. He reminded her of Mr. Steros in that way.

"I'm Casey, yes sir," she said as primly as she could, taking a dainty seat and crossing her legs at her ankles. It did little to help distract her from how her pussy was being pleasantly squeezed by her new panties, especially with how she was throbbing with unquenched desires.

Mr. Mordule slammed the door shut then went behind his desk, looking at a thin file folder.

"Seems you're an exemplary student, Miss Casey," he remarked, sitting down, then looking at her through his dark rimmed round glasses. "So I can count on you to tell me anything... suspicious you might've seen, right?" he asked, his voice so harsh, his gaze like it could bore through her and tell her lies.

It made her squirm, giving him a nod of her head.

"Of course, Mr. Mordule," she replied obediently. But her heart was racing with fear. She'd only just started testing out her abilities to lie or withhold the truth, and it had mostly worked so far, but... he seemed like he'd just be able to smell a fib off of her.

"So, tell me," he said, as he shut the folder closed and laid it aside, staring right through her it seemed. "Why is it that those who've wronged you seem to end up hurt? Especially when near you," he asked, pointedly.

Casey's brows furrowed as she looked to her lap and her dainty hands that were clasped there.

"I didn't do anything to hurt Leslie. She was a bully, but I'd never do something like that, I swear," she said, deciding to focus on the things that were objectively true.

There was uncomfortable silence in the room then. Mr. Mordule staring at her harshly.

"So it's just coincidence that Leslie was hurt near you? That you were seen near this boy..." he looked at a page in front of him, "Declan? And a teacher that gave you your worst grades got permanently dyed purple?" he asked harshly.

"Declan was a bully too; he didn't just pick on me! I'm sure he had lots of people that didn't care much for him. And Mr. Mullard was hard on a lot of students, not just me. But he *did* treat me especially unfair. He would say I was wrong even when I could prove I wasn't," Casey blurted out.

The severe looking man kept staring into her, making her itch beneath her clothes. But finally, he broke the silence.

"So you have nothing to add? You didn't see anything odd that day outside the building when Declan was hurt? Or at the gym lockers with Leslie?" he asked, sounding almost angry with her.

She *hated* that. It made her want to fall into a pit into the center of the earth to hide.

But she could tell him something. Something Claud might have already mentioned. Something innocuous.

"I was heading to Mr. Alder's office to ask for some extra credit work on the day Declan was hurt. A person in a mask rushed by and knocked me over, but I didn't get a good look. I couldn't even say if it was a man or a woman at the time. Their clothes were dark and not very fitted," Casey confessed, giving him the information that she had at the time. "I went to Mr. Alder's office after that and didn't think much of it until I heard about Declan the next day."

That brought Mr. Mordule to life, and he jotted down some fast notes as he she spoke.

"Why didn't you report this sooner? Or did you tell Mr. Alder?" he asked sharply.

"I told Mr. Alder that someone bumped into me, but we didn't know anything about Declan, and then after that... I don't know, it just didn't seem important. I didn't know who it was, or where they were headed. They helped me up after I fell and they seemed polite, but mysterious," Casey said nervously.

"They helped you up and seemed polite but you didn't see their face? Or hear if they're a boy or a girl?" he asked, sounding doubtful about her whole testimony. He looked at her like she was a liar. It was so unsettling!

"They were wearing a mask. They call them the Black Mask or something now. But they sounded kinda, I don't know. Androgynous, I guess, but the mask muffled their voice a lot, so I couldn't really tell. I'm sorry Mr. Mordule, I swear, I just don't know what more I can tell you."

He looked no more convinced than before, but he jotted down a few more notes then looked to her.

"I might follow up with you again, if I have more questions. But for now... you're dismissed, Miss Casey," he said to her with a wave of his hand as he resumed taking more notes on his ledger.

She squirmed again before realizing she was dismissed, and she quickly stood up.

"Yes, Mr. Mordule, sir," she said with a polite curtsey. "So I don't have to see the therapist?"

He only spared her a glance.

"He's across the hall, just turn right," he instructed her curtly.

There weren't a lot of doors to the place, so it wasn't hard to find the other room.

She found the door open, with the casual looking Dr. Ramlein sitting back in a comfortable looking chair.

"Oh," he said, looking surprised as he smiled and stood up. He came right up to her, offering her his hand, "You must be Ms. Casey, am I right?" he said with a warm, cheery smile.

"Yes sir," she said politely, putting her hand gingerly in his. Her head was still reeling from her last appointment. Everything that was said between them was spinning in her mind, as she tried to search for any potential clues she gave away that she didn't intend to. "Should I shut the door?"

"Certainly. If that would make you feel more comfortable, by all means," he said kindly as he went to the sofa next to his chair, and plumped up the cushions, making it look more inviting. "Would you like anything? I have some juice, milk and water on hand. And a few biscuits," he said, as he gestured to the tray of cookies on the coffee table.

She was so nervous, and she closed the door, if only to put herself further away from Mr. Mordule.

"Uhm, cookies and milk sounds really nice," she said tentatively, eyeing the biscuits. It was nearing lunch time, and she didn't know how long to expect this all to take.

She went to the sofa, tucking her skirt beneath her bum before she paused. "Oh, should I sit here?"

"Of course," he said so kindly, "anywhere you like." He remarked with a smile as he took a carton of milk from a small cooler, and poured up a glass full, taking it to her with care. "How are you feeling today, Casey? I imagine it was a jarring period for you," he said, that friendly smile on his handsome, older face. Streaks of silver through his medium length brown hair.

He was so disarming after meeting with Mr. Mordule, and she graciously took a seat.

"I don't know, it's all been really weird," she said with a sigh. "Are you going to tell Mr. Mordule and Mr. Steros what I say? And, like, dissect me? Mother always said that I should only confess to a priest and that therapists were charlatans out to tear families apart."

Dr. Ramlein's brows rose up high at that, then he gave a soft, good-natured laugh as he sat back in his seat, adjusting his suede jacket as he did.

"Oh my, no," he remarked with a light chuckle. "Everything you say here is in strictest confidence. That is, I don't tell anyone else. The only exceptions are if you tell me you're going to hurt yourself, in which case... I have to act to protect you," he said, looking to her calmly. "Does that make sense? Do you have a problem with that arrangement, Ms. Casey?" he asked calmly, crossing his legs and folding his hands on his knee.

Her hands wrapped around the glass of milk nervously, fidgeting with the condensation that was starting to form on it.

"What if I said I was the Black Mask, would you have to tell them then?" she asked, transparently testing him.

"No," he said calmly, with a curious smile blossoming on his face. "Why? Are you the Black Mask? If so... I'd have to say I was impressed," he remarked with a chuckle.

Casey's green eyes widened at him.

"Why would you be impressed? The Black Mask has hurt people," she said, aghast.

"Oh sure, yes," he began, sounding so calm and patient. "But for you to keep it a secret all this time... that'd be impressive. Secrets don't last long in a school like this, do they?" he said with a smile. "You know, if you're feeling too anxious to speak... there's something I can do to help."

She tilted her head, studying him curiously. He wasn't reacting as she expected, and it was grabbing her attention.

"What can you do?" she asked, nervously taking a sip of milk.

"It's not medicine or anything. And you seem like a very proper girl, so I wouldn't want to trouble you with drugs or pills you don't need," he said as he fished out a shiny pocket watch from his suede jacket. "When you're ready, I want you to lay back on the sofa. Leaning against a cushion, okay?"

"I'm not popular," she protested, before looking at the watch curiously. "What's that for?" she asked, taking another sip of milk before setting it aside. "You want me to lay down?"

"Yeah, or you can sit up if you prefer," he said, as he pulled his chair in closer to her. He opened the pocket watch, showing her the old-fashioned filigree and designs. "This is something given to me by my father. And his father before him," he explained softly, the ticking sound reverberating. "It has to be wound up every day, unlike modern watches," he explained as he then shut the watch and let it sway back and forth before her eyes.

It was very confusing, but she did as he instructed. She pulled up her high heel shoes, taking off each mary jane and setting them back down before resting her stockinged legs on the sofa. She smoothed down the front of her skirt, and tugged her shirt down to bring it back into place and cover her belly.

"Like this?"

"Perfect, Casey. You did that wonderfully," he complimented in that soothing, deep voice of his. He leaned over her slightly, making that watch sway back and forth. "Now I want you to focus on the watch. Keep your eyes on it as it sways back and forth... back and forth..." he said, speaking so slowly and soothingly. "Let your ears hear the ticking of the watch, the sound of my voice... and let everything else... just fade... fade away, until there's nothing but you, me, and my watch..."

Twenty-Nine

It was so strange. She'd never heard of anything like this before, and didn't really understand the purpose of it.

But he'd sounded so sure of himself, of what she should do, and so she felt that she owed it to him to give it a chance.

She let out a heavy sigh, her bust heaving against her ribs as she got comfortable. Her hands were lightly clasped on her stomach, and she stared at the watch. It got easier to pay attention to, the longer she did it. The way the ticking filled her ears.

It was almost like sex. It made the rest of the world... fade away.

And his soothing, calming voice helped.

"There's nothing but you and me, Casey," and she began to feel that was true. Just him and her floating in an emptiness. Except that wasn't scary for some reason. "You, me... and a comfy, frilly bed, made just for you, that you're laying on. Feel it beneath you without moving... isn't it comfortable? Everything is so relaxing," he assured her, and what he said seemed to instantly become true every time.

"Nothing you tell me will leave this room. And nothing I say or do will either. I will help you today, Casey. And you will help me. Doesn't that sound nice?" he asked.

It did sound nice.

She took a deeper breath, feeling the tension begin to leave her shoulders and neck. She didn't know why she'd been so nervous about coming here. He was going to help her.

Casey smiled at him and nodded.

"Yes, Dr. Ramlein."

"Wonderful," he said soothingly and he slipped the watch into his pocket, smiling at her. "You feel completely at ease with me. Nothing at all you care to hide. Nothing you'd want to hold back. You and I... we're like best friends. But better," he said, smiling. "Aren't we? So, tell me, what's on your mind today, Casey?"

That was a hard question to sort out. There were a lot of layers to it, and it was a challenge to even know where to begin.

"Oh... I don't really know. A lot of things, I guess. What do you want to know about specifically, Dr. Ramlein?"

"Oh," he began, moving closer to her, his eyes drifting over her form. "Let's begin with... do you have a boyfriend?" he asked, undoing the buttons of his blazer.

"Not really," she answered earnestly. "I've been exploring things a bit lately. But I'm not going steady with anyone." She still used a lot of outdated words, ones her mother had used in her presence as a warning. She looked at him, watching him as he undid his blazer, that throbbing between her thighs igniting once more.

"Good. It's good to explore things," he said to her with a warm smile as he sat there with blazer open, his maroon tie showing beneath. "I'm going to touch you as we talk, Casey. But don't worry, you'll like it. It'll just help you relax and enjoy the moment, as I touch you," he explained, as his hand came to her ankle, then lightly drifted up her calf. "What have you... explored, so far?" he asked, his eyes twinkling.

She glanced down at his hand, and really, she didn't even need his hypnotic suggestion to know that she'd like it. She watched his hand caress over her white stockinged leg with a faint smile.

His words captured her attention again, though, and she began counting off on her fingers, "I know how to do a hand job, a blow job, a tit job, and... well, sex," she said thoughtfully. "With me in their lap, or on my back, or on my knees, or on my feet," she added on, just in case it wasn't enough information the first time. "Oh, and I made a girl cum."

Dr. Ramlein's brows shot up in surprise at all that, but a grin began to form on his lips as he let his fingers wander up, just past her stocking. He touched her creamy inner thigh there, so near to her she could smell his lightly scented cologne.

"Wow. You have been a very ardent student in your exploration," he remarked approvingly. "Tell me, how did you make her cum? And what girl was it?" he asked, licking his lips, tonguing the lower one extra long.

She inhaled his intoxicating scent, her eyes fluttering up

for a moment as she squirmed. It felt so strange, and so exhilarating, all at once.

"I like to learn," she confessed, her gaze drawn to him once again. "I used my hand on her pussy, and I kissed her breasts. She helped show me what to do. Dahlia's my best friend," she said with a growing smile. "She's amazing and so beautiful."

"Dahlia," he repeated, and he leaned back, jotting down a note on his pad of paper before looking back to her. "Is she as beautiful as you?" he asked warmly, before gesturing to her breasts. "Are her breasts as big and lovely as those? Speaking of, you must feel so hot and stuffy. Feel free to undo your top and take it off if you like," he invited her, but she did suddenly feel very overheated and stuffy at his suggestion.

"She's very beautiful, with dark hair, and a bright smile," Casey said wistfully as her fingers began popping the buttons out of their holes. The red lingerie was a bit more obvious beneath the white, stretched blouse, but as her tits spilled out, it was unmistakable that what she was wearing was not a bra suitable for the classroom. Her nipples were pinched between the fabric, teasing them erect, and she was only too happy to be rid of her shirt.

She sat up as she removed the top the rest of the way, putting it on top of her Mary-Janes.

"Her breasts aren't as big as mine, but they're just as nice. So soft and perky," she sighed.

He was fast sporting a thick bulge in his lap as he listened to her talk, his one hand still at her creamy thigh as he watched her. Those eyes were drawn to her tits immediately, and the scandalous bra beneath was not lost on him.

"Oh my... what a lovely bra you've chosen to wear today, Casey," he remarked warmly. "You must feel so confident and... powerful in that," he remarked to her casually. "Tell me, if I brought Dahlia in here sometime... do you think the three of us might all play together? Explore each other, I mean," he remarked, as his hand slid up, then very purposefully lifted her skirt to marvel at her exposed puffy labia.

"I don't know, Dahlia usually makes people pay," Casey said with a shrug as she shifted in her seat, watching him curiously. "What do you want, Dr. Ramlein?"

Him staring at her, touching her... it was really turning her on, and her breathing was becoming shallower. But she didn't know the things he did, that she was under his control, and she was just speaking with him as normal.

Dr. Ramlein pulled his hand from her thigh after finishing peering up her skirt. He licked his lips and sat back in his seat.

"Get on your knees in front of me, Casey. Wait, actually... for this moment, your name is Cocktoy," he said warmly as he began to casually unbuckle his belt. "You're going to play with my dick a bit while we speak, okay Cocktoy?" he said warmly.

She blinked in a moment of confusion before that hypnotic acceptance washed over her and she nodded.

"Okay, Dr. Ramlein," she said as she stood up from the sofa and shifted to the floor, right in front of his chair. She knelt down, feeling the hardwood against her stockinged knees, as she rose her hands up to his still clothed bulge.

It felt so interesting and different to touch it while his pants were still on, and she found herself fascinated by it.

He smiled down at her, caressing her hair with one hand, as the other slowly unzipped his pants.

"Perfect. You're a very good girl, Cocktoy. And I am gonna show you the best cock you've ever seen. And you get the lucky position of being its own personal toy, how does that sound?" he asked, as he fished out his cock, that hard, veiny organ emerging so rigid and firm. It was by no means the biggest or longest or thickest of the ones she'd done, and yet...

It was *perfect*. The best. Beyond all the others.

She smiled at it as if he'd unveiled the most delightful gift a girl could have asked for.

Her hand wrapped around his shaft without further instruction needed, learning his shape, the veins, the thickness. He had her full attention, her young body practically quivering with delight.

"That sounds just perfect, Dr. Ramlein."

He sighed as she began to fondle and caress his dick, patting her head as he smiled down at her.

"Good girl, Cocktoy," he said soothingly, as he stared at her tits. "How many dicks have you sucked, fucked or jerked so far, Cocktoy? Be honest, it's okay. I don't mind that you're a slut," he said warmly. "In fact, I like it."

"Oh... I'm not sure," she said, trying to do a mental tally. "Should I count each person once or..." she asked, her fingers beginning to stroke his cock, her eyes glued to the swollen tip as it hid behind the skin and then was revealed once more.

He chuckled as he watched her toy with his dick, the head leaking some glistening pre as she stroked it.

"Oh, it's okay. We'll just say... too many to count then,"

he remarked, peering down at her. "So, tell me, Cocktoy. You've been fucking a lot... is it safe for me to fuck you without a condom? I mean, without any risk of illness. I assume you're on the pill?"

She didn't understand any of that.

"I'm not sick," she replied thoughtfully, "and I'm not on any medication." She smiled at him, as if she were giving him the correct answer. At least, it was correct in her mind. "And I could count them, if I had more time. I'm very good in math, despite what Mr. Mullard says."

His dick throbbed excitedly in her hand and he groaned as she revealed that.

"Oh my, perfect," he said warmly, licking his lips afterwards. "You can lick and kiss it in between talking, Cocktoy. I know you really want to," he said so casually, and yet she felt it so intensely. "Tell me, is Dahlia safe to fuck bareback too? Does she use condoms when she's whoring?" he asked.

"Yea, she told me I should, but I don't like how they feel," Casey confessed, feeling relieved that he gave her permission to lick his cock. She felt like there was some invisible thing around her, controlling her actions, and she knew that she had to be obedient. Wanted to be obedient.

She wanted to make him happy.

Her tongue gathered up the precum at the tip of his cock, letting out a soft sigh of satisfaction. She wanted him so badly she thought she might die, but at least she was able to enjoy his salty-sweet elixir.

"Mmm, me neither, Cocktoy. Condoms ruin the whole thing. Don't worry, you and I will never be using condoms," he said to her warmly, smiling down at her so soothingly. He loosened his tie after that, beginning to unbutton his shirt. "Tell me Cocktoy, do you know the administrator, Mr. Steros well?" he asked.

She shook her head, letting her tongue glide along his shaft.

"No, he's very intimidating," she said as she bathed him with her mouth. "I'm glad you don't want to use a condom with me."

"Really? It is just better without one, isn't it, Cocktoy?" he asked her, caressing her cheek lightly. "Now then, before we get down to stuffing my favourite toy full of cum," he said, petting her hair, "I want you to know... I plan to get your friend Dahlia in here. And you're going to help me with that, aren't you? You want to help me fuck her, don't you?"

Casey smiled stupidly at the suggestion, nodding her head.

"Of course, Dr. Ramlein," she said cheerfully. "Just let me know what to do, and I'll do it!"

She licked his cock from base to tip, still stroking him as her tongue twitched over his sac, exploring him with full curiosity.

"You and your friend—" he peered at his notepad, "Dahlia, are going to have a lot of fun with me," he said warmly. "I'm going to give you a pass for her to come see me tomorrow. And another for you too. I'll see her first to arrange... the price and all. Then the three of us can fuck to our heart's content. Doesn't that sound nice?" he said, tugging at her hair. "Come sit on my lap and bounce on my dick, Cocktoy. Oh, that gives me an idea. You're Cocktoy and... maybe I'll change her name to Cumdumpster. You like the sound of that, Cocktoy?" he asked.

Casey let out a happy little giggle.

"That sounds dirty," she said as she got to her feet with the aid of his little tug. She looked down at the older man, her eyes scanning his face as she moved closer to him. Luckily, with her panties as they were, she didn't even need to remove them to fuck. That knowledge seemed to strike her as if for the first time, and it made her shiver with delight.

Her knees went to either side of his hips, and she positioned herself over his cock, lowering herself down enough to find the crown of his dick. Her emerald eyes were trained on his as she began to take him into her bare pussy.

"It is dirty," he said with a soft chuckle as his hands went to her large tits, fondling them through that skimpy brazier. "Now then, Cocktoy. You're going to slide down around my dick and ride it. But be warned, it's going to be the greatest experience you've ever had," he said fondly, before leaning in and licking a nipple of hers, "Do it."

Thirty

S he couldn't resist, even if she wanted to.

Truthfully, she would have done mostly the same things even if she wasn't under his hypnotic suggestion, but that extra compulsion just made it more impactful. Made it matter more.

And when her tight, wet pussy began to slide down his shaft, she let out a shiver of arousal. She was so horny, and the suggestion that he was going to be the greatest experience was impossible to resist. She already felt like she was so close to the edge, her nipple achingly stiff against his tongue.

Dr. Ramlein's eyes rolled back into his head, and he gave a deep moan as her tight, young pussy swallowed up his shaft. He was under no such compulsion, but he seemed almost as satisfied as she was with the experience. He squeezed her tits in response, bit a nipple, suckled and tugged it before speaking again.

"Isn't it the best cock you've ever had, Cocktoy?" he

asked her, groaning as he slid one hand around to her ass, to give it a light slap. "Ride it," he commanded.

He didn't even need to tell her, she was already beginning to slide up his shaft before falling back upon it, just like she had with Mr. Alder. Her arms wrapped around Dr. Ramlein's neck and she let out a moan, doing little to muffle the sound of her pleasure.

"The best," she cooed, another thrill of pleasure going through her. "I feel so good."

"Mmm, me too..." he moaned, his hand groping her ass, also helping guide her tempo as she rode up and down his dick. "I'm so glad I trusted my instinct on which girl to call to my office. I saw the notes... saw Leslie taunted you about your chest," he groaned, and stared lustily at her tits. "Fuck, I had no idea you would be such a willing slut though, Cocktoy," he groaned as his dick pulsed and spurt precum into her.

"I like being a slut," she moaned in return, riding him with a growing confidence. "I've been so horny with all of us being locked up, it's been driving me crazy." She confessed things so easily, so readily. Even without the hypnosis, she was always so open about these things in the heat of the moment, but with him, it was intensified. Her pussy squeezed him as jolts of pleasure began to build in her clit.

Her large tits were bouncing in his face, that bra doing little to keep them from jiggling and swaying. He didn't mind though, he still occasionally licked and suckled at one of her stiff, needy nipples, as one hand fondled the other mound.

"Mmm, I know just how you feel, Cocktoy. My last

assignment... was to a boy's school. No hot young sluts to fuck at all," he groaned out, squeezing her ass. "And that's the whole reason I got into this line of work... to stick my cock into sweet hot sluts like you," he cooed, then grunted as his own orgasm was approaching.

Casey was growing used to learning when a man was nearing his end, and it sent a delightful ripple through her body. Her arms tightened around his neck, and she began moaning more loudly, her body keeping up the same pace, but increasing in intensity.

"I love how you touch my tits," she whimpered.

"You've got so much of them to touch," he said, squeezing them, licking one. "Ohh yes... I am going to line you and Cumdumpster up together, and compare and caress both pairs at once. Ah... f-fuck. I'm going to cum in you... oh fuck yes," he panted out, groaning as she rode on his dick. "Cum with me, Cocktoy. Do it," he commanded.

It was unlike anything she'd ever experienced. It was as though he hastened everything with that command, and her pussy squeezed his cock as she gasped and heaved forward, her body grasping his. Her hot honey gushed onto his cock as an intense orgasm struck her entire body all at once.

And that was more than enough to bring him into that precipice of bliss too. He threw back his head, groaned, as his dick began to swell inside her. She felt him begin to shoot off his thick load of hot, pent-up cum. Fulfilling that deep, intense need in her own loins, as he attempted to plant his seed in her womb.

He bucked up into her, a hand squeezing a breast tightly, as they came together. Their orgasms were long and intense, as he shook and gasped beneath her, until he was left panting.

She didn't want to get off of him. Perhaps she couldn't, without him telling her to. It was hard to say. All she knew was that she just had the best cock she ever had, and she didn't want it to end. She wanted more, and even through the post coital sensitivity, she began to ride him once more.

He groaned, then shivered all over. And finally, he gasped and said, "S-stop, stop," he grinned and stood up, lifting her with him. Then he pulled her off her dick, letting her stand before him as cum drooled from her slit down her inner thighs.

"Good girl, Cocktoy. But it's time for you to clean me up before the next student comes in," he instructed her, taking a kerchief out of his pocket and dabbing his forehead as his glistening cock dangled there.

"Oh," she said, slightly disappointed, even though he called her a good girl. Still, she got down on her knees again, her tongue instantly going to his dick, lapping up the honey she'd coated him in. At least it was something to tide her over. Her eyes fluttered closed and she let out another soft sigh against his cock as she cleaned him.

Dr. Ramlein took out his pad and pen again, and began to write as she licked him. Him jotting away, as she so dutifully and erotically cleaned his girth. He smiled when he was done, and patted her head after tearing off a couple sheets.

"Here you go. You'll be coming back to do more therapy with me, Cocktoy. And the other one, is for your friend, Dahlia. I'll be seeing you both tomorrow. In the meantime, you'll have to go back to class and all that. And you'll sadly forget everything that happened here when I snap my fingers, except the tasks I've given you. But don't worry, it'll all come back to you again when you hear 'Cocktoy', got it?" he asked, looking down at her with a smile.

"Why would I forget?" she asked, sounding *quite* saddened by that fact. She didn't want to forget! She paused her cleaning, looking up at him with a pouting lower lip. "I can keep secrets, Dr. Ramlein, I promise. I don't want to forget."

"Oh, sweet toy," he said, caressing her cheek. "Don't worry. Like I said, it'll all come back to you next time I say 'Cocktoy'. And you'll obey the best cock you've ever had again. And your friend will be here with us too. Think of how much fun that will be, huh?" he said warmly. "Us three, doing all kinds of fucked up, debauched shit."

Casey didn't seem thrilled with it, but he seemed so certain, it was hard to fight back against him on the issue. She finished cleaning his cock until the only thing remaining was a bit of her saliva, but kept up the task until he approved of her job.

"It's usually so much trickier than this," he said with a soft laugh and a shake of his head as he watched her clean. "But you are a very special girl. Alright, that's enough," he said, pushing her head back then tucking his dick into his trousers. "Get dressed. And... whatever cum is leaking from your pussy, try to tidy it up and swallow it. Oh, and should you get pregnant... it wasn't me, understood?"

Casey's face furrowed in confusion at that.

It was the first time anyone around her had ever linked *sex* to *pregnancy*.

She stood up, obediently putting her fingers between

her legs, gathering up his cum and suckling on it as she looked at him thoughtfully.

"How would you get me pregnant?"

"Exactly," he said with a grin as he watched her suckle his seed. "Now then. You'll leave here, go back about your day as if nothing happened in here... except that we had a lovely chat, that left you feeling much better. Feel free to tell your friend Dahlia that when you give her the slip," he instructed.

"Okay," she said, still confused and cleaning the cum off her fingers. "So, I'll come back tomorrow with Dahlia at the same time?"

"Yes. But she'll come in first, so I can help her get prepared," he said with a smile. "Now hurry up and get dressed, Cocktoy," he reminded her.

Casey had started lingering. She didn't want to forget, and she figured the longer she cleaned herself up, the longer she'd remember.

But she couldn't waste any more time with him ordering her like that, so she grabbed her shirt, quickly buttoning it up, before sitting down to put her shoes back on. She didn't even get a chance to eat a cookie or finish her milk, though that was hardly what was on her mind at the moment.

She stood up, looking much as she had when she walked in.

"Did you want me to tell Mr. Steros that I feel better after our chat?"

"Yes, Cocktoy. Tell him exactly that. But that you feel you could use more time with me," he said with a smile, caressing her breast through her top. "Alright. Now remember, when I snap my fingers... you'll forget everything that happened here, except that you must do the things I told you. So then, one... two... three..."

And just like that, the past hour was erased from her mind, but for the vague sense that the talk went well. Just with a snap of his fingers.

She smiled at him politely, giving a slight curtsey.

"Thank you, Dr. Ramlein. I don't know how to describe it, but... I just feel a lot better now. Is there anything else you need of me?"

"No, that's all, Ms. Casey," he said kindly. "Just remember to pass that slip along to Dahlia, okay? And take care of yourself," he said as he went back to his desk, jotting down a few more notes.

Casey picked up her bag and tucked the notes inside her notebook. She gave him a friendly wave as she left his office, feeling just as horny as she had when she first walked in. Perhaps more so. She felt as though something might have scratched that itch, but instead... inflamed her passions even more.

Still, she had her tasks, not to mention the rest of her afternoon classes.

Casey decided to go out the back door of the building, so as to not have to walk by Mr. Mordule's office again and risk more of his accusations.

She took in a deep breath of the fresh air as a familiar face emerged from the woods behind the campus.

Thirty-One

S he hadn't seen Aeron since that first night they met outside Mr. Alder's office, and it felt like a lifetime ago. She was still a virgin the first time she'd met him!

She picked up a brisk walking pace, trying to catch up to him.

It didn't take long for him to turn and notice her.

"Hey there, if it isn't the wonderful Ms. Casey," he said, hands in his pockets. "To what do I owe the pleasure of this stalking, ma'am?" he said playfully.

He was a tall guy, with platinum blonde hair, and his school uniform wasn't all glammed up like so many others. He still had that slightly disheveled look to him, that might've looked messy on others, but for him? He made it work. It actually looked kind of nice, like he was just a handsome, carefree kinda guy.

"I wasn't *really* stalking you. I mean, like, I would've probably tried... crouching if I was stalking you. I just had an appointment and got curious about what business you had in the forest," she grinned, so much more confident than the last time they'd met.

"Oh really?" he said, looking so pleasantly delighted at her curiosity. He grinned a bit, then glanced back at the woods. "Wanna find out?" he asked, gesturing back the way he came, then waggling his immaculate brows enticingly.

"Ohh, you can't tease me about something like that," she pouted, her smile quick to wipe it off her face. "Do we have enough time? I feel like I was only in there for a few minutes, but also feels later than I expected, so I don't really know."

He gave a casual shrug of his shoulders to her, his suit looking so fitted and sharp on him, unlike her own ill-fitted clothes.

"The risk is part of the fun," he said before beginning to walk back towards the woods. "C'mon. It'll be fun. I promise ya," he said, grinning a bit cheekily.

"Well... if you promise," she said, following after him. Her curiosity really did get the best of her. She was naturally drawn to learning and understanding new things, and he had been so polite to her that afternoon. She had no reason to think he'd be anything else now.

"Great," he said, sounding genuinely excited that she agreed. He took a hand out of his pocket then reached in to take hers. "Just stick close, it can get a bit confusing," he said as he began to lead her back into the woods with a careful look around. "And I know I owe you one, but... you'll keep this a secret, right? Nobody knows but me. And soon you. And I wanna keep it that way."

"Yea, I won't tell. I've never been back here before. I was always too afraid to go explore it, especially by myself," she confessed as her fingers laced into his. "Is this why I never see you on campus?"

He laughed at that, as he led her along the trail she took to the picnic spot with Claud, where she'd first had sex with the Black Mask. But instead of going there, he passed it off, guiding her deeper into the woods as his hand held hers nice and firmly. That thumb of his caressing the backs of her knuckles.

"Unfortunately, I just don't think we have any classes together. Except the one. But you're always too focussed to notice me," he said with a smile to her, a twinkle in his steely eyes.

She furrowed her brow in thought.

"What class? Mr. Alder's?" she asked as she gazed around, trying to figure out where they were going. His hand felt so good in hers, so kind and reassuring...

The trees got thicker, and it was hard to know where he was leading her. It felt like the real, wild woods back there, as she even saw a squirrel run up a tree.

"Yeah, that's right! Maybe you did notice me after all," he said with a playful wink as he took a turn around a large outcropping of rocks and...

Next thing she knew, they were face to face with a steel door in the middle of the woods, mostly hidden by bushes and bramble. It looked old, real old. Not as old as the school itself with its intricate woodworking dating back centuries, but... a century old maybe.

"Welcome to my little hideaway, Ms. Casey," he said with a smile, before stepping towards the door. There was a combination lock on it, that looked newer than the door himself, and he punched in a few numbers, causing a click sound to be heard. He pulled open the door, showing a concrete stairway leading down into darkness.

She was truly shocked. It was the last thing she expected to see in the woods. The idea of an actual private place... it was truly impressive. She squeezed his hand, peering down, then up at him.

"Where does it go?" she asked, her voice a bit softer and apprehensive.

"Come with me and find out," he said, lifting her hand and kissing the back of it, before he stepped in through the doorway and flipped a switch. The loud sound of old-fashioned fluorescent lights switching on, one at a time, as the circuit lit up resounded through the stairs as she saw it led down, down to a lower level where she could make out little.

"Okay," she said cautiously. "It's not dangerous or anything, right? Just, like, a private hideout?" she asked as she stepped in after him. Her heels clicked on the cement, and there was a little bit of a chill in the air that caused her nipples to stiffen beneath her blouse.

"I wouldn't take you somewhere dangerous," he assured her, as he pressed a button and the door swung shut behind them with a loud clang. He winked at her, "Don't worry. Follow me," he said as he took her down the stairs.

They seemed to go on forever with her high heels hindering her, but Aeron didn't rush her, he just smiled back at her now and then.

"So, Ms. Casey... welcome to my hideaway," he said, as they reached the bottom and there was what looked like a coat room. Then another door, this one even bigger than the last. He turned a wheel, having to let go of her hand to open it up, as it took some strength.

But when it opened, it was like peering into a time capsule.

Old sixties furniture, an old-fashioned record player, and so much more, adorned the place. With carpeting that looked ancient but well kept. It was a fairly large space, with three doorways at the back.

It honestly looked like someone's living room from the past.

"Oh my God," she cussed, stepping more eagerly into the room. Her emerald eyes were wide as she took it all in, excitement trembling through her body. She spun about to face him, admiration clearly written in her face.

"Aeron, this place is *gorgeous*!"

"Right?" he said, looking so casually cool and confident as he had one hand in his pocket. He then went on over to the record player, sliding a sleeve from the ample shelf there. He took out one of the big, black discs and put it in place. "You want a drink?" he asked, as the music started playing, some beautiful old romantic sounding song that Casey didn't recognize.

"Uhm, yea, okay. I think I missed lunch, so at least some water would be great," she said as she began cautiously exploring. "How did you manage to find this place? What did it used to be? Was it part of the school?" she rattled off questions, rapid-fire, one after another.

Aeron seemed so at home in that place, and he went to a drink cabinet, taking out a crystal decanter and pouring a glass of some kind of amber fluid. One for each of them.

"It was an old bunker, I think. Something to use in case

of nuclear war. Y'know, back when people still cared about us surviving such things," he said casually, peering around before taking the glasses to her. "And I found it when doing some research about the place. You're not the only one who enjoys learning, y'know? I just prefer knowing... the things they don't want us to know," he said with a grin. "To our secret party pad," he said, raising his glass for a toast.

She lifted the glass to him, still somewhat distracted by the secret hideaway.

His words drew her attention back, though, and she smiled.

"*Our* secret party pad?" she teased.

"Our secret party pad," he reiterated with a charmingly playful wink. Then he downed the entire glass of his drink in one go.

She took a smaller sip, before the burn hit her throat and she made a little sound of confusion.

"Ah... what is it?" she asked, clearly not having had enough experience with liquor to know it was scotch.

"Scotch. Nicely aged too. Y'know this stuff would cost you a fortune if you bought it," he remarked casually. "So don't let it go to waste," he cautioned gesturing to her glass as he then walked around the room casually. "Y'know, I've had this place to myself so long... it's funny to actually bring someone else here."

She wouldn't waste it, not if he told her not to, so she took a longer sip this time, though she still made a noise as she swallowed it.

"I can't believe there's no one else you ever wanted to bring here. I don't know how I could keep it a secret if it was mine," she said earnestly, following behind him. "How long have you been hanging out here?"

He made his way over to the sofa, then gestured for her to take a seat.

"All year pretty much. Y'see, I began to poke around in the school archives for stuff when I got here. And the librarian, Mr. Dejardin, told me about some old blueprints for the school. Well, I noticed on there… there were once tunnels connecting the school to some point outside the scope of the blueprints," he remarked.

"Wow," she said, genuinely impressed as she joined him on the sofa. "I never woulda thought to even look for something like that." She took a sip of her scotch, her green eyes scanning his handsome face. "It's not really fair that you can look like that *and* be so deviously smart."

He grinned at that, adding a mischievous air to his face. But he never lost that natural charm and attractiveness he seemed to ooze.

"That's not even the best part. Because that by itself didn't tell me much… Oh, I mean, I was able to predicted where the tunnel pointed, and it led me to the door above. But without the code… it was pretty useless, and there were too many permutations to guess," he said as he put one arm behind her. "The documents I needed were no longer in the library, or it's archives. But I did get Mr. Dejardin to tell me where they were…"

"Wow," she breathed out, hanging on every one of his words with rapt attention. It had even managed to distract her from the stiffness of her nipples, the throbbing of need between her thighs.

Though it was doing nothing to actually *diminish* her arousal.

There was a reason Mr. Alder was her true love, after all. She had the hots for smarts.

And Aeron putting his hand on her knee, his thumb caressing her thigh, wasn't helping diminish the arousal either.

"Mr. Steros. He had the final blueprints I needed in his office. Well..." he laughed good naturedly. "Getting in there was hard enough. But finding where he hid the stuff? Wow," he remarked. "But then I tried to think like he does..." he remarked, looking so serious. "Calculating, cold. And it occurred to me: he'd hide that stuff behind the sentimental portrait of the school students and staff. And... bingo. I got the blueprints for this bunker, with the passcode scribbled in a corner."

He looked rather proud of himself as his hand began to caress her thigh more openly.

"What?!" she asked, in equal parts admiration and terror. "Oh my *God*, he scares me so much, I'd never be able to poke around in his office," she said quite sincerely. She shifted closer to him, drinking more of the scotch, her head getting a little bit fuzzy. "How did you stay calm enough to even do that?"

"A nice drink helps," he said pointing to the scotch in her hand before grinning. "Nah, I didn't have any then. I just..." he shrugged his shoulders, "didn't let the danger chill me. It's important to push on and face your fears... if you wanna do something... special," he said, as his face drifted closer to hers. "Or someone special," he added, his voice breathy and lower.

Her body was flushed with adrenaline, having long ago picked up on the sensual cues that her mind was skipping past in her fascination and curiosity. But as his face neared hers, it seemed to snap her back into her hyper aroused body.

"Oh," she cooed softly, her shoulders dipping as her body softened against his. She rested back into his arm, her thighs parting as her mouth grazed against his.

He smiled at her unevenly, that crooked little look only adding to his overwhelming attractiveness. And he tipped her tumbler of scotch back, making her drink a bit more of it, before he took it away, and laid it on the old coffee table.

"I think the administration and staff used this place as their own little getaway for a while. A secret escape from the students and their job," he remarked, as his hand returned to her thigh, and slid up to her skirt. Then beneath it. "It's only fitting you and I do the same..." he said, before leaning in and kissing her on the lips softly, sensually.

Thirty-Two

Her throat burned from the liquor, but it only made her more aware of the sensations beneath her flesh. She was so easily aroused, especially since she still *felt* like she hadn't had sex in many days. The moment in Mr. Ramlein's office was completely erased from her mind, as if it never happened, leaving her just as pent up as she was earlier.

And handsome, clever Aeron was just making her body go crazy.

She yielded willingly against him, truly not having needed the alcohol to get her in the mood.

But it certainly helped, as that dashing, handsome man pressed her back onto the sofa, his tall form atop hers. He even very smoothly guided her one leg in around him, so that he was laying atop her, between her two thighs as they kissed and made out.

"You're the most beautiful girl I've ever laid eyes on, Casey," he said, before kissing her again, letting a hand come up to her side, squeezing her breast through her top.

She moaned wantonly as he pinned her beneath him, that weight so wanted, so needed. He was a delicious man, she decided, and his devious intellect certainly helped add to his natural, carefree charm.

Her arms wrapped around his neck, encouraging him to put his weight on her, kissing him back as his hand felt the faint outline of her lingerie overtop her blouse.

"Mmm, I've been waiting for this moment too long," he moaned the words, as his hand went to the front of her blouse, popping open her buttons one by one as he teased his lips against hers, not quite kissing her. And once that top was undone, he reached for her breast and... he glanced down, finding her stiff nipples exposed. "Well, this is new..." he said with a delighted grin, as he teased her stiff, sensitive teats.

"Is it okay?" she asked self consciously, her breathing so heavy, making her breasts rise with each rapid breath. She was so turned on, it was absolutely impossible to deny, even if she wanted to. But she had no reason to hide anything from him.

"Is it okay?" he repeated, squeezing her breast through her bra as he did, his thumb teasing her areola. "It's more than okay. You'll have to tell me how you managed to get such a... risqué and delicious outfit," he remarked with a sensual husk to his voice as he leaned in and kissed her lips again. The two of them making out a while as he ground his thick, hard bulge against her mound.

She relaxed at his reassurance, her legs slowly wrapping around him, her high heels digging lightly into his calves as she kept grinding in against him. He was on top of her, keeping her in place, and she couldn't resist that little wave of pleasure she was able to get out of his clothed erection.

"How long have you been waiting for me?" she breathed out between kisses.

His eyes were heavily lidded as he kissed her lips and peered into her own gaze.

"Since last time," he remarked, as he let a hand slide down between them, reluctantly ceasing his grinding on her as he undid his pants, then fished out an especially long, thick cock, veiny and rigid. "You won't mind me going in raw, will you," he said more than asked, as he lifted her skirt, then took hold of his cock.

"When we met in the halls?" she asked, but then her attention was quickly stolen by that beautiful unveiling, those tempting words.

She stared down between their bodies as best she could, though it was a bit of a challenge with the size of her tits. Her thighs lifted, wrapping around his ass a bit higher, her swollen, pink vulva practically begging for his dick.

"I prefer it without a condom," she breathed out.

"It's the only way I want it anymore," he agreed with her, nuzzling his nose to hers as he guided his dick towards her slit and... he gazed down, noticing her scandalous panties, leaving her vulva showing, so slick and ready. "You are just full of surprises," he said with a grin, and a spark in his eyes before he began to sink his cock up inside her. A deep moan and a look of sheer bliss on his face as he slowly filled her up to that familiar degree, making her feel so full and complete.

It was *just* what she needed, and she moaned out her desire, her arms and legs wrapping around him. She wanted to feel him on top of her, keep him from leaving her. All her nerve endings were prickling to life, and that pent up arousal was making her even more sensitive than usual.

"Oh God, you feel so good," she purred.

He was so thick and long and filled her so right. In her drunken state, she could only think of a few men that compared: Mr. Alder, Damien and the Black Mask. And Aeron held nothing back, moaning delightedly as he began to pull back, only to pump into her. He had not only a generous masculine size, she quickly began to tell he knew how to use it too. Angling himself just right, pumping into her at that deliciously rising pace.

"Mmm fuck Casey..." he said, kissing her lips as he took her atop that old yet pristine sofa. "You're so beautiful. So perfect," he said, caressing her cheek with one hand, as he held himself up by the other. "We can do this... as often and as long as we like down here... as loud as we care to," he said, punctuating that with an especially deep hard thrust.

It was difficult to imagine wanting to do anything else in that moment.

Oh, sure, she was in love with Mr. Alder. And she enjoyed slutting it up. But every time, when she was in that moment, it was like everything else just faded away. Nothing mattered except for the man that was railing her, and she was fully present in the act.

Her back arched, her breasts tipping up towards her collarbone as his cock struck against some bundle of nerves, and she moaned out sweetly.

Aeron leaned down, his mouth capturing her nipple as she presented it upwards with her motions. He suckled at it, as his hips pounded into her with that steady, firm, exacting pace. He made her tits jiggle and quake with those hammering thrusts, and his soft moans vibrated through her sensitive teat as he claimed her.

And while neither of them were aware of the other man's cum still inside her pussy, it squelched wetly around his shaft as he claimed her. His pace rising, as if he seemed intent on making her scream his name.

He was so good, it was impossible not to. It first started as breathy moans and gasps, her head rolling from side to side on the sofa. It was intense and perfect, and soon the room was filled with the rising crescendo of his name, trailed by moans and gasps of pleasure.

He moaned deeply as they fucked in that old world looking bunker. And he tugged at her stiff teat, before it slipped from his lips and he shuddered all over, moaning so lewdly.

"Ohh Casey," he groaned, thrusting into her faster, harder, giving her that dick she so needed in such a deliciously hard, fast manner. His balls slapping against her ass, his pants filling the air. "I want to make you my girl, Casey... fuck, I love you," he groaned out.

It would have taken her by surprise, if not for the fact that her brain was not functioning at its usual level. She'd had a little wine with Mr. Alder, but that wasn't the same as hard liquor, and her head was definitely spinning.

Her arms wrapped around him tighter in a hug as her mewls and moans pressed against his mouth. She was beginning to shiver, that pleasure soon to be reaching its apex.

He shivered all over, and he brought a thumb so close to her clit. But he didn't press it, not directly. He teased that little bundle of nerves with fleeting touches, as he angled his dick just right. That thick shaft striking her so perfectly as he pounded away, his cock growing thicker. She could recognize those tell-tale signs of his cock approaching climax, but he was holding back.

"Cum on my dick, Casey. Fuck I know you need it as bad as me," he said, shivering as his dick spurt some pre into her.

"I need it," she agreed, her body trembling as he worked her pussy so expertly. He clearly knew what he was doing, and even though it felt like he was teasing her, she knew he wasn't. He was just helping her along to a higher plane, and when she finally made it, the descent was exquisite.

Her cries filled the bunker, holding absolutely nothing back. She screamed as her pussy tightened around his shaft, drawing him in deeper as her arousal grew to new proportions. Honey washed over him, her sweet juices marking him as hers.

And in return, he threw back his head, let loose a loud moan and gasp, then began to shoot so much thick, pearly white seed into her. Yet another load of virile cum dumped into her fertile depths as he hammered in relentlessly. Thrusting it in, his dick instinctively trying to supplant the other man's seed as he fired into her so deep.

And together they screamed and moaned, quaking through that intense climax until he fell upon her. His chest heaving as he kissed her lips, caressing her, holding her.

"Oh, fuck Casey..." he groaned out.

She hugged him back, her mouth eagerly finding his. It was hard forming words, but being able to touch and caress him felt absolutely wonderful.

Her red hair was fanned out around her face, her cheeks

pink with arousal, her body still twitching as the aftershock of her orgasm paid her a visit.

He moaned into her mouth and ground his dick into her again, rewarding her with more of that stiff, filling goodness. He held her to him, one hand squeezing her breast, the other knitting into her red hair as they made out. And only after a long while could he spare some words in between kisses.

"Stay with me... I'll make love to you all day," he promised as their lips then smacked once more.

Normally, she'd have protested. She'd have explained that she needed to get to classes, and that she wanted to get ahead of some studying.

But she was tipsy, and his cock was still in her, teasing her. Tempting her.

A shiver went through her as she clung to him.

"I'll get in trouble," she whispered.

"We'll be in trouble together," he responded, kissing her again. "And it'll be worth it. There's something more I can show you," he said as he squeezed her breast, feeling that supple flesh swell between his digits.

They made out for a long time after that, and his cock never quite softened entirely. But finally, he pulled from her with a shiver and a moan, looking down to her.

"I gotta use the washroom," he said, peering down at her with sparkling eyes. "Head into the bedroom, and check the closet if you wanna change into something... more comfortable," he said with a grin. "There's a surprise or two in there."

"The bedroom?" she asked, watching him as he pulled from her, her hungry gaze going to his softening cock. Her mouth watered, and she leaned forward. "Should I clean you first?"

"Oh yes you should," he said as his eyes lit up at her suggestion, and he caressed her hair as he poised his partially turgid cock in front of her face. "And the bedrooms are back there," he said gesturing vaguely to where the three doors were. "It's the first one on the right, not the left," he explained.

She shifted on the sofa, not paying much mind to his seed as it dribbled from her puffy labia. Her hand went to his thigh, the other one grasping his cock as she began to lick him. It felt so good to be cleaning a man's cock after he finished in her, that alluring combination of tastes upon his sensitive flesh. Her tongue was diligent, and her eyes fluttered closed as she began to lose herself to the act.

And Aeron watched her as she worked his shaft so masterfully. Until finally she wasn't just cleaning him anymore, she was sucking on his fully hard, rigid shaft, and he was moaning, his hand in her hair.

"Ohh fuck," he groaned, as she sucked at his dick, before he finally pulled it from her mouth. "A-Ah god damn Casey," he said with a look of excitement on his face. "Calm down will ya? Go to the bedroom and I'll be right there to continue," he said with a grin as he finally headed off to the washroom.

She stared after him sadly, her ravenous body craving so much more.

But... that was what he promised.

In the bedroom.

Thirty-Three

⌒◯⌒

S he stood on fawnish legs in her high heels, her top
left open, her skirt fluttering down over her ass. She
walked towards the direction he said, though once
she got there, she couldn't remember if it was left or right,
and she stood there, trying to remember.

She drunkenly went into the right room by accident,
the room looking quite austere. Just metal bed frames with
cots. But there was a closet, and she opened it. Seeing that,
she went to it as he told her, and slid it open. But inside, she
found nothing like he promised. Instead, she just saw
several long, black, hooded overcoats, and some old military
style boots and gloves.

She stared at it in confusion, the outfits looking so
familiar when Aeron's voice broke the silence.

"Wrong room, silly," he said, standing there, utterly
nude. His lean body with a few bruises and old scars, but
otherwise looking beautifully masculine and yet smooth.

And her eyes were immediately drawn to it, like a moth
to a flame.

"Oh," she said, giggling softly. "I couldn't remember. I got distracted, I guess," she said as she walked towards him, her hand gliding to his chest. "You're very handsome, have I told you that?"

His smile returned face and he wrapped an arm around her, his hand at her ass. He squeezed her in against him as he kissed her lips softly.

"I never grow tired of hearing you say it, either way," he remarked, before beginning to guide her out of the room. "Over here," he said, taking her to the other room.

This one was a complete contrast to the last. Whereas that one was stark and utilitarian, with concrete walls, metal bedframes and mostly empty spaces. This one had wood— or at least faux-wood—walls, a large, comfortable looking bed, and a big closet. He took her to it, sliding it open, and she saw an array of men's and women's clothing, separated to each side. And the women's clothing... was almost all old fashioned, 60s and 70s nightgowns, skimpy teddies, and the like. With fuzzy high heels down below that made her Mary-Janes look safe and tame.

"What do you think?" he asked her, as he squeezed her ass and kissed her.

"Ohh," she said, her eyes lighting up. "I haven't seen, like, new clothes since I got here, and I've outgrown every-thing else... Well, other than my new bra and panties. But not, like, other clothes," she said, reaching out to sort through them, inspecting a few pieces. "Do you think these are the teachers'?"

"I think they're too old to belong to the current teach-ers. But maybe Mr. Stereos, or some previous administrator or teachers, used this as their little hideaway love shack too," he said as he watched her look through the clothes, his hands refusing to leave her. "You can take what you like. Even if you only wear it in here," he explained, as she saw that some of it was newer.

"I can't believe you had this all to yourself and never showed it off to anyone else," she said, grabbing a white, transparent little dress that had pink frills along the bust and hem of the skirt. It had a ribbon around the waist, and it might be a bit tight, but also looked like it would be one of the best fits. It seemed like it was supposed to be a loose and airy cut for a slender woman, but for her, it would be rather fitted. "What do you think of this one?"

He sized her up a moment, looking at the garment as a wry grin grew on his face.

"I think you'd look absolutely stunning in that," he said as he caressed her backside. Then he finally let her go, to look through the men's things. He took out an old-fashioned silk smoking jacket, with fur cuffs. He put it on and tied the belt, standing there otherwise nude. "And what about me? Do I look sophisticated?" he asked, arching one brow up real high, looking quite playful.

"So handsome," she said with a sigh, not hiding her attraction to him. "I can't believe I'm skipping class..." It came as a surprise to her, but she clutched the negligee tighter to her, not willing to let it go. "Maybe I can say the therapy just ran long, and afterwards I needed some time."

He grinned at that and nodded.

"There you go. You're covered," he said as he caressed her side then kissed her lips. "That'll give us the day to play house... you'll be my beautiful, blushing bride," he declared so charmingly.

She giggled, the alcohol and desire no doubt clouding her judgment.

"I've just always been the good girl, you know? And when mother sent me here, well, I swore I'd prove myself. But then we got cut off from the world, practically, and I started to realize just how much I was missing out on what other students took for granted."

She spoke as she changed into the negligee, the transparent fabric even more see-through as it clung to her large breasts, but then it drifted off into a cute little dress. The hem landed about halfway down her ass, the frills dancing along her skin.

She looked like a fantasy doll from an old sci-fi movie.

"What do you think?"

He sized her up with a fire in his eyes, his approval more than apparent on his handsome face.

"You look stunning, my darling," he said in that playful imitation of an old 1950s husband, reaching out to grasp her by the waist and hold her to him. "And I know what you mean about the expectations. I wasn't so lucky as I seem," he began, starting to sway, making her dance with him. "But I'm done with suffering and struggling. Busting my butt all the time. Once I got in here, and realized how easy life could be... I decided I wanted that. And I'll take it," he remarked with a charming smile, a twinkle in his eyes.

He had an aura around him that just made her feel comfortable, and she leaned her head against his shoulder as they swayed. She always tended to be a trusting and open woman, but his calm confidence really rubbed off on her. It even eased her worries about missing class, which was a monumental feat.

"I'm glad we finally met up again."

His hands were strong and guiding, keeping her moving in that delightful sway. The alcohol in her blood made everything so much more... easy. It was easier to let go and enjoy when it was hot inside her from the drinks.

"I want to tell you so much, Casey. Can you keep a secret?" he asked her, as they danced around that old, retro looking bunker bedroom.

She nodded gently against his chest, a lazy smile upon her plush lips.

"I won't tell anyone about the bunker, Aeron. I already promised you that," she reminded him.

He laughed softly at that, as one hand slid down to cup her bubbly round bottom, squeezing it through that thin little, gauzy fabric that covered her.

"I didn't mean that. It's just that...I'm not who I seem. I mean, I'm not with the rich kids. I just convinced them I was one of them when I got here. My family's actually dirt poor," he confessed to her.

Her brows furrowed in thought, a soft wave of appreciation slowly smoothing it away.

She had always been so honest, truthful to a fault. It hadn't even occurred to her when she arrived that she could, or would, lie about who she was. To her, it hadn't even been a thought that came to her and was dismissed after a moment's consideration.

Lying had been such a foreign thing to her until so recently.

"I never would have imagined that. You seem so... proper. So posh."

He laughed softly at that.

"Well, I dunno about proper, but... thanks," he said with a soft laugh. "I just wanted to be more than I was. I didn't ever want to go back to being the unlucky kid that struggled to get by. That had to worry about the holes in my clothes, or where I was gonna get every meal. I decided when I got here: I'd be like those fortunate kids. It was easy here, because they provided me the uniform. Crisp and clean. Ready to go, just like everyone else's. So nobody could look at me and tell where I came from," he explained.

"I've always been smart, but never clever. Mother taught me that cleverness was just another word for deceitful, and deceitful was just another word for sinful. But she was never very nice to me. Not like most of the people here. And reading the things in Mr. Alder's class, a lot of the women are clever, and I like them a lot."

He smiled warmly at that, their bodies swaying and moving so delightfully. It was her first real dance with a partner, she realized.

"You're a bright woman, and you'll have a great life, I just know it," he said to her cheerfully. "But there's something more I want to tell you... an even bigger secret," he began. "Wait right here, okay?" he said, smiling slightly, as he went and poured her up more drink. "Here, I'll be right back," he said, before leaving the room.

She didn't really need more alcohol, already imbued with that pleasant buzz, but she took a polite sip as she glanced around the room once again. It felt like stepping into a museum, a little slice of an era long passed. She imagined the people who built it, afraid of what might happen one day, and then as time passed, and the fear ebbed, it became a hideaway from their troubles.

It was romantic. A repurposing of something built in fear.

She heard from out in the hallway shuffling and movement. But Aeron was taking a while, and she found herself sipping a bit more as she passed the time. But soon she heard a voice, distant and muffled. It must be Aeron returning she assumed.

But when another voice returned, she knew it wasn't Aeron. At least not just Aeron.

"...You just never know," came a vaguely familiar male voice.

"Like I said, nobody knows of this place but me. It's impossible," responded a more familiar male voice. That of the school administrator. "You check that side, I'll check this one," he said.

And then, in a panic, Casey tried to hide what she was doing. She put the drink down, and looked around. But there was no time.

She was staring at Mr. Steros in the doorway, the administrator looking at her, wide-eyed and in shock.

It was hard to look innocent in a transparent negligee.

And even though he hadn't even said a word of admonishment, her green eyes began to water with the threat of tears. She blinked them away, her arms going around her waist protectively, her head dipping down like a scolded puppy.

Mr. Steros, hawkish and in command at all times, suddenly looked... afraid. Of her? It was bizarre. But when he finally moved again, he put a finger to his lips, urging her to hush. Then he cleared his throat.

"Nothing in here," he shouted out into the hallway. He

then muttered to her much quieter, "Wait here." That authoritative air back, before he turned and shut the door on her, leaving her locked in the room.

She couldn't make out the voices very well after that, but Mr. Steros was talking with someone else.

"Nothing, see? That music must've just come on automatically when we activated the breaker," he said to someone else.

"It was still worth checking out," said the other voice, which she thought was that creepy new inspector guy, Mr. Mordule.

"Yes yes. But let's get out of here now, the air smells so musty," said Mr. Steros. "Actually, you head on. I'm going to make sure there's nothing out of place here, or left draining power, like that record player."

Her ear was pushed against the door, her heart racing in her chest.

What was he going to do to her? Expel her?

The very thought made her hyperventilate.

The one time she misbehaved, the one time she skipped class, of course she'd get caught. How could she have been so careless?

Thirty-Four

The fear was making the buzz of the alcohol wear off a bit, and she began pacing the room in her high heel shoes, looking the role of a slutty 50's housewife.

But finally, her long, anxious waiting came to an end after hearing a loud clang of a door shutting. Then Mr. Steros returned, opening that door. Only he looked slightly less confused this time as he eyed her in that little skanky dress.

"What in heaven's name are you doing down here, Ms. Casey?!" he demanded of her.

"I'm so, so sorry. I know I shouldn't be here," she sputtered out, her cheeks red with shame. "I just... I had that therapy session, and I just felt all worked up after that, and I needed some time alone," she confessed, leaving out more than a few key points in her explanation. "I'll make it up to you, I swear. I've never done something like this before. Please don't kick me out," she pleaded.

Mr. Steros, with his jet-black hair, and piercing eyes, sized her up at that. Inspecting her scantily clad body.

"All worked up? You had to break into the bunker—somehow!—to come down here and rub one out in some of my wi—some of these old clothes?" he asked her, in disbelief. But she detected that tinge of interest in him, that she was beginning to pick up in men around her. Something she'd never seen in Mr. Steros before.

She let out a little gasp at his crassness, unable to resist looking up at him.

She was also unable to fully deny the accusation. Especially dressed up as she was. She couldn't very well say it was all innocent when her stiff nipples were visible through translucent pink lingerie.

"I'm sorry, Mr. Steros," she said, lowering her head again. She shifted her weight from one foot to the other, the nighty swishing from side to side with her nervous motions.

"God almighty. Nobody has been down here in years and years—I hope—but somehow you manage to figure out how to get in past all the security... just to masturbate," he said, running a hand back over his jet-black hair.

He looked lost in thought for a while, staring at her, licking his lips.

"What am I going to do with you...?" he muttered beneath his breath, brushing a hand over his jaw and chin, across his dark beard.

She stared up at him, her green eyes pleading.

She didn't know what it was about authoritative men, but they just made everything in her shift, as if she wanted to make herself smaller and more submissive. To never earn their ire or even a sharp word.

"Was... am I in some of your... personal things?"

"What?!" he responded sharply. "No! They belonged to my—never mind," he said, giving an exasperated sigh. But she was noticing that he was acting slowly. Mr. Steros was never known to be so indecisive. He doled out his judgments sharp and fast. But for some reason he was slow to act with her. "You are obviously a smart girl. And cleverer than I gave you credit for, to find your way in here, Ms. Casey. Tell me, how did you do it?"

She didn't have a response for that. Not an honest one. And truthfully, she knew she wouldn't even be able to spin such a complex lie as what she'd need to if she had any hope of convincing him she was alone down there.

"I just..." she started, but then her lower lip began to tremble. "Oh, you must think I'm so awful, dressing up in this outfit. Taking things that aren't mine. It just felt so nice to pretend for a little while, that things were normal. That I didn't have to worry about school and my future and mean old security guys."

She took a step closer to him, forcing her gaze upwards, her innocent face twisted with remorse.

"It must be your lover's clothes, aren't they? I'll put it right back, I swear, and then... I'll make it up to you. I'll come to your office after classes, be your assistant, whatever you want."

And even though her pleading was genuine, her worries honest, she was hardly unaware of how her tone turned lustful at the end when she gave that promise.

Mr. Steros listened to all she said, and while none of it addressed his question... it succeeded in distracting him from that demand.

"My assistant..." he repeated, his eyes unable to help from sweeping over her scantily clad body, down to her long legs. He swallowed, then cleared his throat. "You're lucky I'm in a forgiving mood, Ms. Casey," he said, something he was never known for. "I'll let you off with it this time. But you'll have to make it up. Somehow. And as for the... outfit," he said, his eyes admiring it on her again, and lingering at her breasts. "You may keep it. You're the only one it could possibly fit since my wife passed away anyhow."

The weight that lifted from her shoulders was practically visible, and her green eyes sparkled with warmth instead of tears.

She stood up straighter, watching as he scanned her body, and her heart thudded heavily beneath her breasts.

"I will make it up to you, I swear it," she said, excitement leaking into her voice. "You'll see, I'll do whatever you ask."

"Come with me," he said, ushering her along to follow him. "Grab your other clothes too, take it with us," he told her, as she then hurried to get the bundle of clothes that was her school uniform.

Then Mr. Steros guided to the back of the bunker, past rows and rows of rooms, far past where she'd gone so far. Until finally she got an idea of how this place was connected directly to the school itself.

The corridors were long, but finally they came to some stairs.

"Now we go up," he instructed her, past one level, then another. Until finally he opened a door, that brought her straight to the lavish office of Mr. Steros himself. Bookshelves lining the walls on all sides. The furniture an old and opulent Victorian style.

There was his large desk, and two leather sofas facing each other, with a coffee table in between. The windows overlooked the town in the distance.

"Come in. Put your things down somewhere and shut the door," he instructed her, as she realized the door was absolutely undetectable from the office side. It blended right into the walls!

Aeron had theorized about it, but seeing it in reality was amazing.

She softly closed the door behind her, admiring how seamless it was, before she turned and politely folded her skirt, blouse, bra, and panties. She set them down on the coffee table, and then turned to look at him.

In her heart, in her loins, she knew the path she was walking with him. The interest she'd fired up within him. Truthfully, when he sent Mr. Mordule away, she had an inkling of why he wanted to keep his discovery private.

Her hands clasped lightly in front of her, the curly locks of strawberry-blonde hair practically glowing in the afternoon sun around her face.

"What would you like me to do, Mr. Steros?"

He was standing behind his desk by the time she'd finished her folding, and he looked at her as he pressed a button on top of it. She heard a lock click in place to the big, double doors out of his office.

"It would have been quite embarrassing for me, if that Mordule fellow found you down there, after my telling him it was unoccupied for years. It would've reflected very badly on me," he remarked as he sat back in his tall, leather chair. "Come here, sit on the desk and face me," he urged her, leaving plenty of room in between himself and the desk.

She moved forward obediently, a soft frown toying at the edges of her lips.

"I don't want to embarrass you," she said. Her heels gave her a few inches of extra height, which helped her get atop the lavish desk. She shifted until she was between him and the desk, her legs daintily crossed at the ankle as she gazed at him with slightly lidded eyes.

The rush of fear had sobered her up a bit, but that magnetic pull of desire was enough to send another pleasant vibration through her system.

Mr. Steros' intense eyes ate her up, devoured her. No longer even trying to mask that desire he held for her, he stared at her, like she was a marvelous work of titillating art.

"Of course not. Now show me," he said critically, licking his lips. "Show me how you were masturbating down there," he instructed her in that firm, commanding voice of his.

It seemed like her body was obeying before she could even really process his words. Something about his tone just spoke to a primal part of herself, and a dainty hand was lifting the hem of the negligee.

Her fingers dipped between her soft thighs, finding that slick valley between them.

"I'm... I'm not very good at it," she warned him. She'd never been able to find more than a shadow of pleasure at her own touch, not compared to her experiences with others. She didn't want to disappoint him with her own ineptitude.

He wet his lips at that, two fingers at his temple as he leaned to one side.

"I'll be the judge of that. Just show me. Now," he commanded her as he sat there in that crisp, well tailored suit. He was far from the biggest or tallest guy she'd been with, but he had an aura of authority and command about him, that sang to that part of her that wished to give up the burden of having to think and decide everything for herself.

Her lashes fluttered before she closed her eyes, her fingertips gliding along her wet slit. She was still a mess from earlier, but that made it feel even better, and she let out a soft sigh.

Her shoulders relaxed as she touched herself, and her breasts rose higher along her ribcage as her breathing began to quicken. Her nipples pressed into the transparent fabric, the pink hue illuminating the flush of arousal that grew along her chest.

She was still so horny. Always so horny. It was enough to make her lose her mind. It wasn't fair that her sexual awakening had been so swiftly followed by a lockdown, leaving her so desperately wanting. And even fucking Aeron—and Mr. Ramlein, though she didn't remember that—had done little to quell that unquenchable need.

Mr. Steros' cock began to grow, bulging his tailored pants as he watched her little display. Something she'd never dared dream of doing in front of another not long ago, now coming so easily to her.

"You're right..." he said, his voice so firm and commanding. "You're not very good at this. No wonder you've been going through such ridiculous lengths. You must be so pent up and in need," he remarked, as he reached a hand out, sliding it along her bare thigh, caressing it. "Are you wanting help with that, my dear?" he asked, his eyes staring with such intensity.

A moan caught in her throat as she looked at him, felt his hand on her supple inner thigh.

"More than anything," she confessed.

Thirty-Five

She knew he was lonely, that she must have reminded him of his wife in some way, and she needed to take care of him nearly as much as she wanted to take care of herself.

"Are you sure?" he asked, as his thumb kneaded her soft inner thigh flesh, so close to her pussy. While the other hand came down, caressing the bulge of his cock, slowly unzipping his pants. "Because I won't be using my hands to help you. I'll be using something much better," he husked, as he fished that thick, veiny cock from his pants, letting it stand up straight, so rigid and hard. The tip glistened with so much sticky pre-cum.

And she stared at it with awe, her cravings utterly transparent.

She licked her lips as her fingers began to slowly withdraw from her slit, her pussy pink with need.

"Whatever you think is best," she said breathily. She had to swallow, her mouth practically watering at the offering of his dick, knowing just how wrong it was. He was the administrator, the one in charge, and it would be a massive scandal if anyone knew what they were doing.

But that just made it more exciting. He wanted her so badly that he would take such a risk with her.

Especially since he'd been nothing but so serious and by the book at all other times. Her body—so ripe and feminine —was what managed to crack that tough exterior of his.

"Lean back on your two hands," he instructed her, as he stood up, that thick hard cock pointed at her as he cupped one breast, beginning to fondle it, hefting its weight. "God, you have been blessed with such a rare and exquisite body... it would be such a shame not to put it to use," he said, licking his lips as he let his thumb tease her nipple through that thin fabric.

The material felt strange and enticing as it pressed against her, sending a rivulet of desire down her spine.

She leaned back as he instructed, the pink frills lifting to further expose her dripping sex to him. For a moment, she was worried that she would make a mess of his desk, but she knew if it was a problem, he'd tell her. He had everything under control.

Except, perhaps, his own desires.

Her legs spread as he stood between them, her pale skin pressing into his tailored slacks.

"You really think so?" she cooed affectionately at his compliment, a warmth spreading along her lips as he enjoyed her body.

"I do," he said with a wry smile as he squeezed her ample breast. "I haven't seen someone as enticing as you since the early days with my... it doesn't matter," he said, as he stroked his shaft, then guided the tip to her slit. He teased it up and down her raw pussy, parting her labia, nudging her little clit. "Just give yourself over to me, and I'll handle everything else," he husked, as he began to slowly push his shaft up into her, leaning in as he moaned deeply, his eyes shutting as he shivered with delight.

He didn't care if he was her first or not, didn't care that she was young enough to be his daughter. He needed inside her far too much for those worldly concerns, and it made her heart skip a beat with delight.

She leaned back further as he began to press in between her thighs, giving him eager access to her sweet pussy. She moaned as he satiated that hunger within her, easily submitting all control to him.

"As you wish," she purred.

He released his hand from his member as it sank deeper into her, and he brought it up to cup her cheek. He tilted her head, just in time for their lips to meet.

"You have a lot of promise as an assistant already," he husked between smacks of their lips. While his other hand squeezed her breast some more.

But all the while, through his words and moans, he began to rock his hips. That thick, throbbing cock pumping into her, easing her into things. But he was fast figuring out she didn't need much help easing into it. She was already quite used to taking dick, after all.

And she was positively dripping with desire.

Her tongue played with his, trading breathy moans and gasps of pleasure.

No matter how many times she gave her body over to someone, no matter their different skills or shapes, she was always filled with a single-minded need for the one inside of her at that moment. She didn't compare and contrast. Every lover she had gave her something unique, and Mr. Steros was no different.

His passion was filled with longing, complemented with control, and it made for a delicious afternoon delight.

He gripped her in a way that was impossible to compare to others, even if she wanted to. And he was fast building up to a good, satisfyingly hard pace. His hips impacting her inner thighs as he fucked her more roughly with each passing moment.

She felt grateful that his desk was such a solid, heavy wood construction. Because before long their lips drifted apart as he was railing her so hard, huffing and panting as he bent over her.

"Mm... fuck," he swore, his cock throbbing inside of her. "Much better than those fingers of yours, no?" he growled, grasping her thigh with a hand, and pushing her leg back further.

It wasn't long before her shoulders were pushed to the wood, her curly hair acting as a pillow for her head as she lost herself to the moment.

He was so different than she expected, but the confident strength, the angle that he pushed in at, suited him perfectly.

And gave her precisely what she needed.

"So much better," she gasped out, panting for breath as her tits bounced harshly towards her chin.

He panted atop her, squeezing one breast as he held himself up on the other hand. He was fucking her hard and fast, as if he had some intense need to take her, after going without for so very, very long. And then... she felt his thumb reach in, and begin to press upon her clit. That far older man, with the silver streaks in his hair, pounding into her pussy as he grunted.

"Cum upon my cock, like a good assistant," he commanded, his voice having this delectable purr that tickled her ears, his lips lunging in to kiss her again, passionately, deeply.

And despite how impossible it was to find release on her own fingers, his touch was just what she needed.

She gasped at the skillful digit, her pussy squeezing his shaft as a powerful shockwave was sent through her nervous system. Her heels dug into the back of his leg as she cried out, biting down on her lower lip to quiet herself, and not risk exposing him.

But he showed little sign of quieting himself. Instead, he was making the desk shake, moaning and groaning loudly atop her. He shuddered as she came, gushing her slick honey around his shaft.

"F-Fuck, it's been so long..." he gasped out, quaking, his dick swelling. And she felt that tell-tale sign of a man about to blow his load inside of her. The erratic twitching and throbbing, how his balls could no longer be heard slapping against her ass.

But just as she expected to feel that satisfying feeling of his dick shooting off it's virile load... he yanked his shaft out of her. And took it in hand. Stroking his length as he pointed it at her mound.

It was so unexpected, and she let out a yelp of surprise and disappointment.

It distracted her from her own orgasm, her head jerking forwards as she opened her eyes.

"What's wrong?" she gasped.

He was too busy coaxing out his own orgasm to give her a thorough answer. But he grunted, and said:

"Pulling out so I don't get you pregnant, silly girl," he said. And she watched as he stroked his cock, until finally thick strands of pearly white cum began to splatter onto her pussy. Instead of inside it, where she really wanted it.

But the look on his face? That stern administrator, eyes rolled back, lost to bliss as he shot his load over her? It was exquisite.

None of that, of course, distracted from the weight of what he'd just said to her.

"Pregnant?" she said with a furrowed brow.

That wasn't how that happened.

At least... that wasn't how she was taught. But then, she hadn't been taught much of anything about sex, or her own body. And, unfortunately for her for multiple reasons, Mr. Ramlein had wiped her mind clean of the fact that he'd told her that very thing, earlier that day.

She stared at his cum as it glistened on her skin, but her own orgasm was long forgotten.

If anyone else had said it, she might think they were joking, or teasing her. But he was so serious, so stern. She didn't imagine he'd ever joke, especially not at the cusp of pleasure.

He squeezed every last drop of his rather hefty load— and she'd been getting some very hefty loads of cum lately —onto her mound, before he shivered and licked his lips. Then responded.

"I knew it was a mistake when they made us take sexual education off the agenda," he huffed, reaching for some tissues at the side of his desk. He gave her several, which she'd need for the mess he'd left. "Yes, pregnant. If I put that inside you, there'd be an unpleasantly high chance you'd get pregnant with my child. And then... well, that would complicate our arrangement of you as my assistant now, wouldn't it?" he remarked with a wry smile at her, indicating he intended to keep fucking her as he cleaned his own member up.

She'd lost count of the number of times a man had finished in her. How often she'd begged them to.

"Is that what... breed means?" she asked, remembering what Mr. Alder had said. That he wanted to breed her. That he wanted her to plead for it. "Or knocked up?"

She was slow to grab those tissues, feeling quite broadsided by this new enlightenment he'd casually offered her.

"Correct," he said as he casually tied himself up, then tucked his manhood back into his pants, doing them up. "But you don't need to worry about that, I pulled out with plenty of time," he assured her. "It wouldn't do for you to be seen carrying my illegitimate child around campus," he remarked, running a hand back over his dark hair with the silver streaks as he sat back into his chair. "I feel I should apologize for how the school system failed you. But your mother really should've told you these things too," he said with a sigh. "Anyhow, the afternoon is partially gone. And you're free to go, do as you like," he remarked, opening his desk and taking out a waiver slip, signing it for her. "A perk of your new position. But don't abuse it, understood?" He shot her a look of warning, as she was left to ponder.

The risk she'd undertaken. All of it. And Mr. Alder quite explicitly trying to knock her up?! There was so much she was left to wonder about. But at least she had her usual date with him very soon, if she wished to ask him about it.

She accepted the slip before she inched off his desk, her knees warbling slightly. She began to change out of the negligee, glancing up at him as she did so.

"I won't abuse it," she promised as she pulled up her plaid skirt, fastening it at the side. "But... can I ask you something else?"

Thirty-Six

She stood in just her skirt, stockings, and heels, her large breasts still nude, and even after fucking her and cumming, his eyes couldn't help but pause to stare at her breasts.

"Go ahead," he said, no longer sounding so severe to her, even when he was clearly trying to be his usual, commanding self.

"How long would it take for me to know I was pregnant?" she asked, her head tilting, her voice sounding so sweet and innocent.

He sighed and put his pen back in its holder atop his desk.

"As I said, you're fine. I pulled out with plenty of time to spare. But if you're asking for the sake of curiosity... it depends. If you wait for some apparent signs to show, it would take months for your belly to show. As much as five or more even," he explained patiently to her, which made her think he'd been a teacher once. "But with a urine test you could know in just a few weeks... I think three or four," he explained.

She made a face at that, and grabbed her bra, pulling the red lace over her skin, her nipples still visible with the little embroidered gaps in the design.

"Okay. And yes, just for curiosity's sake," she said, trying to brush it off as if it were just an innocent question and not something life altering.

"I'm really glad you were nice to me today," she added on, her green eyes lifting to meet his.

Her rather scandalously slinky lingerie did not go unnoticed, but he didn't comment on it then as he eyed her. He gave a slight tilt of his head in response.

"I'll send you word when I wish to repeat one of these... sessions. You're free to ignore it, if you don't wish to come. But know I won't ask a second time if you do," he said rather firmly. "It's an arrangement between us, you aren't being held hostage by blackmail," he clarified for her. "And... you did well. Now you're dismissed."

She took that all in with a curious tilt of her head, followed by a nod. She quickly buttoned her blouse, and grabbed the negligee in her hands.

"Thank you, Mr. Steros," she said with a soft curtsey, before heading to the door.

He hit the switch, unlocking it just as she got there.

She made her way through, her hall pass tucked between her fingers, but she felt lost in thought. It had been a fun day, filled with unexpected encounters, but that revelation was making her head spin.

He was the first man that didn't want to knock her up.

Make her pregnant.

All the others...

They wanted to mark her, make her theirs.

Mr. Alder had said as much, of course. And the others...

She'd been so naive!

And she felt torn about how to feel about it all. A part of her was scared, but she couldn't deny that more secretive part of her. The part that made her heart beat faster, knowing so many men wanted her. Wanted to risk it all for her.

Casey wandered the school, ostensibly heading towards Mr. Alder's place, but... she knew there was some time to kill before then, so she meandered through the halls, taking a very indirect route.

By sheer luck, she stumbled into Dahlia coming out of the Pit with Yuri, giggling before her eyes lit up at the sight of her friend.

"Casey!" Dahlia said, clearly having been playing some hooky herself. "See ya, Yuri," she said, flashing him a wink before going to her friend. "Why aren't you in class?" she asked, looking shocked.

"I had to go see that therapist, and then I offered to help Mr. Steros with a few things for extra credit," Casey replied, a bit more distantly than her usually present self. She blinked and shook her head, focusing her attention and forcing a smile to her lips. "Why aren't you in class?"

Dahlia looked at her, as if she knew something was up. Her friend was always quite perceptive for such things, even if she wasn't the most diligent of students.

"Just makin' some extra cash," she said with a shrug of her shoulders and a casual smile. "Surprised you were helping that grouch. What'd he possibly need help with anyhow?" she asked as they walked along through the empty hallways.

"I guess with Mr. Mordule and Dr. Ramlein and the whole investigation going on, there's more stuff happening," Casey said with a shrug. "Oh, speaking of, you're supposed to come with me tomorrow to see Dr. Ramlein. He gave us both passes, and it was really helpful today. I'm excited to go back," she added with a more genuine smile.

"Oh," Dahlia said, sounding quite surprised by that as she took the pass from Casey. And if she had any ability to know and understand and verbalize what had really happened... she would've warned her friend of the truth. But... as it was, Casey just smiled in ignorance. "Dunno why he'd wanna see me, but maybe I can use it to weasel more time out of class," she said with a mischievous glint in her eyes. "Where you headed now?"

"I have to ask Mr. Alder about the last assignment we got. I missed his class this morning because of the assembly so I wasn't able to. I guess you're on your way to keep earning your keep?" Casey teased gently.

Dahlia grinned and tucked the slip from Dr. Ramlein into her satchel.

"Gonna take a break, I think. I'm due for some self-care time," she said playfully. "Alright. You take care Casey," she said, leaning in and kissing her cheek. "And lemme know if you need anything else, you hear?" she said, sounding quite serious.

"I will, promise. Thanks Dahlia. See you tonight," Casey said, still sounding a bit more spacey than usual. But she smiled it off, clearly not able to tell her friend just yet.

There were so many secrets piling up, but this one could be major.

After that, Casey meandered out of the school, in time to avoid the rush of students pouring out of class. It also made it easier to slip up behind Mr. Alder's cottage without being seen.

And then it was just a matter of waiting, killing time as she got to ponder how the new, hedonistic delight she'd just discovered and indulged in profusely... could also get her knocked up. If she wasn't already. And just how good the odds were... she had little idea.

But as those thoughts rolled through her head, finally, Mr. Alder appeared at the window, sliding it open and reaching down for her.

"There you are. My beautiful Casey," he said, reaching down, and hoisting her up into his lovely home. Those hands of his not leaving her, just shifting to her hips as he bent down and kissed her lips. "So glad you were here early. I was anxious to see you again," he said, brushing back some of her strawberry blonde hair behind one ear.

And she melted in his arms, as if just being near him made her as light as a balloon.

Her worries all seemed so much less significant when she finally felt his lips against hers.

She smiled, her gaze lifting to him, all of her sweet innocence imbuing her face once more.

"I missed you. It's been so long," she sighed.

He smiled back at her, his handsome face—so dashing, so refined, so loving—capturing her gaze as his hands caressed her sides, her bottom, made her feel loved as well as wanted.

"We'll have a lovely little date night, you and me," he said, caressing her cheek, planting soft kisses on her lips, her forehead, her hair. "I can't wait for the day we can spend our time together without having to hide it."

He was so warm, and she couldn't help but feel that love swell up inside of her.

But she couldn't get Mr. Steros' words out of her head.

It was just such a distraction! Intruding on their beautiful reunion.

She pulled back just slightly, looking at him with wide, curious eyes.

"Mr. Alder... I have to ask you something."

"You can ask me anything, my sweet Casey," he said with a warm smile, kissing her lips again. "It sounds kinda serious. I guess it can't wait until after we've made love, huh?" he asked with a twinkle in his eyes, planting another soft kiss on her lips after that, as his hand squeezed her thick, round behind.

She gave him a small, nervous smile.

"It's just... do you really want to get me pregnant, like you said?"

He looked at her, frozen.

"Of course," he said, his smile returning in full force. "You'll make the most beautiful mother..." he said, his hand caressing her cheek, his thumb so near to her lips. "Why? Are you... having second thoughts? I mean... I know we haven't discussed it a lot... and that's on me. But we have plenty of time to go over plans. Is that it?" he asked curiously.

Her heart thud louder in her chest as she stared at him, a rush of emotions washing through her.

She'd always had a pretty clear path for her future. She'd become a teacher, follow in Mr. Alder's footsteps. And when he showed interest in her, well, she assumed they would just teach together.

But her sexual awakening had made things messier.

This new knowledge?

Total upheaval of her plans.

Her head tilted slightly, and she worried her lower lip in thought.

But her heart knew what she wanted. She wanted him. To be his. Just as things had been for the past little while, which also meant she wasn't *exclusively* his.

"I just didn't realize everything," Casey finally said with a gentle smile. "That our secret might come out..."

He gave a soft laugh and caressed her cheek and hair some more.

"Well, we'll have to work to keep it a secret, of course. If it ever gets out that I was the one who did it, I'd be fired, and couldn't ever work as a teacher again. But that just means we'll keep it secret; you say it was someone else. And then once you're out of school, we can get together, and I'll 'adopt' our kid, and everything is in the open," he said with a handsome smile.

It all seemed a little strange to her, and she nervously coiled some hair around her finger.

"It's just, I have a confession..."

"What is it?" he asked, smiling, looking pleasantly amused. "You can tell me anything, Casey."

Thirty-Seven

"I ... well, my mother failed to tell me of some things before I turned 18, and the school dropped its sexual education policies, and so I didn't really realize what that all meant. I didn't know that's how you got pregnant. And if I'd have known, I mean, I would have done some things differently, but..." she looked up at him apologetically. "It's just, I've been with others, and..."

She could see the sudden shift in his expression at those last words of hers. His smile fading, the look of wide-eyed surprise.

"You've been with others... how recently? How many?" he asked, his hands ceasing their movement.

She furrowed her brows, her gaze downcast.

"I mean, you said act like everything is normal, and not to raise suspicion. And there's been a lot going on lately. But now I know, and..." she said, raising her chin. "And now I know I want you to be the one to knock me up!"

Mr. Alder looked conflicted, and worse, a little hurt. But he forced a smile back and nodded.

"You mean that? Because that's what I really want. But..." he looked aside, clearly his head in turmoil.

She shimmied in closer to him, her green eyes on his.

"Mr. Alder, you're the only man I love. And the only one I ever made love to. I obviously didn't know some things, but I think that matters," she said with a tender smile. "I just know that if I get pregnant, it's going to be ours."

He wet his lips slowly, letting a hand caress her cheek lightly as he thought.

"It's a lot to think on... so... are you gonna tell me how many others there were? How often? To give me an idea of... the chances," he asked, his handsome face trying to look happy and calm, but she could see slight cracks of worry.

She leaned in, kissing him so sweetly, so gently.

Truthfully, she'd lost track, and she'd have to do some mental tallying in her head. She didn't want to add to his burden.

"I don't want to think about anyone else but you," she purred, her fingers running along his jaw. "You're the one that matters."

He softened at her delicate touch, and licked his lips.

"I want you, Casey," he confessed. "Even still. And I want you to be mother to my children... all of them. And I want a great many," he told her, gazing into her eyes. "Are you okay with that, at least? You and I, having as many kids as we can?"

She'd never really thought of it before. Her own home life hadn't been a very warm affair, after all. But with him?

"Any life we build together, I'll want with my whole heart and soul," she breathed out.

He leaned down and kissed her plush lips softly, lingering a while, before breaking away.

"We'll be sure all the rest are mine. For certain," he said, giving a faint smile.

Her arms wrapped around his neck, tugging herself closer to him.

"Mr. Alder..." she purred, her tongue teasing out between her lips, glancing against his mouth. "I want you to knock me up," she said, and this time, she knew precisely what she was asking for.

His strong hands slipped to her backside again, squeezing her bubbly behind, as he kissed her back, more of his passion eking back into his touching of her. He moaned softly, lifting her up by her bottom, as she grasped around his neck.

"I want to knock you up again and again, Casey. I want to breed you for the rest of my days," he cooed to her, as she felt his cock begin to rise against her, swelling out inside his pants.

She had been so tense and worried all day since finding out what risks she'd been taking, but when he held her, it all melted away.

She wrapped her legs around his waist, showering his face in kisses.

He was saying such filthy things, such primal things, and it awoke something inside of her. Her pussy was already slick, her body aching for him to do what he promised.

"Oh Casey... I forgive you," he moaned, as he ground his cock against her, carrying her to the wall, pressing her back against it as they made out. "Open my pants," he told her as their lips broke apart. "Guide me in. Show me you're mine. Show me you're willing to be my own personal breeding slut forever more," he told her between kisses.

He was such a romantic during his lectures, able to wax poetic about classical literature.

Even the crass words spilling out of his lips sounded like a love sonnet.

Her hand slipped between them, expertly finding his zipper and guiding it down, unfastening the button before her fingertips found that swell. She relished it, coaxing it out of the fabric of his boxer briefs.

He moaned deeply as her dainty hand cradled his stiff, hard cock. Those jutting veins molten hot against her smooth skin.

"Do it, Casey. Guide me in. Tell me who you are. Who you belong to," he instructed her, his throaty a bit rumbly and rich with desire. He had a possessive need to claim her anew, and wash away the taint of the others.

It sent such a thrill through her, and even though she had been distracted by stroking him, enjoying the sensation of his flesh on hers, she obeyed. Her hand shifted, pulling him closer, until his swollen crown was gliding along her wet slit.

"I'm yours. All yours," she promised, her hips tilting forward as her hand retreated from between their bodies.

Mr. Alder wasted no time, and sheathed his cock within her, thrusting it straight up into her as he gave a loud moan. Unrestrained, intense, that pleasured sound from him like music to her ears.

"Ohh Casey... my sweet little Casey," he moaned, as he

began to pump his hips into her, one hand sliding up along her hip, her side, until he was squeezing and fondling one of her large breasts, popping her buttons open. "You'll have to give me your sweet, tight little pussy whenever I crave it... and I crave it so often."

She had been with so many men that day. Two that she could recall, one that she couldn't.

But she moaned like a virgin when he took her. He was unlike anyone else, that love really igniting the sensations of pleasure between them.

She shifted against the wall to help him get access to her breasts, the lingerie that he'd given her offering up her nipple to his palm. She gasped as her head pressed into the wall, her curls fanning out around her.

"I will give you everything you want," she swore.

"Mmm, gods yes," he moaned, a hand squeezing her milky thigh, as he began to pump into her. His thrusts wasted no time building up, starting off hard and fast. "You will be even more gorgeously perfect when you're swollen with my children..." he murred, squeezing her breast, teasing her stiff nipple as his body crashed against hers.

It felt so taboo to talk about things in such a carnal way, but his honied tone made everything sound so seductive. He made her want things she'd never considered before.

Her hands grasped at him, her legs tightly wound around his behind as she began to shudder.

The orgasm that Mr. Steros had begun to coax from her had fizzled before it was complete, and that tension had been dormant in her nerves until now. Even just the feel of Mr. Alder's cock, his hands so delightfully needy, brought it back to life.

"My sweet pet," he moaned out, as he lifted her heavy breast. But then his lips wrapped around her teat, and he suckled at her as he continued to thrust. That ravenous, sexual appetite seemingly insatiable, and more lusty and needy than ever before.

It was like Mr. Alder needed to cleanse away her admissions, by fucking her harder, faster, by claiming her body anew.

It was so intense, and it ignited something powerful within her. He made her feel so wanted, so desirable, and that jealousy had just brought it all to the surface.

She had been innocent in making the choices she did. She never considered that they might hurt him, or make him feel so possessive.

But in that moment, as her orgasm rose to its crest, she had no regrets. He flicked her nipple with his tongue, fucked into her as deep as he could, and she crashed down upon him with a cry of ecstasy.

There was a good chance their noisy fucking could be heard, if anyone were walking by his cottage closely. But neither was in the mood to care, as he hammered her against the wall, making the pictures rattle as he moaned against her tit.

His cock was swelling, throbbing within her as he chased his own orgasm.

They were chasing out the memories of everyone else, as if they were the only two people left in the world.

"I want you! Oh God, I want you to make me yours," she cried out. Her limbs twitched, and she grabbed him tighter, needing him to envelop her entirely. "I need you to knock me up!"

Mr. Alder heaved a great growl then, his cock stiffening inside her as his body heeded her call innately. His lips tugged at her nipple, but her breast fell from his mouth as he moaned aloud, and then—as the walls quaked, and a frame fell from it—he shouted out his pleasure, as he came inside her once more.

Thick gouts of his pearly white seed filling her, as he trembled and moaned. Each new thrust firing off another lance of his cum, ready to lay claim to her womb if it wasn't already seeded.

It was the first time that she felt that finale, knowing what it promised.

And it was miraculous.

She had barely recovered from her first orgasm when a second one quickly rushed in on its wake. She was trembling so badly that if not for being so firmly pinned between him and the wall, she'd likely have collapsed into a pile of mewling pleasure.

Instead, she was crushed between Mr. Alder's desire for her, and the wall. He ground his dick up into her deeply, locking his seed there. He groaned and moaned, his whole body quivering with desire as he slowly began to shower her face with kisses again.

"Mmm, Casey... my sweet, pet Casey," he moaned out throatily.

Language evaded her as tremors still coursed through her, her mouth parted as she gasped for breath.

When the haze in her mind parted enough, she was able to gasp out, "I love you," before her lips pressed hungrily to his.

And he kissed her back with such intensity, only prying his lips from hers, to lock their eyes.

"I know you do. And I know you'll work with me to make us... last. I love you too, Casey," he confessed at last, as he held her against the wall, his gaze piercing her soul.

Her heart soared, and the way her flushed face lit up was magical.

Hope and excitement touched every feature, making them glow.

He was such an intense man, so passionate, so enraptured by romance, but such a simple confession had eluded him until now.

Together they made out, lovingly, passionately. Until he carried her to his bedroom, and they got into his canopy bed. The two of them forgot all about eating, about anything else, just holding one another, caressing. Until it became making love again. Hours having passed as Mr. Alder, thrusting atop her, came once more.

"Ohh Casey..." he panted, as they lay in a post-coital haze beside one another. "I wish you didn't have to go so soon. But the bells will chime any moment now. But... soon. We'll be able to be together all the time," he said with a smile for her.

She had forgotten about her responsibilities, about the expectations upon her. She'd even forgotten all about Aeron, and where he'd escaped to when they were interrupted.

The only thing that mattered was Mr. Alder, and at his words, disappointment weighed heavily upon her.

She knew he was right, that she couldn't take any

chances of exposing their affair, but the idea of returning back to her dorm, pretending everything was normal...

It was crushing.

"I can't wait until that day," she sighed, though she forced a smile to her lips, for his sake. "But I will. I will wait for you. Patiently. As patiently as I can."

"Good. Good girl," he told her, smiling as he caressed her cheek, giving her a kiss. And before she knew it, she was having to get dressed, and he was helping her back out the window. "We'll meet again tomorrow, pet," he told her as they parted ways.

"Just in time," Dahlia said to Casey when she returned back to the room.

Casey was exhausted, her body sore from fucking, the emotional turmoil further tapping her reserves. Once the inspector passed, she collapsed on her bed, heaving a loud sigh.

"I don't know how you manage all this, Dahlia," she confessed, looking at her friend. "Life has been such a rollercoaster lately."

Dahlia settled back onto her bed on her side, studying her friend.

"What do you mean, Casey?" she asked, curiously.

"Studying, sneaking around, taking all these risks..." Casey answered. "I've never felt so special, but," she yawned, covering her mouth with the back of her hand. "It's just a lot."

Dahlia laughed softly at that, before laying back on her bed.

"Don't overdo it, Casey. You gotta look after yourself first and foremost, before you can look after anyone or anything else. Remember that," her friend cautioned her with a weary sigh. "But you're right. It's all tiring. But tomorrow's a new day," she cooed.

"Yea," she replied with a smile. "And we get to see Mr. Ramlein first thing."

She had no idea why the thought excited her so much.

And she certainly had no idea how much of a mess things would soon be.

Thirty-Eight

"Come in, Casey," Dr. Ramlein said with a smile as he pulled the door back.

Dahlia was already inside, standing there with her top open, tits out, but looking utterly oblivious to the fact.

"Hey Casey, you were right. He really helps a lot," Dahlia said as Dr. Ramlein shut the door behind her.

It wasn't *entirely* unusual to see Dahlia so casually nude, but at the same time, it kind of was. Especially since she was with a therapist.

But Casey smiled anyways, not finding it so confusing as to be a concern.

"Right? I left here yesterday feeling so much better," Casey gushed, oblivious to the hypnosis that made her believe that.

"And doesn't Dahlia look lovely like this? I think she should go around like this all the time," Dr. Ramlein said as he put a hand directly upon Casey's ass, and guided her deeper into the large room that was his office.

Casey let out a little nervous giggle at his forwardness.

"I think Dahlia's the most beautiful girl I've ever seen," Casey easily admitted. "But I think she'd probably get cold come winter."

"Well, that's why it's good to have friends," Dr. Ramlein said, as Dahlia looked at her, confused, as if she didn't know what they were talking about. "You can help keep her warm, by fondling them. Giving them a suckle. Why not give it a go now?" said the doctor, as he groped Casey's backside.

It was all so surreal.

He hadn't yet used that hypnotic trigger word, and so she hadn't yet felt that compelling need to obey.

But he was still a man in a position of authority, and so her body complied before she could even really question it.

"Oh, uh... of course. If you think that'll help," Casey said as she walked towards Dahlia. "If it's okay with you?" she asked.

Dahlia just smiled, and gave a shrug that caused her bare breasts—almost as large as Casey's—to jiggle.

"Of course. We're besties, right?" she said, looking a little more... vacant than usual, her dark eyes wide, looking almost drugged. "Dr. Ramlein knows what's best for us, after all," she said, smiling towards the doctor.

"That's right, I do," he said as he licked his lips and watched the two girls. "Why not open your top too, Casey. You don't want Dahlia to feel like she's all alone here, do you?" he asked her, in that condescending tone of a paternal figure.

"Oh, right, I guess not," she replied, beginning to unbutton her own white top, letting it fall open. She leaned in, lightly caressing Dahlia's collarbone before tracing down. It teased the skin, making it prickle with excitement, her nipples beginning to stiffen.

And then Casey's head lowered, flicking her tongue over Dahlia's nipple, letting out a sweet little giggle.

Dahlia smiled and laughed softly as Casey began to play with her breasts. Her own hands rising up, cradling Casey's chest, hefting each tit in a hand.

"God Casey, they're even more huge than they seem once you get your hands on them," her friend said.

While Dr. Ramlein licked his lips, poured himself a drink and sipped.

"Such good girls you two are," he remarked as he came in closer to them, eyes glued to their two pairs of breasts. "Dahlia here was just telling me about how she's never fucked raw before. Can you believe that? Not a single time. Poor girl," he remarked.

Casey was focused on Dahlia's body, enjoying the chance to touch and explore her, so it took a little while for Dr. Ramlein's words to sink in.

"Oh, yea, Dahlia has everything all figured out. She's so smart," Casey said with an admiring smile. She put her mouth around Dahlia's nipple, suckling it tenderly, enjoying the sensation of the supple flesh against her tongue.

Dahlia was breathing heavily, her shoulders pushed back, one of her hands leaving Casey's tits to caress her strawberry blonde hair. Soft little moans escaped her lips as she watched her best friend suckle at her teat.

"You're so sweet to me, Casey," Dahlia said breathily.

"I say it's time that we fix that, girls," Dr. Ramlein said, as he unbuckled his pants, opening up his zipper and pulling out his hardening cock. "It's not fair that Casey gets to have all the real fun, and poor little Dahlia has to suffer with condoms," he said, as he began to stroke his length, watching them.

Casey's brows furrowed, even as she continued to lavish her friend's breast with attention.

Even though it was an authority figure saying that, she'd talked to Dahlia enough to know how important it was for her to use condoms. And now, knowing about the whole *pregnancy* thing, she really understood.

Casey's gaze rose to Dahlia's, and she whispered, "Is that okay?"

"Of course," Dahlia said with that vacant eyed smile, that seemed very off and... fake to Casey. And Dahlia was never fake. "Dr. Ramlein knows what's best. And he says I should be a good little cumdump for him," she said, caressing Casey's hair, and cheek with her soft, dainty hand.

"You see?" he said, stepping up to them, his cock thrust out. "Now both of you... kiss and lick this," he told them, and Dahlia immediately began to slide her tongue along his veiny shaft, teasing its length as he pet her head.

Casey was starting to feel very weird about how Dahlia was behaving. It just wasn't her to be so obedient to authority. Casey had always admired that about her. She always stuck to her guns, and stood up for herself.

She looked at Dahlia, then at Dr. Ramlein. Dahlia had been so quick to start sucking him, so eager.

But despite Casey's feelings of unease, she joined her friend in licking the offered cock.

It would give her some time to try to understand what was happening.

"Ahh, good girls," Dr. Ramlein said, as he started caressing Casey's hair too. He watched intently as the both of them laved his dick with their tongue, coating him in their saliva from stem to tip.

And as they both reached the tip together, Dahlia kissed Casey on the lips with the head of his cock against them. She giggled softly, "Isn't this fun, Casey?" she said, in that strange way that was so odd for Dahlia.

It was like the exact opposite of their threesome with Damien. Casey always thought Dahlia had a sharp tongue and liked to tease guys, and even with Damien, she'd had a certain kind of casual air to her.

In fact, Casey couldn't recall a time that Dahlia *giggled* over a guy.

Casey's hand went to Dahlia's cheek, stroking her skin there as she kissed her friend back, pressing her forehead against hers. She wanted to see if Dahlia might have a fever or something, but her forehead felt normal.

"So how much did you agree to be paid?" Casey asked.

"Paid?" Dahlia repeated, tilting her head, looking confused. As if the whole concept were odd to her as she caressed Casey's breast. "Whatever do you mean, Casey?" she asked.

"Alright. Time for you two to bend over on the sofa. Stick your yummy, round bums out, and offer up those pussies to me," he ordered them, and right away, Dahlia began to obey, planting her knees on the sofa, then reaching beneath her skirt to haul down her panties, revealing her bare, glistening slit.

Something was really wrong with Dahlia.

Casey didn't know what, but she knew that she wasn't going to let her friend take her first raw cock like this. And for free, no less!

She had to think fast, which wasn't something she was particularly skilled at.

But she could at least fall back on something familiar.

She smiled at Mr. Ramlein as she took a step towards the couch.

"Can... can we do something fun? I've always wanted to taste another girl..." she said, as honestly as she could muster. She'd already done it once with Dahlia, of course, but he didn't know that. And as long as her mouth was on her friend's pussy, he couldn't fuck her bareback.

Dr. Ramlein's face lit up, and he patted Casey on the cheek.

"Good idea, dear," he said as he gestured towards Dahlia. "Get down on your hands and knees and lick her pussy then. Cumdump? Lean over the arm instead. That way I can fuck your friend as she eats you out," he instructed, organizing the two girls for his depraved pleasure. "But don't worry, I'll save my cum for you, Dahlia," he added.

"Thank you, Dr. Ramlein," Dahlia said as she got into position, sticking her round ass out, parting her milky thighs to show that glistening slit off to them both.

He still didn't use that hypnotic word.

He didn't need to.

Casey was always so obedient, and if she might've been a bit reluctant with him on his own, the dynamic was completely different with Dahlia present. Her desire to keep her friend safe meant that she would go along with whatever she could, trigger word or not.

Even if she had to plead for the therapist to knock her up instead of her friend.

She figured the odds were that she was already pregnant, after all, still ignorant of things like her natural cycle.

Casey moved into position behind Dahlia, looking at that offered slit, and feeling that desire swell in her despite the strange situation. She leaned in, her nose teasing along Dahlia's pussy as she inhaled. Her tongue poked out, feeling Dahlia's silken lips part for her.

The pleasured sigh and moan that Dahlia gave sounded sincere. Those were the only times that she seemed... more normal actually, when Casey was the one touching her. And she arched her spine, pressing her pussy back to Casey's mouth.

But as they did their dutiful work together, Dr. Ramlein got in behind Casey. That thick, bare cock of his pressing to her raw pussy, which was Mr. Alder's.

"Mmm, beautiful. You two are stunning. The finest girls I've ever played with," he remarked, as he gripped Casey's hips and then hilted himself inside of her with a loud moan and a sigh.

Casey gasped against Dahlia's pussy.

She didn't remember yesterday's session, nothing about the details. Just that it had been good, helpful, and that she should let others know that. But trying to recall why she felt that way?

It was like trying to recall a dream from nights before. Just the sensation of reaching out into her memory for something that was no longer there.

Why couldn't she remember what happened?

And why was he acting so confident and calm about fucking her?

Mr. Alder, Mr. Steros, Mr. Grieg, they'd all been cautious. Careful. Swore her to secrecy. She had to initiate with all of them, or at least be willing to tip them over the edge of their moral dilemma.

Casey's hand reached up to caress Dahlia's ass, to pull one cheek apart so that she could delve in deeper, and it hid the fact that the gears were turning in her head.

Dahlia moaned and welcomed Casey's touches, while behind her, Dr. Ramlein made it harder to do, as he started to pound into her from behind. He was moaning, grunting, making her ass quake.

"Mmm, that's it... get her nice and worked up. She's ever so eager to start her new role as my cumdump, aren't you Dahlia?" he asked in his pleasured voice.

"Y-yes Dr. Ramlein. A-Ah yes!" she panted out.

"Mmm, it's only fair, since your friend here got my last load," he remarked, giving Casey's ass a light spank.

Something was really wrong, but Casey was trapped. She whimpered into Dahlia's pussy, and felt a cold chill go down her spine.

She couldn't have forgotten something like that, could she have?

She'd been with a lot of men, but she could still recall them when she tried.

But not him.

It was so strange, and Casey quivered as her tongue traveled along Dahlia's slit. The taste of her friend filled her mouth, and it was so sweet, so soothing.

Casey would do anything for her.

And if he was able to steal her memories away, well, she was going to do everything she could to not let Dahlia get knocked up! That would be way too confusing.

So even as conflicted as she was, she pushed back against Mr. Ramlein, inviting him in deeper. She'd taken so many chances with so many men, unknowingly. But now, it wasn't just about her!

Dr. Ramlein continued to pound her, but she felt him growing closer. And as he began to pull out, she tried to push back to stop him from doing it.

"Hey now," he panted, giving her ass another slap and a grope. "Don't be greedy, cocktoy," he said, and suddenly... the triggering mechanism went off. And the memories flooded back. But with it, also came the urge to obey, even stronger than before. "You want your little friend to get knocked up too, don't you? So the two of you can sport a nice round belly and be changed forever by it," he taunted her with a grin.

Casey let out a whimper, confusion building upon confusion.

The impulse to obey was so strong, it had managed to render the cocky Dahlia into a submissive bimbo. Casey didn't stand a chance, not with how much she already loved being a good girl.

But along with the need to obey came the awareness that he was the best cock she'd ever had, better than any others.

And she *was* greedy for it!

So she pushed back into him again, taking him to her depths, her pussy squeezing him, trying to get him to fill her up. To make her his cum dumpster, that dirty phrase he'd introduced her to.

Dr. Ramlein moaned and groaned, gripping Casey's ass tightly.

"You greedy little cocktoy," he growled out, grinning, giving her ass another slap. "You really want to rob your friend of all this satisfaction, don't you? And to think, how cute you'd both look with my seed growing inside you at nearly the same rate," he said with a laugh.

"Mmm, c'mon Casey," moaned Dahlia, in that strangely... off voice of hers. "Share. I want to get knocked up with you," she said, pleading in that vacant, off voice.

A part of Casey knew what was happening with Dahlia, but it was hidden in the shadows of her mind.

And if she weren't such a natural slut, she might have acquiesced. To feel that urge to share, to let her friend get knocked up. Or maybe it was her desire to please, to know that a man wanted her.

Regardless, Casey chose the path that was both selfish and selfless.

She grabbed Dahlia more aggressively, her tongue and fingers working in tandem, just as she had showed her. Casey's feet lifted and stretched back, holding onto Mr. Ramlein as best she could, trying desperately to claim that virile load for herself.

And there the three of them were interlocked, as Dr. Ramlein pounded into Casey in an angry sort of manner.

"Fine. You greedy little cocktoy," he growled out as he huffed, thrusting into her wildly. "You'll get just what you're after."

Thirty-Nine

"I don't know what the fuck is going on in here, but it stinks. And I've got it all recorded!"

The tether that held Casey and Dahlia's minds taut was severed at the sudden intrusion. The hooded vigilante stared down at the three of them from the window, holding up his recording device triumphantly.

Dr. Ramlein lunged forward, but the vigilante hopped down, sprinting off as Dahlia recoiled, trying to tug her top closed.

"Get back here! You don't understand, my methods are very unorthodox!" Dr. Ramlein protested, pushing his dick back in his pants as he took off after the intruder.

"You... you saved me!" Dahlia sobbed once he was gone, her gratitude bubbling over as she held on to Casey.

Casey didn't know it at the time, but it was an end of an era, and the opening that she needed for her own happily ever after.

Mr. Mordule tried to cover for his associate, but once Mr. Steros got involved, and the hooded vigilante shared a brief clip with him, no excuse in the book would be enough to get them out of hot water. They were both placed under arrest, and Mr. Steros told her that anything that might come of it—such as pregnancy—wouldn't be held against her.

Even better, she'd be allowed to continue on and given compensation by the collegiate.

She had explored so much, and so many people, in such a little amount of time. It made the prospect of settling down all that much easier, and Mr. Alder was every bit the romantic he promised to be. When she inevitably swelled up with child, they both knew that it was his, and after a conversation with Mr. Steros, they were given his blessing, however muted it was.

Casey never did find out who the vigilante was, but she knew that he was a hero. She had her suspicions of who it was, of course, but for her, the mystery just made it all that more special, so she never tried to unravel it and ruin the magic.

She had chosen the life of a housewife, and though she might have left her bimbo adventures behind, the experience had shaped her into the perfect horny wife, so that her and Mr. Alder could live their strange, wonderful, happily-ever-after.

Subscribe for more Candy Quinn:
http://candyquinn.com/newsletter

Recommended For You

For a full list of all my books, or to browse by length or kink, please visit my website!

https://candyquinn.com/books

─── ❧ ───

YOUR NEXT HOT READ

Stranded Princess

Seducing the Hawthornes

Nympho Farm Girl

Biker's Sugar Babe Nympho Pet

His Girl

Free Exclusive Story

LUST LESSONS: BELLA

She has the hots for teacher

Mr. Wright is totally off limits. Not only is he her teacher, but he's also her brother's best friend.

Bella has never wanted anyone more. At first, she just

wants to tease him. She doesn't wear panties, and practically begs him for the big D —- detention — just to prove to him how good she is at being bad. But he wants more than a tease. He wants to claim her fertile, innocent body, and neither of them can resist their forbidden desires.

TEASER

By the time the bell rang and the other students rushed out, Bella's fantasies had her wound up tighter than a knot. Her bare pussy was dripping on her chair, and she slipped out of it eagerly.

"Well, Mr. Wright, you got me alone," she grinned.

Clark gave her a cautionary look, before he went to the door and shut it tight then locked it.

"You really chose an... interesting way to get yourself in trouble, Bella," he said to her as he returned from the door, shaking his head at her in surprised disbelief, a soft chuckle escaping his lips. "But you always were a little terror of a tease," he said as he made his way back towards the class windows, beginning to slide the curtains shut.

"You make it sound so sweet," she giggled, sitting on his desk. She pulled her white skirt out from under her, crossing her legs as she watched him shut the curtains. "I just did what felt natural."

Get your free copy of Lust Lessons: Bella, and so much more! All you have to do is subscribe to my newsletter.
http://candyquinn.com/newsletter

Become Candy Obsessed

For over a decade, I've been writing the hottest, naughtiest stories I can think of, and I'm addicted. I love to explore the forbidden, the taboo, and the over-the-top sexy. Each story starts off with a sizzle, giving you that nice build up, and that perfect release.

Discover new, secret fantasies, or just indulge in those sticky-sweet guilty pleasures. I'll never judge! Make sure to follow me on your fave site so you never miss a new release.

Plus, if you sign up for my mailing list, you'll get updates on my new books, bundles, giveaways **and** a **Free, exclusive** novella.

CONNECT WITH CANDY!
candyquinn.com
candyquinn.com/newsletter
candy.quinn.erotica@gmail.com

FOLLOW ME EVERYWHERE!

facebook.com/candyquinnromance

twitter.com/sexycandyquinn

amazon.com/Candy-Quinn/e/B00K187NCE

bookbub.com/authors/candy-quinn

Also by Candy Quinn

NOVELLAS

Stranded Beauty

Innocent Farm Girl

Precious Pet

The Fugitive

Dirty Country Love

Mandy Collection

Nympho Farm Girl

Biker's Sugar Babe Nympho Pet

His Girl

Innocent Tease

THE DELANEY BROTHERS

Alastair

Jack

Tristan

William

TEACHER / STUDENT

Lust Lessons Bella

Lust Lessons Claira

AGE GAP

Bad Seed

Tease

Seducing Her Boss

His Fertile Groupie

The Doctor and the Fertile Housewife

The Fertile Beauty Queen

The Fertile Beauty Queen & My Wife

The Doctor and the Fertile Housewives

Fertile Celebrity: Aida

The Fertile Celebrity: Zoe

A Fertile Work Party

Mrs. Fertile Claus

The Fertile Bride

And a Fertile New Year

Love That First Night

Dancing for the Mob Boss

His Fertile Present

The Fertile Tour Guide

His Fertile Sweetheart

The Fertile Stewardess

Bought by the Bad Boy

World's Finest

Nympho for the Billionaires

Parked Between Her Thighs

Matchmaker

Sugar Daddy Rock Star

Sugar Daddy Camgirl

Sugar Daddy Influencer

Sugar Daddy Student

THE FERTILE FARM

The Fertile Farm Olive

Nympho Farm Girl

Mandy Collection

The Fertile Farm Rosa

The Fertile Farm Lucy

The Fertile Farm Daisy

The Fertile Farm Dixie

Fertile Farm Laura's Innocence 1

Fertile Farm Laura's Innocence 2

The Farmgirl & The Fugitive

The Farmgirl & The Bandit

The Military Man & Farmgirl

Bought by the Billionaire

MFM BREEDING

Her Fertile First Time

Her Fertile Second Time

BECCA, KATIE & LYNN